MODERN HUMANITIES RESEARCH ASSOCIATION
CRITICAL TEXTS
VOLUME 62

ENGLISH SERIES EDITOR

JUSTIN D. EDWARDS

THE BLIND BOW-BOY
BY CARL VAN VECHTEN

The Blind Bow-Boy

by

Carl Van Vechten

Edited with an Introduction and Notes by
Kirsten MacLeod

Modern Humanities Research Association
Critical Texts 62
2018

Published by

The Modern Humanities Research Association
Salisbury House
Station Road
Cambridge CB1 2LA
United Kingdom

Copy-Editor: Simon Davies

First published 2018

ISBN 978-1-78188-290-0

CONTENTS

INTRODUCTION

The Blind Bow-Boy:
'A Great Forgotten American Novel
of the 1920s'

The Blind Bow-Boy (1923) is a quintessential Jazz-Age novel, celebrating the spirit of an age that its author, Carl Van Vechten (1880–1964), dubbed 'the Splendid, Drunken Twenties'.[1] Certainly, it is as deserving of this honour as its more famous contemporary — F. Scott Fitzgerald's *The Great Gatsby* (1925). It may seem presumptuous to claim this for a forgotten novel by an author who is virtually unknown outside of academia — and little known within it. The book, however, lives up to the claim. Indeed, it bears striking parallels to its canonical counterpart. Both novels originated and are set in 1922, that talismanic year for modernism; both figure New York as the centre of decadent modernity; both capture the sybaritic lifestyles of wealthy and bohemian pleasure-seekers; and both have been considered modern-day *Satyricons*.[2] Where Fitzgerald, however, treats the superficiality of the world he portrays in tragic terms, Van Vechten celebrates its glittering artifice. Though it is *Gatsby* that now occupies a position in the modernist canon as *the* quintessential Jazz-Age novel, *The Blind Bow-Boy* merits recuperation, as does its beguiling author.

Van Vechten was a major cultural figure of the period, whose friends

---

[1] 'How I Remember Joseph Hergesheimer', *Yale University Library Gazette*, 22, 3 (1948), 87–93 (p. 87).

[2] Fitzgerald originally intended to title *Gatsby* 'Trimalchio in West Egg', Trimalchio being the vulgar upstart from Petronius's *Satyricon*. Critics have made much of this connection. Van Vechten's novel was deemed a modern-day *Satyricon* in reviews of the period. See, for example, Ernest Boyd, 'Van Vechten's New York', *Nation*, 5 September 1923, pp. 244–45; Edmund Wilson, 'Late Violets from the Nineties', *Dial*, 75 (October 1923), pp. 387–90; L. Stuart Rose, 'Petronius in New York', *Brentano's Book Chat* 2, 5 (Fall 1923). This last review was sourced from an unpaginated clipping in Scrapbook 13 in the Carl Van Vechten Papers, Manuscripts, Archives, and Rare Books Division, New York Public Library. Hereafter reviews derived from this source and lacking page numbers will be referenced by Scrapbook number, Van Vechten Papers. Other material from this collection will be cited as from Van Vechten Papers.

included Gertrude Stein, George Gershwin, Langston Hughes, Eugene O'Neill, Wallace Stevens, Charlie Chaplin, Georgia O'Keeffe, and Man Ray, to name but a few. His accomplishments, meanwhile, were many. In addition to writing novels, he was a notable critic of modern dance, music, and theatre, the first to champion Igor Stravinsky, George Gershwin, Isadora Duncan, and other emerging modernists across the arts. As a photographer, he captured images of the most important figures in the arts in the first half of the twentieth century. As a collector and patron, he established major institutional collections related to the modern arts. His novels were acclaimed by influential critics of the day, including H. L. Mencken, Edmund Wilson, Burton Rascoe, and Carl Van Doren, in reviews that compared him to James Joyce, Oscar Wilde, Aldous Huxley, Max Beerbohm, and Ronald Firbank. They were heralded, too, by modernist contemporaries, including Fitzgerald, Gertrude Stein, Sinclair Lewis, and William Somerset Maugham. Today, however, of his seven novels, only one — *Nigger Heaven* (1926) — is reliably in print,[3] leaving Van Vechten at the margins of modernist scholarship and disproportionately represented by a single novel.

This edition of *The Blind Bow-Boy* is designed to encourage further study of and research on Van Vechten and to enable contemporary readers to make the most of the novel. The introduction, textual annotations, and suggested readings contextualize author and work in relation to the key literary and cultural ferments of the day. The introduction provides biographical information and offers suggestions for critical approaches to the text based on its position vis-à-vis 'high' modernism; its relationship to *fin-de-siècle* decadence; its importance as a study of queer identity; and its status as a 'realistic' novel of New York. Publishing information, meanwhile, is provided in the Note on the Text. The edition recuperates an important example of the literature of America's Jazz Age — one that Van Vechten's contemporary, Sinclair Lewis, deemed 'a superb novel', and that his most recent biographer has declared 'one of the great forgotten American novels of the 1920s'.[4]

Carl Van Vechten (1880–1964)

Van Vechten was born in Cedar Rapids, Iowa, in 1880 and grew up in prosperous circumstances. A highly precocious and imaginative child with a strong

---

[3] Carl Van Vechten, *Nigger Heaven*, ed. by Kathleen Pfeiffer (Champaign: University of Illinois Press, 2000). This edition contains a critical introduction but no annotations. Reprints, lacking critical apparatus, of *Firecrackers* (Mondial, 2007) and *Parties* (Sun and Moon Press, 2000) are available through Amazon, but the publishers are now defunct.

[4] Letter to Van Vechten, 27 September 1923, Box 16, Van Vechten Papers; Edward White, *The Tastemaker: Carl Van Vechten and the Birth of Modern America* (New York: Farrar, Strauss and Giroux, 2014), p. 150.

interest in the arts, he was, from an early age, in revolt against the small-town environment of his upbringing. University provided a means to escape this world and, in 1899, he left Cedar Rapids for the University of Chicago. He never looked back. Following university, Van Vechten embarked on a journalistic career, eventually leaving Chicago in 1906 to pursue a career and interests in places even more congenial to him for his cultural development: New York City and the capitals of Europe. In the years leading up to the First World War, Van Vechten continued his journalistic work as a music critic, Paris correspondent, and drama critic; he married and divorced his childhood sweetheart; and began circulating within a number of interconnecting transatlantic cultural networks that included writers, artists, musicians, dancers, and stage and screen stars. These were the networks that would nurture him. In 1914, he married his second and lifelong partner, actress Fania Marinoff. Theirs was an intense relationship, often fiery, and most certainly unconventional. Van Vechten was bisexual and carried on relationships with men throughout their marriage, which Fania knew about. Such arrangements were not unusual in their networks, where homosexuality, lesbianism, bisexuality, interracial sexual relationships, sexual promiscuity, cross-dressing, exhibitionism, and voyeurism were part of the socio-cultural fabric. In career terms, the years between 1914 and 1920 would see Van Vechten establishing a reputation as a critic of modern music, dance, drama, and literature, moving from the realm of newspapers to high cultural and avant-garde magazines and essay collections.

None of this work, however, was very lucrative. It was not until 1920, when he was forty, that he took up the novel-writing that would prove profitable for him. His first novel, *Peter Whiffle* (1922), was published by Alfred A. Knopf, a prestigious trade publisher with a high-quality list and beautiful, well-designed volumes. *Peter Whiffle* is a semi-fictionalized *Künstlerroman* and *roman-à-clef* about a shadowy artist figure who strives all his life to write a great work but dies, having completed nothing. While Peter is fictional, the context is a real one in a novel that provides insight into the post-war transatlantic avant-garde realms in which Van Vechten circulated. The novel was a surprise success, and was nearing its tenth printing when *The Blind Bow-Boy* was published in 1923. Two more books followed in quick succession: *The Tattooed Countess* (1924) and *Firecrackers* (1925). *The Tattooed Countess* was a fictional homage to his Midwest upbringing, a satirical take on the popular literary theme of small-town America made famous in this period by Sinclair Lewis and Sherwood Anderson. *Firecrackers*, meanwhile, revisits characters from *The Blind Bow-Boy* and *The Tattooed Countess*, bringing them into the orbit of a new Van Vechten creation, the enigmatic Gunnar O'Grady, who exerts a transformative effect on them. In 1926, Van Vechten would publish his most famous and controversial novel, *Nigger Heaven*, a story of Harlem life, influenced by his involvement with, and interest in, the Harlem Renaissance movement. The novel achieved international success and was translated into many European languages. It drew the attention of the white market to black artists, an achievement welcomed by some in the black community but resented by others. Van Vechten's two final novels were *Spider Boy* (1928), a send-up of Hollywood life, and *Parties* (1930), a bittersweet swansong to the 1920s, featuring characters based on F. Scott and Zelda Fitzgerald.

Van Vechten occupied a unique position in the modernist cultural field of his day, circulating amongst a range of literary and artistic networks, among them the Algonquin Round Table, the Harlem Renaissance, the Lost Generation writers, and various New York salons, including his own, where he controversially hosted mixed-race parties, a taboo social practice in the period. His cultural positioning was reflected in writing that drew from across his diverse knowledge of the modern arts of the period, both high and low. He was a popular, critically acclaimed, and commercially successful author. His commercial success set him apart from high modernist contemporaries such as James Joyce and his friend Gertrude Stein. This success, however, needs to be qualified. He did not achieve the mass-market level of bestselling contemporaries such as Gene Stratton-Porter and E. Phillips Oppenheim, whose works sold in the millions. Neither did he achieve sales constituting the next level of bestsellerdom, sales in the hundreds of thousands per year, as did writers like Ethel M. Dell and Sinclair Lewis. Van Vechten was situated just below this range, with an appeal as a fashionable, sophisticated writer. His readers included the bohemians, avant-gardists, and wealthy cosmopolites that were part of his transatlantic social networks, as well as men and women, young and old, from all across the country and internationally, who wanted to be up-to-date. His novels were well publicized and reviewed, achieving sales in the tens of thousands within the first few months of publication, and continuing to be issued regularly in new editions through the decade. If not mega-bestsellers in national or international terms, they did make local bestseller lists in cities like Chicago and New York, and appeared as 'in demand' titles at city libraries. He was a favourite of booksellers, who often featured window displays of his works. Further, he was counted among living authors whose works were sought out in a period that witnessed a strong interest in book collecting. With *Nigger Heaven* he reached a zenith, achieving sales of over 100,000, and international and long-lasting success.

Van Vechten, however, wearied of novel-writing, retiring from the field in 1930. An inheritance from his brother enabled him to pursue independent interests and, through the 1930s and 1940s, he developed two passions: photography and cultural patronage. From this period to his death, he took up photography as an amateur interest, taking tens of thousands of photographs of notable people across the arts, sharing them with his subjects and friends, and organizing them into collections for institutions. At the same time, he devoted himself to the creation of institutional collections related to the modernist arts, including the James Weldon Johnson Collection at Yale dedicated to African-American culture and the George Gershwin Collection at Fiske. Van Vechten's public profile necessarily waned in these decades from its high point in the 1920s. His literary reputation was in decline from the 1930s, in part because he was no longer active, but also because of the marked shift in literary trends away from the preoccupations of the 1920s — Jazz-Age high jinks and avant-gardist experimentation — to documentary realism and high seriousness. His style would not fare well as the formalist contours of high modernism were consolidated in the 1940s and 1950s, and academics assumed the consecrational powers formerly held by journalist critics. Van Vechten would accrue some attention with the shift in academia to cultural and political approaches from the 1980s on. In this context, he has been recuperated primarily within African-American, Black, and LGBTQ+ studies, where he exists as a controversial figure, often represented as an opportunistic and exploitative 'patron' in cultural and sexual terms. This focus has been reinforced by the prominence of *Nigger Heaven* in his oeuvre and by his photographs and scrapbooks of black subjects. By moving beyond this material, however, it becomes possible to consider the many other ways in which Van Vechten was engaged with, and central to the development of, modernism. *The Blind Bow-Boy*, for example, engages productively with the interests of New Modernist Studies in remapping the modernist literary field; with recent re-evaluations of the legacy of *fin-de-siècle* decadence on modernism; and with current trends in LGBTQ+ Studies.

Reading *The Blind Bow-Boy*

This 'great forgotten American novel of the 1920s' is, on the surface, simple. The plot centres on Harold Prewett, a naïve young man who has led a sheltered life, and his initiation into a life of pleasure-seeking. Upon graduating from college, he is summoned to meet his father — whom he has never met — who informs Harold that he desires him to gain experience of the world. Mr Prewett, a conventional man at heart, has a deceptive plan. In an attempt at reverse psychology, he sets out to expose his son to the corrupting influence of worldly man-about-town Paul Moody. His idea is that Harold will be disgusted by the experience and will enthusiastically take up his role in his father's cloak and suit business. The plan, however, backfires and Harold falls under the spell of Moody and his pleasure-seeking set, including the ultra-sophisticated and enigmatic Campaspe Lorillard; Zimbule O'Grady, a louche Coney Island snake charmer turned film actress; Bunny Hugg, an avant-garde jazz composer;

Drains, an inscrutable butler with a past; and the Duke of Middlebottom, a British, monocle-sporting, bisexual dandy. Harold seems, at first, to desire a conventional life and he abandons his rowdy friends for a marriage to a nice young woman. Ultimately, however, he finds in the lives of his carefree friends a greater authenticity than in the bourgeois life he has been destined for.

The surface simplicity of this plot obscures the greater complexity of the novel's treatment of important themes and topics, and its position both within a literary tradition and in relation to contemporaneous modernist fiction. As Van Vechten himself said of the novel to British author Ronald Firbank, 'everything is so clear that no one will understand it'.[5] Though Van Vechten may be underestimating readers here, there is no question that background information and contextualization aid in the development of a rich reading of the novel. While readers will undoubtedly find their own frameworks for understanding and interpreting the novel, what follows are four possible approaches, informed by considerations of its reception in its day and/or by recent critical and theoretical methodologies suited to its themes: *The Blind Bow-Boy* as i) a novel of 'arched brow' modernism; ii) a novel of queer identity; iii) a novel of the new decadence; and iv) a 'realistic' novel of New York.

A Novel of 'Arched Brow' Modernism

While Van Vechten's positioning between the realm of mass-market fiction and the high culture avant-gardist or experimental novel might suggest he be considered a middlebrow author, such a categorization ignores the particular conditions of the 1920s literary field and the interventions he made in asserting the authority of his own modernist aesthetic. In this period, the hierarchies of what would emerge as the modernist canon were not yet established. It is not unusual, therefore, to see critical reviews discussing Van Vechten alongside James Joyce or Gertrude Stein. Indeed, some reviews of *The Blind Bow-Boy* specifically invoke *Ulysses*. Similarities are noted in the manner in which these texts scrutinize 'segments of life'.[6] One critic goes so far as to declare Van Vechten's novel more 'consistently entertaining' than Joyce's.[7] In his day, then, Van Vechten's work was accorded highbrow status. Fellow writer and friend, Sinclair Lewis, for example, found his brand of highbrow unique, commending *The Blind Bow-Boy* in the following terms: 'you slap the tradition that highbrow American novels must be either lugubriously and literally "realistic" [...] or else

---

[5]   Letter, 12 July [1922], in *Letters of Carl Van Vechten*, ed. by Bruce Kellner (New Haven: Yale University Press, 1987), 46–47 (p. 46). Letters from this collection hereafter cited as from *Letters*.

[6]   Boyd, 'Van Vechten's New York', p. 244.

[7]   Lawrence Stallings, review of *Blind Bow-Boy*, in *New York World*, 15 August 1923, Scrapbook 13, Van Vechten Papers.

acrobatically "original" like Waldo Frank and all the others who are deriving from the solemn theology of a Gertrude Stein'.[8] Van Vechten did, indeed, eschew forms of highbrow writing that would come to characterize canonical modernism — Freudian psychological approaches, for example, and a stylistics of abstraction and difficulty. In order to account, then, for the distinctive nature of Van Vechten's mode, it might be useful to particularize it as 'arched brow' modernism: modernism that approaches serious subject matter in a blithely sophisticated manner typified by characteristics associated with the body language of the arched brow — knowing, wry, cynical, and sardonic. Beneath an easy manner and arched brow, Van Vechten was serious. Explaining his approach to friend Emily Clark, for example, he said: 'My formula consists in treating extremely serious themes as frivolously as possible'.[9] To another friend, Mabel Dodge Luhan, meanwhile, he revealed one of the consistent serious themes across his books: 'They seem to me to be books about a man who is alone in the world and is very sad'.[10]

The Blind Bow-Boy exemplifies this 'arched brow' modernism, approaching the subject of the sad, lonely man, represented by Harold, from the perspective of the knowing observer. As Van Vechten told Hugh Walpole, it is a 'tremendously serious book with a sardonic approach'.[11] The 'arched brow' modernism manifests itself in a novel privileging, as Bruce Kellner argues, 'brilliant scenes and dialogue' over 'plot'.[12] On the one hand, it is written in a sleek, sophisticated, accessible style. On the other, it is laden with references, allusions, and lists covering literature, art, theatre, music, interior design, decorative arts, and fashion, a characteristic feature of Van Vechten's style that contributed to its highbrow air of sophistication and led reviewers to comment on the encyclopaedic qualities of his work. In this sense, the novel, as Burton Rascoe insisted, was an invaluable directory for the 'up-to-date modern young man or woman'.[13]

Van Vechten was characteristically coy about his fiction. He was outspoken in his defiance of the high seriousness of much modern art, outwardly promoting an aesthetic of pleasure. In the dustjacket blurb he wrote for The Blind Bow-Boy, for example, he adopts an 'arched brow' tone, Wildean in manner:

> The author has sworn before a notary public that his only purpose in creating The Blind Bow-Boy was to amuse. Readers, therefore, are especially

---

[8] Letter to Van Vechten, 27 September 1923, Box 16, Van Vechten Papers.
[9] Letter to Emily Clark, July 1922, as cited in Clark, Innocence Abroad (New York: Knopf, 1931), p. 134.
[10] Letter to Mabel Dodge Luhan, 8 October 1924, in Letters, 71–72 (p. 72).
[11] Letter to Hugh Walpole [circa 25 August 1923], in Letters, 54–55 (p. 54).
[12] Carl Van Vechten and the Irreverent Decades (Norman, OK: University of Oklahoma Press), p. 145.
[13] Review of Blind Bow-Boy, New York Tribune, 26 August 1923, Scrapbook 13, Van Vechten Papers.

warned against the danger of comparing this work with other books, written, apparently, in a somewhat similar form, for it should be obvious that no purpose, beyond that just noted, actuated its construction, and no ideas are concealed beneath its surface.

This messaging, alongside Van Vechten's subject matter, style, and treatment, led many to discount any possible depth in the novel. This perspective characterized many reviews of *The Blind Bow-Boy*, which often quoted from the blurb to reinforce this assessment. While such an understanding is not invalid — it *is* a fun book — it belies the more serious aesthetic philosophy that he claimed for this novel and his work more broadly. Disappointed that so many reviewers took him at his word, he complained to Walpole that no one had understood his purpose, revealing that it is Campaspe who 'sums the whole thing up'.[14]

Campaspe is indeed Van Vechten's mouthpiece, providing the key to understanding not only this novel, but his 'arched brow' modernism more generally. Her pages-long reverie in chapter eight is central to elucidating an aesthetic that conceals seriousness beneath a seemingly superficial style. Campaspe, inspired in her philosophy by Nietzsche's first principle of aesthetics — 'what is good is easy; everything divine runs with light feet' (p. 95) — elaborates her aesthetic in the following manner:

> How was it possible to read an author who never laughed? For it was only behind laughter that true tragedy could lie concealed, only the ironic author who could awaken the deeper emotions. The tragedies of life, she reflected, were either ridiculous or sordid. The only way to get the sense of this absurd, contradictory, and perverse existence into a book was to withdraw entirely from the reality. The artist who feels most poignantly the bitterness of life wears a persistent and sardonic smile. [...]
>
> A book [...] should have the swiftness of melodrama, the lightness of farce, to be a real contribution to thought. [...] How could anything serious be hidden more successfully than in a book which pretended to be light and gay? Plot was certainly unimportant in the novel; character drawing a silly device. [...] In life we never know anything about the families and early lives of the people we meet; why should we have to learn all about them in books? Growth of character in a novel was nonsense. People never change. Psychology: the supreme imbecility. The long and complicated analyses that serious writers give us merely define the mental limitations of these writers. (pp. 94, 96–97)

In the midst of these reflections, Campaspe goes on to offer an analysis of the state of contemporary literature, contrasting good and bad practice. Her examples often undermine conventional wisdom, rendering the high low and the low high, including a critique of Joyce that reflected Van Vechten's own view: 'Works like *Ulysses*', she declares irreverently, 'are always out of date.

---

[14]   Letter to Hugh Walpole, *Letters*, p. 54.

At first too modern, they soon grow old-fashioned' (p. 97). 'Arched brow'
modernism is thus manifested in the novel in theory. But how in practice? What
is the 'serious' subject matter hiding in this 'book [...] pretend[ing] to be light
and gay'?

A Novel of Queer Identity

One of its serious subjects is, in fact, revealed in Campaspe's rhetorical question
about hiding seriousness beneath a 'light and gay' surface. For, if the novel is
gay in the sense of 'brilliant', 'showy', and 'carefree' at its surface, it is gay, in
the sense of 'homosexual', underneath.[15] The use of gay as a code word was
emerging in this period in the homosexual and bohemian circles Van Vechten
circulated in.[16] This double meaning in Campaspe's reverie is undoubtedly
intentional, an interpretation reinforced for the attentive reader by the novel
that prompts Campaspe's irritation about 'author[s] who never laugh' and her
subsequent philosophising: Waldo Frank's *Dark Mother* (1920). *Dark Mother*
is a psychoanalytic and mystical study of repression, about a naïve young man
who comes to New York, where he struggles to come to terms with his sexuality.
This subject, of course, is precisely the same one that Van Vechten takes up with
a sardonic, playful approach.

While 'gay' is thus being used in a coded way in this text, Van Vechten's work
lends itself more readily to the more expansive term 'queer' in its approach to
gender identity and sexuality. Indeed, in other contexts he used the term 'queer'
in coded ways to mean both 'odd' and 'homosexual',[17] this latter connotation, one
more restricted than current uses of queer, in circulation in homosexual circles
in the 1910s and 1920s.[18] Because the term 'queer' encompasses homosexuality
(in Van Vechten's era), as well as a broader spectrum of sexual and gender
identities (in our day), it is a more useful term than gay for the challenges the
novel presents to normative sexuality. For both these reasons, it is useful to
consider *The Blind Bow-Boy*, and Van Vechten's work more generally, as queer,
rather than strictly homosexual. As articulated in queer theory, queer disrupts
the binaries that underpin not only heteronormative culture but also gay and
lesbian identity. This anti-essentialism, a resistance to heteronormativity, and
an interest in challenging binaries are all central to Van Vechten's thinking.

---

[15] 'Gay, adj., A1a, A3a and A4d', *OED Online* (Oxford University Press). Accessed 12
December, 2017.
[16] George Chauncey, *Gay New York: Gender, Culture and the Making of the Gay Male
World 1880-1940* (New York: Basic Books, 1994), pp. 14–21. Van Vechten's scrapbooks
devoted to queer subject matter and desire provide further evidence of his interest in visual
and textual coding and play.
[17] Carl Van Vechten, 'Ronald Firbank', in *Excavations*, by Carl Van Vechten (New York:
Knopf, 1926), 170–76 (p. 172).
[18] Chauncey, *Gay New York*, pp. 15–16.

Queerness in its historical and present-day sense inhabits the novel well beyond Campaspe's reverie. The novel abounds with references to sexual and gendered otherness in the way of subplot elements and in literary and artistic references. The most overt element of queerness is embodied in the bisexual Duke of Middlebottom, who provides comic distraction at the surface level. The serious sexual theme percolating below, however, concerns the protagonist, Harold, Van Vechten's 'man who is alone in the world and is very sad' in this novel. The novel traces Harold's dawning realization of the truth of a 'never say never' parable provided by Campaspe, one prefaced with a reference to cross-dressing and lesbianism in Zola's *Nana*, and ending with the proverb 'it is not good to say fountain — out of your basin I shall never drink' (p. 130). This lesson leads Harold to abandon his conventional bourgeois marriage for an affair with Zimbule and, ultimately, to his departure for Europe in the company of the Duke of Middlebottom. Readers seeking a psychologized tackling of queer sexuality will be disappointed, however, as, unlike Campaspe, whose thoughts are revealed extensively through free indirect discourse, Harold's are less fully realized, and the novel ends ambiguously, leaving us only to surmise that his homosexual experience is beginning.

Corinne E. Blackmer criticizes this ending, arguing that it reinforces the 'ideological compliance and self-erasure' demanded in heteronormative societies in which 'homosexuals must disappear from sight in order to be free'.[19] Many readers will concur, but it is useful to recall the contexts and constraints of a period in which works such as *Ulysses* and *Lady Chatterley's Lover* were banned and Van Vechten himself had to agree to expurgations to secure British publication for the novel (see Note on the Text). What to Blackmer is a disappointing ending, for example, was, for its time, subversive. T. R. Smith, a notable editor of the period, thought the ending 'so clever and so wise. It opens up the possibilities of a new life — a new pleasure for people who are different from so many other people'.[20] Heywood Broun similarly credited the novel with 'propagandiz[ing] for all those brave beings who seek, in spite of tyranny, to follow their own inclinations'.[21] It was true, however, that most reviewers did not see — or pretended not to see — its deeper meaning beneath the playful surface, which disappointed Van Vechten.[22]

Perhaps the best means of bringing out the queerness and subversiveness of *The Blind Bow-Boy* is through the lens of camp. Indeed, Van Vechten's

---

[19] 'Selling Taboo Subjects: The Literary Commerce of Gertrude Stein and Carl Van Vechten', in *Marketing Modernisms: Self-Promotion, Canonization, and Rereading*, ed. by Kevin J. H. Dettmar and Stephen Watt (Ann Arbor: University of Michigan Press, 1996), 221–52 (p. 239).
[20] Letter to Van Vechten, 14 August 1923, Box 16, Van Vechten Papers.
[21] '*The Blind Bow-Boy* Hits a Chrome Yellow Target', *New York World*, 19 August 1923, Van Vechten Papers.
[22] Van Vechten, letter to Walpole, *Letters*, p. 54.

'arched brow' modernism might be understood as a precursor to camp style
in the interest it shows in artifice, extravagance, irreverence, frivolity, play,
and transgression. Van Vechten has, in fact, been acknowledged by some
queer studies scholars as a pioneer of camp.[23] Though camp itself has long
been viewed as an apolitical aesthetic, recent theorizations have insisted on its
disruptive status as an aesthetics of social critique. Moe Meyer, for example,
defines Camp (capitalization his) as 'the total body of performative practices
and strategies used to enact a queer identity, with enactment defined as the
production of social visibility'.[24] Van Vechten may not have been explicit in his
treatment of queerness, but his work played an important role in developing a
language and strategies of communication for the expression of queer desire
and identity in this period. This achievement is attested to by letters from queer
readers in his papers at the New York Public Library, pressing Van Vechten with
questions as to his intentions and coyly revealing their identification with his
characters. Thus, while the novel was widely touted as a guide to fashionable
modern culture for sophisticates, it was also, clearly, as much a guide for
non-heterosexual men and women seeking articulations of their feelings,
experiences, and desires.

A Novel of the New Decadence

Another key feature of Van Vechten's writing is its indebtedness to British and
French decadent literature of the *fin de siècle* by Oscar Wilde, Max Beerbohm,
J.-K. Huysmans, and others. This appropriation of decadence is integral to
his 'arched brow' resistance to other forms of high modernism. At the same
time, it can be said to feed into his development of a language of queer desire,
precisely because Wilde and his decadent style were touchstones for queer
identity in this period. At a time when modernists ranging from Ezra Pound
to Ernest Hemingway were promoting concision and 'hardness', Van Vechten
cultivated excess through the hallmarks of decadence: a jewelled style; an
emphasis on ornament and artifice; a penchant for lists and cataloguing;
an interest in outré subject matter; and high wit and a deft, satirical touch.
Literary histories of modernism have tended to overlook the influence of 1890s
decadence on modernism, privileging the 'make it new' mantra of Pound
and his ilk who professed an antipathy towards the antecedent movement.
The interest in decadence, however, was strong at this time and had cultural
cachet. Van Vechten, meanwhile, was by no means its only proponent. Others

---

[23]   See, for example, Fabio Cleto, 'Queering the Camp', in *Camp: Queer Aesthetics and
the Performing Subject*, ed. by Cleto (Edinburgh: Edinburgh University Press, 1999), 1–42
(p. 9).
[24]   'Introduction: Reclaiming the Discourse of Camp', in *The Politics and Poetics of Camp*,
ed. by Meyer (London: Routledge, 1994), 1–22 (p. 5).

included James Gibbons Huneker, James Branch Cabell, Joseph Hergesheimer, Edgar Saltus, Ben Hecht, Henry Blake Fuller, Ronald Firbank, Aldous Huxley, and Michael Arlen, writers who were described variously as the 'exquisites', 'the sophisticated school', and the 'new decadents'.[25] This new decadence was deplored by high modernist purists such as Wyndham Lewis, who railed against such writers as 'that fearful, sophisticated ninetyish mob'.[26] As Van Vechten's fame grew, he would be regarded as a leader of new decadence, his name invoked in reviews of other authors as a shorthand for the style, as in the following descriptors: Van Vechtenites, the Van Vechten school, the Van Vechten manner, and disciple of Van Vechten.[27]

While *The Blind Bow-Boy* is less explicitly steeped in 1890s decadence than *Peter Whiffle*, it nevertheless bears hallmarks of the aesthetic. Significantly, it owes a debt to Wilde's *Picture of Dorian Gray* on a number of levels. First, it concerns the corruption of an innocent youth, with Harold as the Dorian Gray figure and Paul, Campaspe, and the Duke serving as reflections of Lord Henry. Second, it offers elaborate descriptions of furnishings, decoration, dress, and cultural tastes as a means of delineating character. Third, this preoccupation with material possessions results in a narrative interrupted by compulsive cataloguing, a feature not only of Wilde's work, but also of that of Huysmans and other decadents. Van Vechten, too, employs an epigrammatic style derived from Wilde and Beerbohm.

This decadence was widely noted in American and British reviews of the novel. Burton Rascoe, for example, characterized its genesis as

> by Robert Hichens's 'The Green Carnation' out of J. K. Huysmans's 'A Rebours'. It is Dorian Gray and Des Esseintes cracking jokes at their own expense. It is a better written book than 'The Green Carnation' and it is quite innocent of that book's high moral purpose of satirical intent. And though it does not precisely epitomize the modernity — the decadence — of 1923 as 'A Rebours' epitomized the modernity — the decadence — of 1889 (for Mr Van Vechten has not Huysmans's critical flair and catholicity), it does aim to designate that which, for the moment, is chic, and to point out just wherein that quality is to be found between the too, too and the not quite.[28]

---

[25]   The term 'exquisites' is Alfred Kazin's, from *On Native Grounds: An Interpretation of Modern American Prose Literature* (New York: Harcourt Brace, 1942; Boston, MA: Houghton Mifflin, 1995). 'Sophisticated school' is a term used widely in the 1920s as, for example, in Wyndham Lewis's attack on popular writers, 'The Blessings of the Sophisticated School of Literature', *The Enemy* 2 (1927), pp. 111–12. Decadent was a term frequently bandied about to describe writers like Van Vechten, while the more specific term 'new decadence' appeared in a British review of *Peter Whiffle*, 'An American Decadent', *Observer* (London), 25 March 1923, p. 4.

[26]   Wyndham Lewis, 'Blessings', p. 111.

[27]   Van Vechten's scrapbooks are an excellent resource for gauging his influence for they contain reviews not only of his work, but of that of authors who are deemed to be like him.

[28]   Review of *Blind Bow-Boy*.

British reviews were more likely to regard the book as derivative for employing this style, as did the following from the *London Daily News*: 'The style is brilliant and vivacious, but the cataloguing of names and precious objects went out in this country with Wilde. Its tone, too, will appear to a reader in this country as very old-fashioned, for shocking as a fine art all happened in the eighteen-nineties'.[29] For Americans, however, there was a decided newness to this new decadence. Edmund Wilson, for example, recognized Van Vechten's innovations. His decadence, Wilson says, lacks the 'conviction of sin' that characterized the work of his 1890s counterparts and he makes the 'corrupt [...] amiable.'[30] Van Vechten's fiction, then, was less an exercise in nostalgia than an adaptation for the new decadent moment of the Jazz Age. As I have indicated above, however, this aesthetic was of interest beyond Van Vechten alone, such that reviewer Stanley Babb would describe *The Blind Bow-Boy* as a composite of writings of 1890s and 1920s decadent writers:

> It seems to be the sort of thing that James Branch Cabell, in collaboration with the late James Gibbon [*sic*] Huneker, Anatole France, George Moore, Max Beerbohm, Arthur Schnitzler, Aldous Huxley, and Ronald Firbank, could turn out — if such an odd collaboration can be imagined. It seems to be a piquant pasticcio reminiscent of such books as 'Jurgen', 'Zuleika Dobson', 'Crome Yellow', 'Reigen', 'Valmouth', 'Painted Veils', and 'Under the Hill' [Aubrey Beardsley].[31]

These reviews suggest, then, that the novel merits comparative analysis not only with the works of 1890s British and French decadence from which it derives, but also with contemporaneous instances of new decadence. Like *The Blind Bow-Boy*, many of these works have lapsed into obscurity but, in recuperating and re-examining them, there is much to learn about the wider field of modernist literary production than our current canon allows for.

A 'Realistic' Novel of New York?

One of the curious aspects about the reception of *The Blind Bow-Boy*, both in critical reviews and in feedback Van Vechten received from friends, was the degree to which some insisted on the 'realistic' nature of this seemingly fantastical tale. Realism in literature, of course, is always tricky to define but, in this period, was applied especially to psychological realism and experimentations in the representation of consciousness. That Van Vechten was resistant to such realism was precisely what appealed to Sinclair Lewis in his

---

[29]   [Anon.], review of *Blind Bow-Boy, London Daily News*, 29 November 1923.
[30]   'Late Violets from the Nineties', p. 390.
[31]   Review of *Blind Bow-Boy, Galveston News*, 23 September 1923, Scrapbook 13, Van Vechten Papers.

praise of the novel. Not all shared Lewis's view, however, and it is worthwhile considering more closely how and why one might posit Van Vechten's novel as realistic. One important aspect of Van Vechten's realism — in both literal and symbolic terms — might be said to exist in his representation of New York in 1922. Such was Ernest Boyd's view when he declared *The Blind Bow-Boy* 'the great realistic novel of contemporary New York life' and likened Van Vechten to the famed nineteenth-century realist Émile Zola: 'He does not accumulate detail like Zola, yet one turns from *The Blind Bow-Boy* with as definite an impression of New York in 1922 as one gets of Paris under the Second Empire from the endless tomes of the Rougon-Macquart series'.[32] Certainly, Van Vechten's realism is not Zola's. His characters are fantastical, though they are situated in a New York that would have been recognisable to a contemporary New Yorker of a particular class and type. He achieves this familiarity through an attention to realistic detail that Boyd intuits, but does not quite pinpoint; for though Van Vechten does not 'accumulate detail like Zola', the novel, nevertheless, provides a remarkable documentation of New York social and cultural life in the early part of the twentieth century and, more especially, in the years just preceding and through 1922. Van Vechten's highly allusive and cataloguing style is not only an aspect of his decadence, but is also a means through which he achieves a kind of documentary realism, with references situating the novel firmly in its time and place. As the annotations to this edition attest, the novel is a storehouse of knowledge regarding contemporary, fashionable, and popular culture, ranging across authors, artists, musicians, fashion designers, department stores, boutiques, home decoration and interior design, New York neighbourhoods and real estate, and so on. So set is it in its moment, that when characters refer to news items, these are almost always directly traceable to newspapers and magazines of the day.

This evocation of New York is realistic, too, in symbolic terms. For Edward Leuders, New York is so strikingly represented by Van Vechten that it often emerges as 'one of the most remarkable characters in his books, sometimes separate as a physical entity, more often present as a state of mind and spirit'.[33] Van Vechten himself was entranced by the city and its infinite variety, and was eager, as he said in his essay 'La Tigresse', to 'correlate [his] impressions [of the city], force them into a common note, adapt them to the form of a fictional symphony'.[34] His work represents an important contribution to the mythologisation of New York, giving truth to Wilde's central paradox that life imitates art more than art imitates life.[35] Along these lines, for example,

---

[32] Boyd, 'Van Vechten's New York', p. 244.
[33] *Carl Van Vechten and the Twenties* (Albuquerque: University of New Mexico Press, 1955), p. 127.
[34] Van Vechten, *In the Garret* (New York: Knopf, 1920), p. 269.
[35] This is the central argument of Wilde's 1889 essay, 'The Decay of Lying'.

Alice B. Toklas declared Van Vechten one of the 'creators of modern New York'.[36] *The Blind Bow-Boy* was key to this creation. In the decade in which New York would assume its position as *the* iconic modern city, the novel, as Sinclair Lewis insisted, was proof 'that New York is as sophisticated as any foreign capital'.[37] F. Scott Fitzgerald, meanwhile, who has achieved far greater fame for his depictions of Jazz-Age New York and its flappers, gave credit to Van Vechten for his skilful symbolic melding of the iconic modern woman of the period and the city: 'In Campaspe', he enthused, 'you suggest so much more than you say — she is the embodiment of New York, mysterious and delecate [*sic*] and entirely original'.[38] *The Blind Bow-Boy*'s realistic portrayal of New York has literal and symbolic aspects, then, and is both ephemeral and eternal. On the one hand, the documentary realism of its cultural references and allusions made the novel ephemeral, causing Rascoe, for example, to suggest that its up-to-dateness risked it being 'outmoded tomorrow'[39] — in danger of becoming part of the list the Duke of Middlebottom rattles off in chapter seven of things that a year or two ago were 'modern' but now are 'old-fashioned' (p. 74). On the other hand, its eternal quality lies in its recognizable manifestation of a New York Jazz-Age zeitgeist, part of the imagined reality of the defining mood of the era that we recognise through our knowledge of other, more famous, texts.

It is time now to get into this mood and to make acquaintance with *The Blind Bow-Boy*. So dress yourself in white flannels or an Erté gown; spritz yourself with Bichara's Ambre or Guerlain's L'Heure Bleue; grab yourself a Bacardi cocktail in a Venetian glass goblet, or a gin and ginger beer in a Jacobite ale-glass; put some Gershwin or Berlin or Stravinsky on the phonograph; and settle down to enjoy this 'literary cocktail, compounded of wit, fun and cynicism [...] "shaken" by a competent master of the titillating art'.[40] Welcome to Van Vechten's 'Splendid, Drunken Twenties'.

---

36 From a 1951 letter to Van Vechten, quoted in Lueders, *Carl Van Vechten* (New York: Twayne Publishers, 1965), p. 127.
37 Letter to Van Vechten, 27 September 1923, Box 16, Van Vechten Papers.
38 Letter to Van Vechten, Fall 1925, in *The Letters of F. Scott Fitzgerald*, ed. by Andrew Turnbull (London: Penguin, 1982), p. 506.
39 Review of *Blind Bow-Boy*.
40 [Anon.], review of *Blind Bow-Boy*, *Daily Chronicle*, 1 November 1923, Scrapbook 13, Van Vechten Papers.

NOTE ON THE TEXT AND
ACKNOWLEDGEMENTS

Van Vechten began *The Blind Bow-Boy* in May 1922, completing a first draft, entitled 'Daniel Matthew's Tutor', on 8 June. He completed a second draft on 6 August, with its new and final title, and a third draft on 28 October. This pattern was typical for Van Vechten, who wrote with ease and who always produced three drafts, with further changes made on galleys. An attempt at a pre-publication serialization with *Harper's Bazar* (title changed to *Harper's Bazaar* in 1929), a popular sophisticated magazine of the period, failed on the grounds that it was 'not a serial for a general magazine, even one of the character of *Harper's*'.[1]

The novel was published on 15 August 1923 by Alfred A. Knopf, and was dedicated to 'my publisher and my friend'. Profiting from the interest in, and continuing sales of, his first novel, *Peter Whiffle*, *The Blind Bow-Boy* achieved advance sales of about 10,000 copies, running through four printings by publication date.[2] Total sales were 14,000 by October and there was a fifth printing that year, a sixth in 1924, and a seventh in 1927. The price was $2.50. Published simultaneously with the first edition was a signed limited edition (tall paper edition) of 130 copies at $10. Due to its popularity, the novel was also issued in cheap format as a Borzoi Pocket Book in 1925 (3000 copies) and 1926 (1976 copies), priced at $1.00. The novel was issued in a trade edition in Britain in October 1923 (print run unknown) at a price of 7/6, and as a Borzoi Pocket Book in 1928 (print run unknown), priced 3/6. The British version was expurgated, and deleted passages are noted in this edition in the annotations. The novel was subsequently out of print until AMS Press issued a reprint in 1982, priced at $24.50, after which the novel again fell out of print.

Knopf was famed for the beautiful design of his books and Van Vechten was always involved in this aspect of his publications. The first printing of the trade edition featured paper boards with a red, green, and white design by British artist Fraser Lovat. When this paper ran out, Van Vechten chose another decorated paper, in different colour schemes, such that there were at least five colour variations in the first and second printings. The third printing featured

---

[1]   Henry Sell, Letter to Carl Van Vechten, 18 September 1922, Box 16, Van Vechten Papers.
[2]   Further bibliographic information is available in Bruce Kellner, *A Bibliography of the Work of Carl Van Vechten* (Westport, CT: Greenwood Press, 1980).

blue and magenta boards, while subsequent trade editions were issued in green cloth boards. These editions all featured a dust jacket with decoration by Robert E. Locher, designed in consultation with the author, which also served as the frontispiece. The image corresponds to the description of Campaspe's garden in the novel. It features a fountain dominated by the titular blind bow-boy, Eros or Cupid, kneeling, with a nymph prostrate in front of him. In the left foreground is Campaspe's tortoise, Aglaë, eating a butterfly. The Borzoi Pocket Book edition and British editions would feature different book designs and dustjacket illustrations.[3]

The novel inspired some notable artistic responses: first, a parody by Samuel Hoffenstein, *The Tow-Headed Blind Boy*, which served as his review of the novel in the *New York Tribune* and was also issued as a privately circulated pamphlet; second, a series of visual realizations of the novel's characters in the manner of Aubrey Beardsley by Alastair (pseudonym of Hans Henning Voight) in his book *Fifty Drawings* (New York: Knopf, 1925), which included an introduction by Van Vechten.

This edition is based on the first edition, first printing of the novel, with some corrections. It adopts one correction made by Van Vechten for the fourth printing, changing 'blue stars' to 'gold stars' (p. 72) and corrects the following glaring errors, changing Dopo to Doppo (p. 55); Pysche to Psyche (p. 58); beseiged to besieged (p. 62); Sacré Cœur to Sacré-Cœur (p. 94); Pathé to Pathe (p. 123); al-always to always (p. 127); al-already to already (p. 136); legs, to legs. (p. 139); cupids to Cupids (p. 141, first instance); br-eaks to breaks (p. 144, second instance); and Dalzant to Delzant (p. 152). Otherwise, the edition retains Van Vechten's idiosyncratic spelling, capitalization, and punctuation; his lack of quotation marks for dialogue; and his lack of formatting for titles of artistic and literary works and foreign languages. Paragraph indentation and other formatting is also retained as in the original.

This edition of *The Blind Bow-Boy* is issued with the permission of the Van Vechten Trust. I am grateful also to the Van Vechten Trust and the New York Public Library for permission to print selections from materials in the Carl Van Vechten Papers, Manuscripts and Archives Division, New York Public Library. Research for this edition has been supported through a Social Sciences and Humanities Research Council of Canada standard research grant and through a fellowship with the Eccles Centre for American Studies.

---

[3]   See Kellner, *Bibliography*, for details.

SELECT BIBLIOGRAPHY

The bulk of scholarship on Van Vechten concerns his relationship to African-American literature and culture, with considerable attention given to his novel *Nigger Heaven* and to his photographs of African Americans. I have omitted this material here to foreground the modernist contexts more relevant to *The Blind Bow-Boy* and Van Vechten's early novels. As there is scant scholarship on this early work, only some of the secondary sources reference *The Blind Bow-Boy*, providing, instead, resources for situating the novel in its broader literary and cultural contexts.

Concerning Primary Sources

Van Vechten's archives relating to his writing career are held in the Carl Van Vechten Papers, Manuscripts and Archives Division, New York Public Library. The Berg Collection at the New York Public Library and the Beinecke Library contain significant holdings of his correspondence with fellow artists. The Beinecke is home also to the James Weldon Johnson Collection established by Van Vechten for African-American writers and artists and to a scrapbook collection documenting his sexual interest in men and his delight in visual and word play. A transcript of an interview with Van Vechten in 1960 is held at the Columbia Center for Oral History. Numerous other institutions across North America hold collections established by Van Vechten, many of them photograph collections.

Bibliographies

CUNNINGHAM, SCOTT, *A Bibliography of the Writings of Carl Van Vechten* (Philadelphia: Centaur Book Shop, 1924)

JONAS, KLAUS W., *Carl Van Vechten: A Bibliography* (New York: Knopf, 1955)

KELLNER, BRUCE, *A Bibliography of the Work of Carl Van Vechten* (Westport: Greenwood Press, 1980)

Select Published Works by Carl Van Vechten
Essays and Essay Collections

VAN VECHTEN, CARL, *Caruso's Moustache Off: And Other Writings About Music and Musicians*, ed. by Bruce Kellner (New York: Mondial, 2010)

—— *The Dance Writings of Carl Van Vechten*, ed. by Paul Padgett (New York: Dance Horizons, 1974)

—— *Excavations* (New York: Knopf, 1926)
—— 'How I Remember Joseph Hergesheimer', *Yale University Library Gazette*, 22, 3 (1948), 87–93
—— *Interpreters and Interpretations* (New York: Knopf, 1917)
—— *In the Garret* (New York: Knopf, 1920)
—— *The Merry-Go-Round* (New York: Knopf, 1918)
—— *Music After the Great War and Other Studies* (New York: Schirmer, 1915)
—— *Music and Bad Manners* (New York: Knopf, 1916)

Novels

VAN VECHTEN, CARL, *The Blind Bow-Boy* (New York: Knopf, 1923)
—— *Firecrackers* (New York: Knopf, 1925; New York: Mondial, 2007)
—— *Nigger Heaven* (New York: Knopf, 1926; Champaign: University of Illinois Press, 2000)
—— *Parties* (New York: Knopf, 1930; Los Angeles: Sun and Moon Press, 2000)
—— *Peter Whiffle* (New York: Knopf, 1922)
—— *Spider Boy* (New York: Knopf, 1928)
—— *The Tattooed Countess* (New York: Knopf, 1924; Iowa City: University of Iowa Press, 1987)

Life and Letters

KELLNER, BRUCE, *Carl Van Vechten and the Irreverent Decades* (Norman: University of Oklahoma Press, 1968)
STEIN, GERTRUDE and CARL VAN VECHTEN, *The Letters of Gertrude Stein and Carl Van Vechten*, ed. by Edward Burns, 2 vols (New York: Columbia University Press, 1986; 2013)
VAN VECHTEN, CARL, *Fragments from an Unwritten Autobiography*, 2 vols (New Haven: Yale University Press, 1955)
—— *Letters of Carl Van Vechten*, ed. by Bruce Kellner (New Haven: Yale University Press, 1987)
—— *The Splendid Drunken Twenties: Selections from the Daybooks, 1922–1930*, ed. by Bruce Kellner (Urbana: University of Illinois Press, 2003)
WHITE, EDWARD, *The Tastemaker: Carl Van Vechten and the Birth of Modern America* (New York: Farrar, Strauss and Giroux, 2014)

Select Reviews of The Blind Bow-Boy

[Anon.], review of *Blind Bow-Boy*, *Daily Chronicle*, 1 November 1923
—— review of *Blind Bow-Boy*, *London Daily News*, 29 November 1923
—— review of *Blind Bow-Boy*, *New York Times*, 26 August 1923, p. 17
—— review of *Blind Bow-Boy*, *Spectator*, 23 February 1924, p. 24
—— review of *Blind Bow-Boy*, *Vogue*, 15 October 1923
BABB, STANLEY E., review of *Blind Bow-Boy*, *Galveston News*, 23 September 1923
BOURGEOIS, MAURICE, ' "L'Archer aveugle", ou l'amour à New York', *Figaro* (Paris), 25 January 1924, p. 4
BOYD, ERNEST, 'Van Vechten's New York', *Nation*, 5 September 1923, pp. 244–45
BROUN, HEYWOOD, '*The Blind Bow-Boy* Hits a Chrome Yellow Target', *New York World*, 19 August 1923

CURTIS, WILLIAM, 'Some Recent Books', *Town and Country*, 15 October 1923

FLANNER, JANET, review of *Blind Bow-Boy*, *New Republic*, 31 October 1923, pp. 259–60

GOULD, GERALD, 'New Fiction', *Saturday Review* (London), 17 October, p. 474

HANSEN, HARRY, 'The Disillusioned Romantics', *Chicago Daily News*, 18 August 1923

HOFFENSTEIN, SAMUEL, 'Book News and Reviews', *New York Tribune*, 2 September 1923. Reprinted as 'The Tow-Headed Blind Boy or, the Blind Bow-Boy's Step-Brother' (Cedar Rapids: Privately Printed, 1923)

JOHNSON, NUNNALLY, 'Speaking of Books', *Brooklyn Daily Eagle*, 18 August 1923, p. 3

LIVERIGHT, HORACE B., 'Carl Van Vechten's *The Blind Bow-Boy*, a Clever Brilliant and Amusing Story', *Philadelphia Public Ledger*, 18 August 1923

MENCKEN, H. L., 'Three Gay Stories', *American Mercury*, March 1924, pp. 380–81

RASCOE, BURTON, review of *Blind Bow-Boy*, *New York Tribune*, 26 August 1923

ROSE, L. STUART, 'Petronius in New York', *Brentano's Book Chat*, 2, 5 (Fall 1923)

STAGG, HUNTER, review of *Blind Bow-Boy*, *Reviewer*, October 1923, pp. 58–60

STALLINGS, LAWRENCE, review of *Blind Bow-Boy*, in *New York World*, 15 August 1923

VAN DOREN, CARL, 'Century Survey of Current Books', *Century*, October 1923

WILSON, EDMUND, 'Late Violets from the Nineties', *Dial*, 75 (October 1923), 387–90

Secondary Sources

ALASTAIR [HANS HENNING VOIGHT], *Fifty Drawings by Alastair*, introduction by Carl Van Vechten (New York: Knopf, 1925)

BLACKMER, CORINNE E., 'Selling Taboo Subjects: The Literary Commerce of Gertrude Stein and Carl Van Vechten', in *Marketing Modernisms: Self-Promotion, Canonization, and Rereading*, ed. by Kevin J. H. Dettmar and Stephen Watt (Ann Arbor: University of Michigan Press, 1996), pp. 221–52

BRONSKI, MICHAEL, *A Queer History of the United States* (Boston, MA: Beacon Press, 2011)

CHAUNCEY, GEORGE, *Gay New York: Gender, Urban Culture and the Making of the Gay Male World, 1890–1940* (New York: Basic Books, 1994)

CLARK, EMILY, *Innocence Abroad* (New York: Knopf, 1931)

CLEATON, IRENE and ALLEN, *Books and Battles of the Twenties: American Literature 1920–1930* (Boston: Houghton Mifflin, 1937)

CRUNDEN, ROBERT, *American Salons: Encounters with European Modernism, 1885–1917* (Oxford: Oxford University Press, 1993)

—— *Body and Soul: The Making of American Modernism* (New York: Basic Books, 2000)

DOUGLAS, ANN, *Terrible Honesty: Mongrel Manhattan in the 1920s* (New York: Farrar, Strauss and Giroux, 1995)

HAMMILL, FAYE, *Sophistication: A Literary and Cultural History* (Liverpool: Liverpool University Press, 2010)

KAZIN, ALFRED, *On Native Grounds: An Interpretation of Modern American Literature* (New York: Harcourt Brace, 1942; Boston: Houghton Mifflin, 1995)

LUEDERS, EDWARD, *Carl Van Vechten* (New York: Twayne Publishers, 1965)

——*Carl Van Vechten and the Twenties* (Albuquerque: University of New Mexico Press, 1955)

MACLEOD, KIRSTEN, 'Making It New, Old School: Carl Van Vechten and Decadent Modernism', *Symbiosis: A Journal of Anglo-American Literary Relations* 16 (2012), 209–24

MCCOY, BETH, 'Inspectin' and Collecting: The Scene of Carl Van Vechten', *Genders* 28 (1998), <https://www.colorado.edu/gendersarchive1998-2013/1998/08/01/inspectin-and-collecting-scene-carl-van-vechten> [accessed 15 January 2018]

MURRAY, ALEX, 'Venice, "sans hope": Reading Decadent New York', in *Landscapes of Decadence: Literature and Place at the fin de siècle*, by Alex Murray (Cambridge: Cambridge University Press 2016), pp. 157–90

OJA, CAROL, *Making Music Modern: New York in the 1920s* (Oxford: Oxford University Press, 2000)

PIZER, DONALD, 'The Novels of Carl Van Vechten and the Spirit of the Age', in *Toward a New American Literary History: Essays in Honor of Arlin Turner*, ed. by Louis J. Budd, Edwin H. Cady, and Carl L. Anderson (Durham: Duke University Press, 1980), pp. 211–29

SCOTT, WILLIAM B. and PETER M. RUTKOFF, *New York Modern: The Arts and the City* (Baltimore: Johns Hopkins University Press, 2001)

SEED, DAVID, 'Party-Going: The Jazz Age Novels of Evelyn Waugh, Wyndham Lewis, F. Scott Fitzgerald and Carl Van Vechten', in *Forked Tongues: Comparing Twentieth-Century British and American Literature*, ed. by Ann Massa and Alistair Stead (London: Longman, 1994), pp. 117–34

SELDES, GILBERT, *The Seven Lively Arts* (New York: Harper and Brothers, 1924; New York: Dover Publications, 2001)

SINCLAIR, UPTON, *Money Writes* (New York: Albert and Charles Boni, 1927)

STANSELL, CHRISTINE, *American Moderns: Bohemian New York and the Creation of a New Century* (Princeton: Princeton University Press, 2000; 2009)

WEINBERG, JONATHAN, '"Boy Crazy": Carl Van Vechten's Queer Collection', *Yale Journal of Criticism*, 7, 2 (1994), 25–49

WILSON, EDMUND, *The Shores of Light: A Literary Chronicle of the Twenties and Thirties* (New York: Farrar, Strauss, and Young, 1952)

WOODS, GREGORY, *Homintern: How Gay Culture Liberated the Modern World* (New Haven: Yale University Press, 2016)

The Blind Bow-Boy

La vie est un jour de Mi-Carême.
Quelques-uns se masquent; moi je ris.
CATULLE MENDÈS*

---

*   French for 'Life is like a Mid-Lent festival day. Some mask themselves; I laugh'. From *Le roi vierge* (*The Virgin King*), an 1881 *roman-à-clef* by French decadent Mendès (1841–1909) about the homoerotic relationship between King Ludwig of Bavaria and the musician Richard Wagner. These lines, spoken by a courtier, the Comtesse de Soinoff, represent her world view. *Mi-Carême* (Mid-Lent) is a French Catholic tradition dating to the Middle Ages that punctuates the austere Lent period with a day of carnivalesque indulgence.

Chapter I

Harold Prewett sat in the broad, black-walnut seat of an ambiguous piece of furniture which branched above, in spreading antlers, into a rack for coats and hats and which below, at either side, provided means for the disposition of canes and umbrellas. The mere presence of these heavy, sullen antlers was sufficiently dispiriting to increase the gloomy atmosphere which environed the young man. The room in which he sat waiting was a hallway. Through a vestibule one entered it from the street, and it served its purpose as the main artery through which the life of the house flowed, by offering entrances and exits to the other rooms on that floor and, by way of a staircase, carpeted in turkey-red and guarded by black-walnut banisters, it led to regions above. There was a high wainscot of the oppressive black-walnut, and the wall from the wainscot to the solid panelled ceiling was covered with a thick embossed paper, bronze in colour, embellished with a grandiose and florid, semi-heraldic pattern. The vestibule door and the door into the street beyond were both open and the warm June light filtered through and somewhat dispelled the moroseness of the 1875 grandeur of the place. On the first landing of the staircase, midway between the two floors, a stained-glass window, of purple and blue and green diamond panes, permitted a little more light to enter. Underneath this window the great pendulum of a high hall-clock swung slowly back and forth, marking the sluggish passage of time with its sharp, tiresome ticks.

Harold Prewett was an attractive young man, with chestnut-coloured hair, brown eyes, a healthy complexion, and a fairly competent build. He looked well in his clothes, a double-breasted brown suit, which any sophisticated person could have told you came from a Fifth Avenue tailor,[1] and the modest shade of his cravat indicated a conservative taste in tinges. The young man had recently graduated from college, but there was nothing in his demeanour to suggest excessive confidence on this account. He fidgeted a good deal; he mumbled to himself, evidently rehearsing words and phrases of which he hoped presently to deliver himself in the presence of an audience. He twirled his straw hat nervously between his fingers and, occasionally, he stood up and walked about, but, after a moment or two of this restless marching, he invariably returned to his seat in the hat-rack under the spreading antlers.

The cause of his perturbation was somewhat grotesque. He had been summoned to a conference with his father. Now, most boys, in good health, well-

---

[1] In the 1920s, as now, Fifth Avenue at mid-town was an exclusive shopping area.

dressed, with no special crimes on their consciences, would be able to face even the most irascible of parents without any great amount of diffidence. The facts in this case, however, were decidedly peculiar. Father and son had yet to meet for the first time. The reasons governing the postponement of this encounter were not unknown to a few of George Prewett's friends, but Harold himself was entirely uninitiated in regard to them. Before going away to college he had lived with an aunt in Connecticut. He had always been provided with plenty of pocket-money and, on rare occasions, he had received instructions on minor points of conduct from his father's legal adviser. During his college years his vacations had invariably been spent at the home of his aunt, who, under orders, probably, never mentioned his father's name, although she was his sister. He had not, indeed, been entirely certain that his father was alive until, on the day that he graduated, he had received a telegraphic summons from the lawyer, bidding him to come to his father's house on West Eighty-second Street in New York.[2] His father, at last, desired to see him.

Now the nature of this unnatural father's plans in his behalf held sinister terrors for Harold. This aloof parent, having footed the bills unquestioningly for twenty-one years, might conceivably have it in mind to take advantage of this fact to make unpleasant conditions in regard to the future. He might wish his son to become a bond salesman or to embark in the cloak and suit business.[3] Harold was a little dubious about the future. He seemed to lack strong desires, but he was conscious of a few strong aversions. The cloak and suit business was one of these, for a reason hereinafter to be noted.

Moodily occupied with such morbid meditations, Harold had been sitting in the hat-rack for ten or fifteen minutes. He sat there for another five before the approach of the man who had met him at the door announced to him that his suspense was presently to be relieved in however unpleasant a manner.

The man spoke: Mr. Prewett will see you now, sir.

The man led the way, Harold following closely at his heels, up the red-carpeted staircase, along the upper hallway to the very front, where he knocked on a closed door. There was a moment of hesitation before a brusque Come in! concluded all this preliminary ceremony. Harold's heart was beating very fast; he was entirely unaware of the opening and closing of the door, the departure of the servant, and his own eventual shuffling to the centre of the room. When he had recovered himself sufficiently to look about, he noted that he seemed to be standing in a vast library. A man, who was, he assumed, his father, sat facing him, bent over a desk, apparently intent on the perusal of a quantity of papers.

---

[2]   Mr Prewett's house is in the Upper West Side of Manhattan, one of the last areas developed during the city's expansion in the nineteenth century. It was a luxury residential area from the mid-1880s, known for varied architectural styles, including High Victorian Gothic and Jacobean, both of which correspond to the decor described.
[3]   Business involving the manufacturing and/or selling of clothing.

Harold became a trifle calmer as he began to realize that the man at the desk was almost certainly as much perturbed and embarrassed as he himself had been. Presently, after a few more seconds of silence, during which the boy stood perfectly still, the elder man (a much older man than Harold had expected to see) rose and leaned over the desk to shake hands with his son.

How do you do? were his first words and his voice sounded suspiciously choked.

Harold echoed this polite cliché.

George Prewett pointed to a chair and then, seemingly entirely overcome by the meeting, by the first words, and by his thoughts of past and future, sank back into his seat and again appeared to busy himself with the pile of papers on his desk.

Completely confident by now that his father was certainly more terrified than he had been at any stage of this strange game, Harold grew steadily cooler. He stared at the rows of books in shelves against the walls, at the steel-engravings above the shelves, at the curtained alcoves framing the windows, and then he ventured to look back at this eccentric figure who seemed to be ostentatiously pretending to be unaware of his presence, a stout, half-bald, rapidly aging man, who wore eye-glasses framed in tortoise-shell, and a suit of purple mohair.

This scene in the comedy was now abruptly terminated. The elder man spoke again.

Fond of athletics, I suppose? he queried, almost sharply, in a voice which was deep but not unpleasant in quality.

Not games so much, but I like to ride and swim, Harold answered.

No football or baseball?

No, I don't care much for those.

Good!

Following this exchange of information there was another brief silence.

Well, what do you want to do now?

I don't know, sir. Your lawyer informed me that I was to make no decisions regarding my future. He asked me to wait.

And you have strictly regarded this injunction? George Prewett seemed almost anxiously eager.

Naturally I have endeavoured to follow the instructions of one to whom I was indebted for my income. Also, quite naturally, I have at times speculated on my future. I must admit that certain occupations appear to me to be extremely distasteful.

Those are? The older man was gruff.

Harold paused and blushed. Then he spoke out: I have no wish, sir, to engage in the cloak and suit business.

It was the turn of George Prewett to blush, but beyond the obvious embarrassment which convulsed his features, it was possible to discern what seemed to be the evidence of a deep and abiding joy and relief.

You are my son! he cried. Embrace me.

He rose from his seat and Harold stood up to meet him. The older man grasped the younger man's shoulders. The son tried to encircle his father's waist. This constrained attempt at a display of affection seemed to exhaust them both, and, dropping their arms, they sank back into their chairs. The father was the first to rally.

You are my son! he repeated. My son! Your answers are music to my ears. You are saying exactly what I would have you say. Then, with an air of suspicion, You haven't been warned?

Warned? By whom? The young man sufficiently showed his bewilderment.

George Prewett was reassured. No, he said, Sanderson would never break my trust, betray my confidence. No more, I think, would my sister. It is fate, he cried, fate, which has given me the son I would have asked for, had I asked for a son at all, he wound up, musing on some hidden grief.

Then, with one of those quick transitions which marked his character, Have you had your lunch?

Why yes, father; it is nearly four o'clock.

So it is. So it is. I never know the time. I have been so occupied today that I have forgotten to eat, but the dinner hour is approaching and one meal a day is enough for any man. Well, I'm pleased with you, delighted would be a better word. Yes, I'm delighted with you.

Harold said nothing.

And now, I suppose that you wish to know about your future, so far as I have any concern with your future. Or would you rather, perhaps, learn something of your past?

It is for you to say, father. Tell me what you feel like telling me.

It is no easy task I have set myself. You may turn against me. You don't know me at all, and it is difficult to tell a boy what I have to tell you. But you must believe that I am pleased with you — he paused for a moment to wipe the moisture from his eye-glasses — or I would not be willing, or able, to tell you what I am about to tell you now.

I do believe it, father.

I am sure you do. You must know then — the hand of George Prewett shook and there were traces of emotion in his voice — that your mother was an extremely beautiful woman, and that she was the only person I have ever really loved. I was past forty when I married her, but she was a young girl at this period. A few months later I learned to my delight that, in the course of time, she would be delivered of a child. The plans I made for the life of that little girl, for it never occurred to me to consider the possibility that I might have a son, were prodigious. I will not take up your time, young sir, in describing them, but you can judge of my supreme disappointment when I learned that my wife had given birth to a boy. My grief and rage were merged in despair when I was informed by her physician that my beloved wife had but a few more hours to live.

At this point in his narrative, the elderly gentleman began to choke. He pounded the desk for a few seconds with an ivory paper-cutter before he resumed his story. Harold, meanwhile, sat perfectly quiet.

I was told that my wife was aware of her fatal condition and wished to see me for the last time before she died. Our meeting for this parting was the saddest moment of my life. I will not dwell upon it — he mopped his brow with his large white linen handkerchief — but upon its results. On her deathbed, my wife, who knew that under such conditions I would promise anything, exacted an oath from me. That oath concerns you. I swore before God over your mother's deathbed that you should have a college education.

But, sir! Harold now began plainly to exhibit his astonishment.

Do not interrupt me! his father resumed harshly. Hear me out. I have no intention of leaving anything unexplained. I have asked you to come here today solely for the purpose of explaining everything. Understand then, young man, that I myself am the victim of a college education. I went to college ... and learned nothing. I left the doors of the university without the slightest preparation for the life to come. Commencement! What an ironic word. It should he called bewilderment. I had studied Latin, Greek, and English prose. I was conversant with the principles of mathematics and chemistry, but I was utterly unfamiliar with life and how to live it. I had no specific talents. I was not an artist. I had no capacity for writing. I discovered, in fact, that, far from establishing any of the laws of existence, my education had completely unfitted me for any sort of intercourse with men. I had been much better off had I never seen a campus.

My people were not poor, but their means were moderate. I had brothers and sisters. The necessity of my making a living for myself was borne in upon me by my well-intentioned parents, who had thrown me in the way of forgetting how to make it. In the face of their hope that I would quickly choose some occupation or profession, I found myself completely helpless. I felt no calling for the ministry, the law, or medicine; nor had my education fitted me for any of these pursuits. My father, therefore, a physician in a small town, could give me no assistance. In my extremity I received a letter from one of my college mates, who had inherited from his father a modest but prosperous cloak and suit business. He, too, was bitterly despondent, and felt himself utterly incapable of undertaking the management of the firm. It had occurred to him, however, that together we might minimize the chances of failure. This opportunity to enter a stray edge of the business world was worse than anything that I had dreamed might happen, but I was forced to consider that no alternatives had presented themselves and that my father, who had generously provided me with what he thought was a good education, could not reasonably be expected to look longer after my welfare. I accepted, therefore, the offer of my friend and engaged in the pursuit of the cloak and suit business.

During this discourse, Harold's eyes dilated with horror, but, obeying his father's expressed command, he refrained from making any comment.

We made a great many mistakes in the beginning, as was but natural, Prewett senior continued, but one grows accustomed to anything, and it was not long before we found ourselves quite capable of running our plant in a satisfactory manner. Had it not been for my sister Sadie, however, the aunt who has brought you up, I doubt if I should have been in a position to marry or to liberally provide for your whims. My sister, who was our head designer, invented the famous Ninon de Lenclos[4] cloak, the sensation of the season of 1897. The fame of this garment swept the country. We sent a model to Mrs. Potter Palmer[5] and, after she had appeared in public in the cloak, its success was made. Our limited capacity proved insufficient to meet the flood of orders and we erected a larger plant. Since then the business has moved ahead triumphantly. Never, however, has this success seemed to me to be deserved; never has it interested me.

Had I not been educated in college, doubtless I should have slipped automatically into my proper niche. I might have been a brakeman on a railroad or a sailor before the mast, but at any rate there would have been some intention or meaning in my occupation. All that college did for me was to unfit me for decision. It unwilled me and threw me forward into the first opportunity that presented itself.

The gloom on the elderly gentleman's face was apparently ineffaceable.

Realizing, he went on after a moment's pause, that with the advent of a boy, my difficulties would be repeated in his life, I wished with all my heart that my dear wife would present me with a little girl. Through no fault of hers, she failed me. Immediately the news of your birth was brought to me, I began to conceive ways by which I might spare you the agony of my own experience. I will never send him to college, I promised myself, never. My wife, who was acquainted with my opinions on this subject, had always pooh-poohed my sentiments. Have you not been successful? she would ask. What more do you wish? You have made plenty of money and your college education has made it possible for you to enjoy the best books, to travel with pleasure, even to marry me. There was, beyond doubt, some logic in this reasoning, but it did not appeal to me. I could

---

4   French courtesan and author (1620–1705), renowned for her wit, beauty, and radical views.
5   Bertha Palmer (1849–1918), socialite, philanthropist, art collector, and businesswoman.

not dispel from my mind the memory of that horrible summer of perplexity and its obvious cause. All I could remember was that a college education had thrown me into the cloak and suit business, which was not, I felt certain, my predestined field. I determined to spare my son, if possible, a repetition of this experience. Aware of my intentions, my wife took advantage of my emotional weakness and made me promise, over her deathbed, that I would send you to college. I gave her the promise. She died, and I closed her eyes.

During the relation of this remarkable history George Prewett had several times permitted his gaze to wander about the room, but now he fastened his eyes securely on his son.

The fact that you were not a girl did not endear you in my eyes; the further fact that you had caused the death of your mother made it impossible for me to entertain the thought of seeing you. The reflection that she had christened you Harold made the alienation complete. I arranged at once for your care. You were brought up first by a wet-nurse, later by my sister, who, amply rewarded for her skill in designing the Ninon de Lenclos cloak, had retired to a life of peace in the country. I have kept my promise. You have been sent to college. And, latterly, I have grown less bitter. After all, it is not your fault that you are a boy, not your fault that you killed your mother, not your fault, even, that you were named Harold. I determined, therefore, to assume the usual paternal relationship towards you, and I began to consider ways and means by which I might possibly counteract the dangerous effects of your education. I believe I have hit upon a method.

There now fell a complete silence, and the young man gathered from the extended pause that his father would raise no further objections to his speaking.

Father, he began, when I told you that I had an aversion for the cloak and suit business I had no idea …

Of course, you hadn't! That's why your remarks delighted me so much. I was expecting opposition, he added, rather ambiguously.

Opposition! But, father, you have provided for me thus far and I understand very well, after what you have told me, how repugnant the idea of meeting me must have been to you. I can see no reason for opposing you, father, especially since you assure me that you have no desire for me to enter the cloak — your business.

Enter it! I would see you dead first! I would give the business away! However, we need not speak of that, since no such contingency has arisen. Our conversation has fortified and delighted me beyond measure. I am relieved to find you so tractable and I have the highest hopes for your future. It had been my original intention to spin this interview out over several meetings, two weeks or a month, perhaps, but it has been so simple to go thus far that I can see no reason for hesitating to go farther. I think I am completely justified in believing that I can make you acquainted with my plans for you at once.

I am waiting to hear them, father.

Know then that I have reasoned that you may be only prepared to struggle with life as it exists by a certain reversal of preparation. You have been prepared … for what? For nothing! But, perhaps, in spite of your present uncertainty, you are not entirely convinced of that fact. You must be convinced. You must see more of life and learn to live; you must learn to discount what you have been taught. In other words, you must learn to think for yourself, and become capable of *choosing* an occupation which will do you credit, which will be a reflection of your own personality and not of mine. I care not what this occupation may be, so long as it represents the results of experience and mature judgment. I have decided, therefore, to make somewhat of an experiment.

If this interview had not been the expected ordeal, at least it had held elements of surprise. This new turn again caused lines of amazement to collect about the young man's eyes.

I cannot, continued George Prewett, throw you out into the world to gain your own experience. You would be as helpless, in that case, as if you were asked at once to choose your future occupation. You have been unfitted for going out into the world. I have determined, therefore, to provide you with a tutor.

Am I to study longer, then?

Study is not the word. You are, as a matter of fact, to do exactly what you please. Your tutor will guide you, however, guide you carefully into the ways of life, and some of its byways. There may be hours for reflection and what you call study. He may conceivably suggest certain courses of reading. I have left him a more or less free hand in this respect, for the young man I have discovered is so uncannily like the ideal I set before myself that I think I am justified in permitting him almost unlimited discretion.

May I ask … ?

Certainly, certainly, I am coming to that. Harold's father betrayed a touch of impatience at this point. This young man is no old and valued friend. I secured him through an advertisement.

An advertisement!

An advertisement. I shall have no further secrets from you. Here it is. Mr. Prewett picked a clipping from the clutter on his desk and began to read:

Wanted: Young man of good character but no moral sense. Must know three languages and possess a sense of humour. Autodidact preferred, one whose experience has led him to whatever books he has read. It is absolutely essential that he should have been the central figure in some public scandal. Age, not above thirty. Right person will receive suitable emolument. Answer BCX.

Harold's stupefaction had merged into terror again; this time something very like panic had seized him.

And you found one … like that? he stammered.

A dozen. At least a dozen. Two hundred replied to my advertisement. With the aid of my very competent attorney, who has succeeded in baffling you in regard to your parentage for twenty-one years, I selected twenty-five of the most promising letters. The writers of these I interviewed personally. Twelve were singled out for future investigation. Many knew the languages and had at least a limited sense of humour, a few were lacking, I am quite certain, in a moral sense, but only one qualified completely as to the public scandal.

But I cannot imagine the advantage …

No more you can, of course. Your education has unfitted your mind for the reception of such ideas. I shall, therefore, make no effort to explain them to you. It will suffice, perhaps, if I inform you that I regard this young man as the apple of my eye. I have conversed with him on several occasions. He has been interrogated by my lawyer, who has made the most minute inquiries into his life. In every respect I find myself entirely satisfied in regard to his manner of living, his past and his present. He is a delightfully irresponsible and unmoral person and I place you in his care without any reservations whatever.

There were several points in these remarks that astounded the young man. He wished to ask many questions, but he judged from his father's expression that he had better limit himself to one, which was:

What is his name, father?

Paul Moody.

The man who went to Ludlow for refusing to pay his wife alimony?[6]

The same.

The papers were full of him a month or two ago!

They were. And now, I think it would be unwise to prolong this interview. You are not as yet prepared to fully comprehend its purport and further conversation might lead us into emotional relations which would be very unfortunate at the present stage of our acquaintanceship. I like you very well to begin with, and I might grow fond enough of you to quarrel with you. I have judged it best, therefore, that for the present we continue to live apart.

The young man opened his mouth to speak again.

Do not interrupt me. To live apart. George Prewett was staring hard at the ceiling. To this end, I have leased an apartment for you on East Eighteenth Street. Moody lives in Gramercy Park.[7] Here is your key. The address is on the

---

[6]   Ludlow Street Jail, nicknamed the New York Alimony Club and famous for housing alimony defaulters. Van Vechten spent time there for this crime in 1915.

[7]   Harold's apartment is located near Moody's Gramercy Park residence (a square situated between Twentieth and Twenty-First Street and Park and Third Avenue). In the early twentieth century, this neighbourhood was popular with artists and underwent gentrification. Rowhouses were transformed into fashionable homes for rich New Yorkers and newly built modern apartments attracted young professionals.

attached tag. You will find the apartment ready for occupancy, and there is a man there who will attend to your wants which, I hope, will not be modest. If you feel inclined to move about, to lease larger quarters, you are your own master. Sanderson will confer with you in regard to such matters, but I may assure you that your means are practically unlimited. Mr. Moody will doubtless inspire you, but when you have ideas of your own, you will discover that he will be only too ready to assist you to carry them out.

In the meantime, we shall resume our former status. A year from today you are to return to tell me what you have learned. Then, having established a proper foundation for mutual intercourse, it will be possible to begin to discuss your future. Thereafter, I have every hope that you will not only be a man of the world but an excellent companion for me as well. That is all. Good-bye, young man.

There was a certain sense of relief in these last words as if this interview had taxed his powers almost to the limits of his endurance.

Good-bye, father, echoed the bewildered Harold.

Chapter II

Harold had been brought up among the flutter of petticoats. That fact had established his character more conclusively than the subsequent college years, His aunt, born Prewett, had never married. Christened Sarah, she was soon dubbed Sadie; after a trip to Europe she herself had altered this to Sadi. The trip to Europe was responsible for other phenomena: one was the aforementioned Ninon de Lenclos cloak, which was a modification of a model she had observed at a famous Parisian couturière's; another was a passion for the method of Delsarte,[8] which, for a time, she had contemplated imparting to New York debutantes; a third was an obsession for the Anna Song from Nanon,[9] which had caught her fancy at a performance of the opera she had heard in Munich and which had held it to the present day. Nearly every morning, indeed, it was her custom to seat herself before her old rosewood square piano, with its thin metallic tone, and perform this waltz, somewhat woodenly, singing the words in her bedizened German and, latterly, in a voice which frequently cracked:

> Anna, zu Dir ist mein liebster Gang,
> > Mein liebster Gang,
> > Mein liebster Gang;
> Anna, Dir tönet mein bester Sang,
> > Mein bester Sang,
> > Mein bester Sang;
> Anna, Annettchen, welch' holder Klang,
> > Welch' holder Klang,
> > Welch' holder Klang;
> Anna, Dir sing' ich mein Lebelang!
> > Ja, mein Lebelang![10]

Long after her visit to Paris, Sadi had succumbed to one more foreign influence. Visiting a New York shop, she had seen a Fortuny gown,[11] one of

---

[8] François Alexandre Nicolas Chéri Delsarte (1811–1871) developed an influential system of movement and vocal expression. It was especially popular in America with upper- and middle-class feminists as part of a broader interest in social empowerment.

[9] Popular 1877 operetta (Richard Genée, libretto by F. Zell), set in Louis XIV's Paris and featuring historical figures Ninon de L'Enclos and the Marquise de Maintenon alongside the fictional innkeeper protagonist, Nanon. The 'Anna Song' is central to the plot, serving as a vehicle for men to woo the main female characters.

[10] Translates as: 'Anna, to thee my fond steps I wend, etc. etc. | Anna, to thee my best songs I send, etc. etc. | Anna, thy name shall ring, etc. etc. | Anna, as long as I live thy praise I will sing, etc.'

[11] Mariano Fortuny (1871–1949), Spanish fashion designer famed for colourful, intricately

those crinkly crêpe robes, knotted at the shoulders with cords of gold, hanging straight like a Mother Hubbard,[12] but belted at the waist with an ornate girdle. She had purchased this garment, and since that date she had never worn anything else. For ten years, two or three times a year, a box arrived with a new Fortuny gown; there had been red ones, blue ones, green ones, and brown ones, old gold and old rose, but the model was always exactly the same. Wearing one of these dresses, Sadi drove along the dusty roads in her surrey, as Louise de la Ramé, in white velvet costumes designed by Worth, had driven along the roads of Tuscany.[13]

Sadi was a large woman, with large bones, large hands, large feet, a large nose, and large eyes. She had a large mole on her throat under her large left ear. Her hair remained a deep, glossy black, and probably would so remain until the day of her death, unless she stopped sending to Buffalo for certain bottles. Every morning she curled it, parted it in the centre, and tied it in a knot at the back of her head.

She had no taste for the kind of New York social life which was open to her; she was too exclusive and eccentric a person for that. Her friends were few, and those few were all women. Consequently, after the success of the Ninon de Lenclos cloak, she had retired to one of those old Connecticut farmhouses, boarded with oiled but unpainted and now weather-beaten shingles. The rooms were all on different levels, and the ceilings were so low that, in the ascension and descension of the slight flights of stairs between the chambers, tall people, like Harold and Sadi, familiar though they were with the contours of the place, frequently bumped their heads. There were stone fireplaces in this house, wide enough to burn four-foot logs, and provided with ovens and cranes, and Sadi had scoured the surrounding country, attending auction sales and persuading indigent country-folk that they were tired of their chairs and tables, in order to furnish her home appropriately. Ever since Harold could remember, Persia Blaine, an old Negress, had been a constant servitor. Other servants, all women, had come and gone, but Persia was a fixture.

Sadi professed a love for children and she was not unkind to them, but it cannot be said that she understood them. She was apparently delighted when fate placed Harold in her hands. After he had learned to speak she lavished affection on him in her own way. She talked to him, as she imagined children

---

pleated gowns inspired by Greek classical styles. His designs defied the dominant corseted styles of the early twentieth century, enabling freer movement, and were popular with progressive, artistic, and bohemian women.

[12]   A long loose-fitting gown that women wore at home in the late nineteenth century.

[13]   Louise de la Ramé (1839–1908), pen name Ouida, a British novelist, noted for her extravagance, who lived much of her life in Tuscany. The Paris-based Worth was a leading fashion house popular with European aristocrats and celebrities from the mid-nineteenth to the early twentieth centuries.

should be talked to, very deliberately, and in words of one syllable, when she could think of them, but solemnly, and often in the third person. Good little boys, etc. Bad little boys, etc. Bad little boys, it seemed, played with neighbouring farmers' sons. Good little boys stayed at home. Sadi never kept a watch-dog: her mere appearance would have frightened a tramp away, but there were pigs and chickens, and Harold was permitted occasionally to visit the pens and scratch the old sow's back with a corn-cob or a stick. Sadi kept a hired man to look after the live stock, but he was never allowed to come into the house — his meals were all delivered to him in the barn where he lived — and Harold was instructed never to talk with him. This and similar prohibitions might have infuriated another boy, might have stimulated a taste for secret disobedience, but in the make-up of Harold's character there was no curiosity, and little initiative. Further, he was conspicuously lacking in imagination. He was proud, and like most unimaginative people, could be disagreeably obstinate. Auntie Persia, as he called her, was his favourite companion. She told him stories which she had heard as a child on a southern plantation, and she sang him old darkey folksongs. They had a game which they played with a song which began, Come on! It's Sat'day night![14] Auntie Persia, indeed, understood children....

Meanwhile, Sadi Prewett continued to live her life, which consisted in rising, dressing, eating a hearty country breakfast, playing the Anna Song from Nanon, eating lunch, taking her afternoon drive, taking her tea, eating dinner, sitting for an hour or so before the fire in the winter, or on the lawn in the summer, and then retiring. These habits were invariable. Other unimportant incidents might be added to her day, however. Sometimes, she read a little, almost always from two little books of poems by Mrs. Hemans and Adah Isaacs Menken.[15] The pale and fragile passion of Mrs. Hemans seemed very moving to her. Tears, indeed, consistently obscured her vision, as she read the lyric narrative of Gertrude von der Wart:

> And bid me not depart, she cried,
>   My Rudolph, say not so!
> This is no time to quit thy side;
>   Peace, peace, I cannot go.
> Hath the world aught for *me* to fear,
>   When death is on thy brow?
> The world! what means it — *mine* is *here* —
>   I will not leave thee now.[16]

---

[14]   Unidentified reference.

[15]   Felicia Hemans (1793–1835), popular British poet, famous also in America. She regularly adopts historical subjects, presenting, especially, the experiences of heroic women involved in male-dominated world events. Menken (1835–1868), actress and nineteenth-century celebrity, famous for her scandalous lifestyle. Much of the poetry in *Infelicia* (1868) is free verse characterized by emotionalism and sensationalism.

[16]   Second stanza of 'Gertrude, or Fidelity Till Death', from *Records of Woman: With Other*

In Miss Menken's Infelicia, she preferred the opening poem, Resurgam,[17] and it was a very easy matter to persuade her to declaim it aloud:

Yes, yes, dear love! I am dead!
  Dead to you!
  Dead to the world!
  Dead for ever!
It was one young night in May.
The stars were strangled, and the moon was blind with the flying clouds of a
    black despair.
Years and years the songless soul waited to drift out beyond the sea of pain
    where the shapeless life was wrecked.
The red mouth closed down the breath that was hard and fierce.
The mad pulse beat back the baffled life with a low sob.
And so the stark and naked soul unfolded its wings to the dimness of Death!
A lonely, unknown Death.
A Death that left this dumb living body as his endless mark.
And left these golden billows of hair to drown the whiteness of my bosom.
Left these crimson roses gleaming on my forehead to hide the dust of the
    grave.
And Death left an old light in my eyes, and old music for my tongue, to
    deceive the crawling worms that would seek my warm flesh.
But the purple wine that I quaff sends no thrill of Love and Song through my
    empty veins.
Yet my red lips are not pallid and horrified.
Thy kisses are doubtless sweet that throb out an eternal passion for me!
But I feel neither pleasure, passion nor pain.
So I am certainly dead.
  Dead in this beauty!
  Dead in this velvet and lace!
  Dead in these jewels of light!
  Dead in the music!
  Dead in the dance!
  etc.

Occasionally, some acquaintance or friend of an earlier day would spend a few days or a week with her. One lady, especially, who, at the time when Delsarte was fashionable, had taught his method, was often favoured with an invitation, and Sadi would converse with her by the hour about the French Master and his Message, as she called it. Then, if it were summer, robed in Grecian garments cut from pale-green cheese-cloth, they would stand on the grass underneath a

---

Poems (1828). This poem imagines the suffering of the wife of one of the alleged conspirators in the assassination of King Albert of Germany in 1308.

[17] Latin, meaning 'I shall rise again'. Van Vechten quotes the first of six sections of a poem that is a passionate expression of suffering following a lover's betrayal.

spreading crab-apple tree, to avoid the direct rays of the sun, and wave their arms and sway their bodies in a manner calculated to give the butcher's boy fits, whenever he passed the gate and saw them. This picture of his large-boned aunt, formidable in appearance but gentle at heart, and the stout Miss Perkins, who reached about to Sadi's arm-pit, delsarting on the lawn was one of Harold's earliest memories.

Until Harold was seven Sadi had kept him in kilts, although the boys of his epoch were usually put into baby-trousers at the age of two. These kilts and his long curls were frequently the object of attention and scorn from passing lads, who, though not over five, sported long and ragged trousers and flannel shirts and wore their hair clipped and frowzy. These boys went by the house with fishing-rods or, in the fall, with baskets to gather hickory-nuts. When they saw Harold in the yard they yelled, Sissy! and Baby girl! at him until he retreated sobbing to the shelter of Auntie Persia's skirts.

When he was seven, Elliot Sanderson, George Prewett's attorney, arrived, and engaged in a long conference with his aunt, the immediate result of which was the purchase of a few suits proper for a small boy, and a hair-cut. Another result was the subsequent arrival of a tall young man with glasses, solemner, on the whole, than his Aunt Sadi, who was to act, Harold learned, as his tutor. At the age of ten, Harold could read and write and do his sums, and knew something of geography, although it cannot be said that he held imaginatively any real sense of this big world. He himself had never been farther than a neighbouring village, whither he was occasionally permitted to drive with his aunt.

There were piles of old bound magazines in the house, Harper's and Godey's and Putnam's,[18] and a few other books besides, left behind by an earlier occupant, Thaddeus of Warsaw and The Scottish Chiefs, Pride and Prejudice, Cranford, Ivanhoe, Pendennis, David Copperfield, The Woman in White, the Poems of Ossian, the Poems of Owen Meredith, The Initials, Charles Auchester, Nothing to Wear, Felix Holt, The Alhambra, Our Old Home, Little Women, Emerson's Essays, the works of Margaret Fuller, Uncle Tom's Cabin, The Pilot, Under Two Flags, Redburn, Two Years Before the Mast, Neighbour Jackwood, and the Poems of James Whitcomb Riley.[19] Harold read all these books, some

---

[18] Genteel middle-class magazines, especially popular in the nineteenth century. *Harper's* and *Putnam's* were general family magazines, featuring fiction, articles on science, art, and politics, while *Godey's* was a woman's magazine with similar mixed content and fashion plates. It was common in the late nineteenth and early twentieth centuries for middle-class subscribers to bind magazines for the family library.

[19] Titles one might expect to find in a middle-class New England home of the day, and which include historical romance and adventure novels, women's fiction, poetry, familiar essays, memoirs, and travelogues. All but one pre-date 1870 and would, therefore, be considered old-fashioned by the time Harold encounters them in his youth. His lack of access to contemporary works emphasises his sheltered upbringing. Authors and dates of publication are as follows: Jane Porter, *Thaddeus of Warsaw* (1803) and *Scottish Chiefs* (1810);

of them twice.

He suffered from the usual slight childish illnesses, but his constitution was good and he was seldom really sick. When he was twelve, a new tutor arrived. He was slightly older than his predecessor and slightly more solemn. These tutors, it is to be inferred, represented the rather sedate taste of Elliot Sanderson, Esq. Mr. Sanderson had strict orders never to mention Harold's name in his father's presence. See that the boy is educated and keep him out of my sight, were his full instructions. With his new tutor Harold began to study algebra, English literature, history, physics, and botany. It was also during this epoch that he learned to swim. The tutor, unaccountably, was an adept at this art and in a small pond near the house, discreetly screened by hazel-brush and cattails, he imparted his knowledge to Harold, who never took more than a languid interest in study of any kind. Harold also began to ride a kind old horse named President McKinley.[20]

When Harold was fifteen a tailor was sent from New York to take his measurements, and this visit was repeated thereafter at regular intervals. From this time on Harold was much too well-dressed for his environment. When, at last, the boy went to college, he had only come in contact with his Aunt Sadi, Persia Blaine, and the other servants, a few female guests, Elliot Sanderson, his two solemn tutors, and his tailor. It is not astonishing, therefore, that his college years were somewhat of a trial. If Sanderson had sent him to one of the big universities, Yale or Harvard or Princeton, it is possible that the lad might have rubbed up against somebody sufficiently sympathetic or altruistic or merely meddlesome to teach him something of the world. The lawyer, however, uncertain how long his rich client's animosity towards his offspring might continue, thought it wise to seclude the boy in a small and rather poor sectarian college where he would scarcely be likely to meet any one who could establish communication or connections with the outside world. In this respect Sanderson's foresight was splendidly justified.

The boy's obviously superior style of dressing, his diffident manner, his rather

---

Jane Austen, *Pride and Prejudice* (1813); Elizabeth Gaskell, *Cranford* (1853); Walter Scott, *Ivanhoe* (1820); William Makepeace Thackeray, *Pendennis* (1848–1850); Charles Dickens, *David Copperfield* (1850); Wilkie Collins, *The Woman in White* (1859); James MacPherson, *Poems of Ossian* (1765); Robert Bulwer-Lytton, *Poems of Owen Meredith* (1869); Jemima von Tautphoeus, *The Initials* (1850); Elizabeth Sara Sheppard, *Charles Auchester* (1853); William Allen Butler, *Nothing to Wear* (1858); George Eliot, *Felix Holt* (1866); Washington Irving, *Alhambra* (1832); Nathaniel Hawthorne, *Our Old Home* (1863); Louisa May Alcott, *Little Women* (1868, 1869); Ralph Waldo Emerson, *Essays* (1841, 1844); Margaret Fuller, *Works* (1860); Harriet Beecher Stowe, *Uncle Tom's Cabin* (1853); James Fennimore Cooper, *The Pilot* (1824); Ouida, *Under Two Flags*; Herman Melville, *Redburn* (1849); Richard Henry Dana, Jr, *Two Years Before the Mast* (1840); J. T. Trowbridge, *Neighbour Jackwood* (1857); James Whitcomb Riley, possibly *Poems by James Whitcomb Riley and Yarns by Bill Nye* (1892).

[20]   William McKinley (1843–1901), twenty-fifth president of the United States.

obstinate pride, natural enough, considering the circumstances of his bringing-up, almost completely isolated him during his freshman year. He attended his classes and studied. Afternoons, he sometimes went horseback riding. He lived in a poor professor's house where there were no other boys. In his sophomore year he made a friend or two, because in any community, however small, complete isolation is well-nigh impossible. The boys who gravitated towards him, however, were solemn souls, semi-ostracized, like himself. This little group discussed and settled many of life's greatest problems.

That sex had something to do with life Harold had vaguely gleaned from the naïve books in his aunt's library. His relations with his new friends were too formal and his curiosity too small for him to add anything very tangible to this knowledge. Presently, however, even among the indigent young students about him, he noted signs of depravity. A grocer's daughter became pregnant and a student disappeared. Bottles were smuggled into respectable boarding-houses in defiance of both college rules and United States laws. Once, out riding, he passed a barn and was horrified at the strident sounds of blasphemy and obscene verse which issued from therein.

In his senior year he had achieved a slender philosophy. He accepted, in his modest fashion, the fact that there were unknown sins in the world. He even became a trifle cynical in an humble and apologetic way: he seemed to be so separated from others by his temperament and breeding. More and more he was alone.

There remains to be told one horrible detail which left its scars. I have noted how as a freshman his clothes by themselves would have prevented any successful intercourse with his fellow students. A raucous junior crystallized the feeling of the college when he shouted at Harold one day, Hello, Cloaks and Suits! The badge seemed appropriate: it had a tremendous vogue. He never, indeed, lost it. It covered him. It labelled him. Later, another boy added a refinement to the insult: His father must be in the business! Harold heard it as he passed, cowered and blushed.

Chapter III

If Harold had entered his father's house cringing, it cannot be said that he left it with his head high. To most boys the promise of a year's freedom under such exceptional circumstances would have opened up a prospect of unbounded bliss, the security of an irresponsible existence. But Harold was not like most boys. He had entertained, it seems probable, some vague expectation that he would be invited to remain.

It was, therefore, a very dazed young man who fairly tottered down the stairs and almost jumped when the servant emerged from the darkness to present him with his hat and usher him through the open doorway. Out in the bright June glare of Eighty-second Street he thought for a moment that he was going to be sick, but he managed to summon enough force to hail a passing taxi-cab, and to give the address of his new home.

Sinking well back into the seat of the cab, he removed his hat and wiped the perspiration from his temples. Freed from the cloak and suit business by this extraordinary father, so much more extraordinary even than he had suspected, Harold seemed committed to a new life which was still more out of his line. He was decidedly alarmed at the prospect before him. This Paul Moody assumed in his eyes a somewhat libidinous character. Even with his limited imagination he could not entirely efface visions of a troubled future from his mind. It was not fair, he began to argue with himself, that he should be dependent on such a singular parent. I am more like my mother, he assured himself. I must be like my mother, and he thought of the pretty miniature of that lady which he possessed. But the possibility of disobedience did not occur to him. All his life he had lived according to the desires of others, and it seemed natural enough to go on living that way.

Suddenly, and for the first time, Harold became aware of his surroundings, for the taxi had come to a full stop. At Broadway, near Twenty-eighth Street, a heavy truck had become entangled with a taxi-cab in so intimate a manner as to completely obstruct the street. A great crowd had already collected. Out of the window of the taxi — for the occupants of neither vehicle appeared to have suffered injury — peeped the frightened and beautiful head of a maiden, a maiden with golden hair and velvet, violet eyes. She wore a blue turban and a simple, blue frock. Out of the violet eyes tears were streaming. A policeman was taking the names of the drivers. The young lady emerged and Harold caught himself staring at her. She approached the policeman.

Is it necessary for me to remain? she asked.

You must give me your name, he replied. We'll need you as a witness.

They were standing directly outside the window of Harold's taxi. He could plainly hear the questions and answers.

But my man was not to blame. The truck-driver turned to the left.

That's what you can tell the judge.

The judge!

The young lady began to cry in earnest.

Your name, miss, and then you can go.

She wiped her eyes with her handkerchief. She was so pitiful and so appealing: Harold felt very sorry for her.

Alice Blake.

Address?

56 East Thirty-seventh Street.[21]

Thank you, miss. You will get a summons. You must be in court tomorrow at nine o'clock.

Isn't there some way....?

No, miss, no other way.

She turned to depart, hoping, doubtless, to find another cab. In the meantime, observing that it would take some moments to clear the street, Harold's driver was attempting to turn about and escape by way of Twenty-ninth Street. At last he succeeded. On the corner stood Miss Blake, timidly bidding for a taxi, but every one that passed seemed to be occupied.

The situation inspired Harold with a hitherto unrealized degree of initiative.

You are going my way ...[22] Can I take you home? he leaned out of the cab, not without embarrassment, to call to her.

I don't know you, sir.

This rejoinder was made quite simply, without rudeness, but it caused Harold to turn red to the full height of his forehead.

I beg your pardon. I thought ...

His confusion seemed to reassure her.

You are very good, she said, as she stepped into his cab. I look such a fright crying, I hate to be seen on the street ... I've been arrested. She sobbed aloud now ... Father will never forgive me.

But you weren't driving the car.

---

[21]   Alice lives in Murray Hill, an exclusive residential area of Manhattan, home to many millionaires from the 1890s on. Though opened up to commercial trade and apartment blocks in the 1920s, it retained an air of exclusivity. Thirty-Seventh Street, for example, was home to banker and philanthropist John Pierpont Morgan, Jr.

[22]   Harold is not, in fact, going her way. Murray Hill is north of Twenty-Ninth, while Gramercy is south.

The chauffeur, as he turned into Fifth Avenue, asked for orders, and Harold gave Alice's address.

You know where I live! she exclaimed with amazement.

I heard you tell the policeman.

You know my name, too?

Yes.... Mine is Harold Prewett.

You see, my father says, she resumed, without seeming to have heard him, that a lady will avoid accidents.

It wasn't your fault. He would be a brute to scold you.

I have disobeyed him. He has told me always to take a cherry taxi.[23] He is very particular about that. I was in such a hurry ... I was late for my piano lesson ... I took a pistache taxi. There was no other about. It is my fault. Father says that the cherry taxis never have accidents.

That's nonsense. The truck ran into you; you didn't run into it. What happened might just as easily have happened to a Rolls-Royce.

Her manner did not indicate that she was ungrateful for his sympathy; nevertheless, she appeared to be inconsolable, and continued to sob intermittently. Nor did she speak again until they reached her door, when with a muttered, Thank you, and the slight flutter of a gloved hand, she descended and disappeared in a brown-stone house, before the diffident Harold had time to give utterance to even one of the hundred different remarks that were surging inarticulately in his brain. He gazed at the closed door. Something seemed to have come into his life and to have gone out of it again. As the taxi drove away he leaned back against the cushions and wiped his temples for the second time that warm June afternoon. He was, indeed, so bewildered by the events of the day that his head began to ache violently.

Presently, his taxi stopped before an apartment house on East Eighteenth Street, and he remembered that he had one more ordeal to go through. The boy in the elevator, a Spaniard, was most obsequious. He had quite evidently been warned of an important arrival. Harold was carried up to the fourth floor, and Pedro ran on ahead to ring the bell of apartment B. The door was opened by a properly uniformed English servant, very tall, very thin, with searching grey eyes, clean-cut, sharp features, a pointed nose, a cleft chin, and very thin hair, embellished with brilliantine and plastered severely over a dome-like head. Harold almost trembled at the sight of him.

Mr. Prewett, I believe, sir. My name is Oliver Drains.

He bowed.

Your trunks and bags have arrived, sir. Mr. Sanderson saw to that.

Harold walked into his new home, not without interest. It was a suite of four rooms and bath. There was a living-room, which was also a library, a dining-

---

[23]   In the 1920s, New York taxis came in many colours, before yellow became the norm.

room, a kitchen, a bedroom, and a bath. An alcove, leading from the living-room, held a couch which could be used for a guest. Harold also noted presently that there were twin beds in the bedroom. The walls were painted, deep blue in the living-room and dining-room, rose in the bedroom. The curtains were of coarse brown linen, bordered with a narrow band of chocolate tape, and heavily lined so that when they were drawn they excluded the daylight. The furniture had slipcovers of the same linen, but such articles as tables, which remained uncovered, were of mahogany, modern-antique in style, but not disagreeable to the eye. Persian rugs made pleasant splashes on the polished oak floors. On the walls were photographs of subjects not unknown to the world: Veronese's Marriage at Cana, Watteau's Pierrot, Ingres's La Source....[24] The selector evidently had been prejudiced in favour of the Louvre.

There were also a few books in a case and on the centre-table in the living-room: Alice in Wonderland, The Way of All Flesh, Ethan Frome, Daughters of the Rich, The Spoon River Anthology, Crome Yellow, The Three Black Pennys, Three Soldiers, Figures of Earth, Gentle Julia, Memoirs of a Midget, and a book of poems by Witter Bynner.[25] There were a few magazines: current numbers of the Atlantic Monthly, the Saturday Evening Post, the Dial, Harper's Bazar, the London Mercury, the Nation, the Cosmopolitan, and the Police Gazette.[26] Harold fingered these periodicals, without much more than taking in their titles. Only the Police Gazette was strange to him, and caused him to wonder why his father had chosen that. For, apparently, every object in the apartment had been carefully chosen.

---

[24]   Paolo Veronese (1528–1588), Italian Renaissance painter whose *Wedding at Cana* (1562–1563), depicts the biblical story of the banquet at which Jesus turns water into wine; Jean-Antoine Watteau (1684–1721), of the Rococo school, whose *Gilles* (1718–19) portrays an actor costumed as the *commedia dell'arte* character Pierrot, standing apart from fellow actors with an air of lonely wistfulness; Jean-Auguste Dominique Ingres (1780–1867), French Neoclassical painter, whose *La Source* (1856) depicts a nude woman holding a pitcher out of which water flows.

[25]   In comparison with the selection at Aunt Sadi's, these books reflect a distinctly modern sensibility. Lewis Carroll, *Alice in Wonderland* (1865); Samuel Butler, *The Way of All Flesh* (1903); Edith Wharton, *Ethan Frome* (1911); Edgar Saltus, *Daughters of the Rich* (1900); Edgar Lee Masters, *Spoon River Anthology* (1915); Aldous Huxley, *Crome Yellow* (1921); Joseph Hergesheimer, *The Three Black Pennys* (1917); John Dos Passos, *Three Soldiers* (1921); James Branch Cabell, *Figures of Earth* (1921); Booth Tarkington, *Gentle Julia* (1922); Walter de la Mare, *Memoirs of a Midget* (1921); Witter Bynner published many poetry volumes between his first, in 1907, and 1922, when the novel is set.

[26]   Like the books in the apartment, these magazines, oriented towards the sophisticated urbanite, represent a more up-to-date selection than those at Aunt Sadi's. *The Atlantic Monthly, The Dial,* and *The London Mercury* were literary journals, the latter two notable for their interest in modernist literature and the arts. *The Saturday Evening Post, Cosmopolitan,* and *Harper's Bazar* were popular general magazines with contemporary fiction geared towards middle-class readers, the last with a women's fashion focus. *The Nation* was a weekly news and opinion magazine with a radical socio-political agenda, while *The Police Gazette* was a tabloid-style men's magazine, covering scandal, sport, and sex.

Drains interrupted his revery.

Will you have a bath, sir? I have laid out your dinner clothes.

What time is it, Oliver?

It is a quarter to six, sir.

And where do I dine?

With Mr. Moody if you like, sir. I was to telephone.

Not tonight, Harold replied in haste, acting by instinct. Telephone Mr. Moody that I will call on him tomorrow afternoon.

Very good, sir. Will you dine at home, sir?

Rapidly Harold was made aware of how much his own master he had become. It gave him size.

Is there anything to eat in the house?

Certainly, sir. What there is not I can get. The markets are open. May I suggest a chop, sir?

A chop? Yes, and …

And green peas, sir; a salad, a sweet, and coffee, sir.

I think that will be all right, Harold replied, awkwardly fingering the Police Gazette.

Thank you, sir, and now will you have your bath?

Drains led the way into the white-tiled bathroom and helped Harold divest himself of his clothing. Water already poured from the faucets and the tub was nearly full. Plunged therein, Harold recalled the events of the day with some confusion, a vague alarm, and yet not altogether without pleasure. After all, his father had been kind: he had permitted him, even requested him, to live as he pleased for a year, and he had already met Alice. He wondered when he would see her again…. But this Paul Moody! Evidently a strange bird.

Ugh! Harold was blushing again. Drains was scrubbing his back.

Am I scrubbing too hard, sir?

N-n-no.

Now, step out on the mat, sir, and I will dry you. Drains enveloped Harold in a vast towel, patting him a few times; then, taking the two ends of the towel, he walked a few feet away and began fanning the bather with the folds. To conclude the adventure he brought Harold a handsome silk dressing-gown with a figured Persian design, and a copy of the Evening Globe.[27]

Would you prefer another paper, sir? I am not yet acquainted with your tastes.

It doesn't matter. This will do.

Very good, sir. Now will you dress for dinner, or dine in your dressing-gown?

I think … Did my father say?

---

[27]   A New York evening newspaper.

Your father's orders were that you were to do exactly as you pleased, sir.

Harold remembered.

I will stay as I am.

Very good, sir. Now, after I have telephoned Mr. Moody, I will prepare your dinner, sir.

Listening to Drains at the telephone in the bedroom, Harold had an inspiration.

Will you bring me the telephone-book, please, Oliver, he said, as the man hung up the receiver.

Certainly, sir.

Starting to thumb the edges nervously, he was aware that the man still stood before him.

Anything else, sir?

No, that's all.

He watched Drains retreat into the kitchen, and then he boldly opened the book at B and began to look for Blake. There, beyond doubt, was the number: Beckford Blake, 56 East Thirty-seventh Street — Murray Hill 0007. Drains entered the dining-room. Pretending to lose all interest in the book, Harold waited until Drains returned to the kitchen. Finally, he mustered the courage to approach the telephone.

Murray Hill 0007, please, he whispered.

Asked to repeat the number, he looked around; Drains seemed very distant. He ventured to raise his voice slightly. This time the operator caught the number. There was a slight noise in the kitchen. Harold dropped the receiver and hastened back to his chair in the living-room, propping himself up behind the Globe. Presently Drains, on his way to market, slammed the front door. Harold returned to the telephone.

Which Miss Blake? queried a woman's voice at the other end of the wire.

Miss Alice Blake.

Just a moment. I will see.

A short silence.

Yes, this is Miss Blake. Who is this?

Miss *Alice* Blake?

Yes. Who is this?

Harold, Harold Prewett. You know, I took you home today.

Oh!

I wanted to know, I wanted to ask … that is, I wanted to inquire if it was all right!

All right?

All right with your father.

Yes.

Well, I just wanted to know.

Yes.

Well — Harold vainly sought for words to continue — , well, good-bye.

Wait … a minute. The voice was faint but desperate.

He waited, much too embarrassed to speak.

A long silence.

I wish … Well …

Is somebody listening?

Yes.

You want me to ask questions?

Yes.

Overjoyed, his mind began to work faster.

Do you want me to go to court with you in the morning?

Yes.

Where shall I meet you?

Silence. Harold groaned. He was entirely unacquainted with New York.

Must I say?

The outside door slammed.

The same thing, Harold ejaculated, almost in a whisper.

What?

You know what you just told me?

Oh!

I'll call you tomorrow.

No, you can't do that! This was positive.

He racked his brain; suddenly a sky-rocket shot up and burst, painting Paul Moody's address in fire against the sky.

Gramercy Park!

Yes.

Eight-thirty tomorrow morning.

Yes. Good-bye.

Good-bye.

Drains was in the kitchen. Had he heard? Harold wondered. He returned to his paper and apparently was buried in the stock reports, but a pair of violet eyes obtruded themselves between his vision and the print. His heart was beating violently. For the third time that day he wiped his temples with his handkerchief.

Drains entered, bearing a tray on which reposed a cocktail.

Dinner will be ready in ten minutes. Try this, sir.

Must I? I do-do-don't drink.

You don't drink? Certainly, sir, you are not obliged to.

Drains appeared to be astonished and a little hurt.

Would my father …? Harold began, and faltered.

Certainly not, sir. Your father demands nothing of you. Only he asked me to see that you had a good cellar.

But it's against the law, protested Harold.[28]

I think, sir, that your father hopes that you will break a few.

Drains was very solemn, but there was a maliciously ironic twinkle in his eyes.

Break the law!

Well, some of them. Everybody does.

I never have…. Then, impulsively, Let me taste it. He sipped the concoction in a gingerly manner. Ugh! It's very bitter.

Drains made something of a ceremony of the dinner. It was served precisely as if there had been eleven guests present, at least one of whom was entitled to a crest on his stationery. There were little attentions. Is your chop too well done, sir? What kind of dressing do you prefer on your salad, sir? Do you drink black coffee, sir? Nevertheless, Harold did not eat much. He was conscious of a growing perturbation in his mind and a continued acceleration in the beating of his heart. When, at length, he had finished — and it had seemed a very long dinner — , he returned to his comfortable chair. He was through with the Globe. He picked up the Nation and read an editorial which seemed very radical to him. What was the world coming to? Anarchists and Socialists. Reds. Bolsheviki. The ex-soldiers seemed dissatisfied.[29] Why didn't they go to work in the cloak and suit business? No one else wanted to. There should be plenty of room for them there. He wasn't sleepy, but he could think of nothing else to do but go to bed. Drains was in the kitchen. Harold retreated to the bedroom where he found a pair of silk pyjamas, striped in two shades of grey, with the name of an English firm embroidered on a label in the collar, lying on the bed. Drawing off his clothes, he donned them, and was just ready to retire when Drains came in. Drains was beaming.

Can I do anything more for you, sir, before I leave?

Leave?

For the night, sir. There is no place for me to sleep here. I shall be in very early in the morning. What time will you have your breakfast, sir?

Seven-thirty … Harold hesitated. Would that be too early?

Not at all, sir. But Drains looked distinctly disapproving. Very good, sir, he added. Breakfast for two?

---

[28]   Prohibition of alcohol was in effect from 1920 to 1933, though drinking remained widespread in spite of the law.

[29]   At this time, *The Nation* was politically and socially radical, expressing pro-Bolshevik and Socialist sympathies. The topics mentioned appear frequently in the publication through 1922.

Two? Certainly not. Breakfast for one. Why two?

You will excuse me, sir, but I heard you telephoning to a young lady and I thought perhaps you had asked her to spend the night with you.

Harold almost fell out of bed.

I was not telephoning that kind of young lady!

I beg your pardon, sir.

Can one ... Is this that sort of house?

Your father owns this house, sir. You are at home.

Then ... he ... This was very difficult for Harold ... he wouldn't object if I, if I ... He achieved the end in a rush and a gulp ... had women here?

Object, sir? Drains raised his eyebrows. Object? Certainly not.

The tone of Drains's reply was profoundly lacking in doubt.

Would he then ... The horror of the idea almost stifled speech.... Would he then be willing?

I can vouch for that, sir. Drains's tone was now both deferential and parental.

Is it ... Harold was sitting bolt upright in bed.... Is it what he wants?

I can only repeat my orders, sir. They are definite. You are to do anything you please. I have had considerable experience, sir, in observing young men do what they please. In London, sir — Drains drew himself up with considerable side — ,[30] I was in the employ of the Duke of Middlebottom. That is why your father engaged me.

Harold's face was a blank.

I perceive, sir, that the name of the Duke of Middlebottom has no associations for you. The name is not unknown in London, sir, especially in certain circles. I left the Duke's service, I may say, sir, for good reasons. I am not a snob; nor am I a puritan. I take great delight in the society of ladies, sir. I like to see a young man surround himself with attractive ladies. I enjoy arranging the pipes for the opium, sir, sterilizing the needles, and running for the doctor when a young lady has overdosed herself with vodka. It is very pleasant to serve breakfast for a numerous party that has forgotten to go home the night before, but I have my personal dignity, sir, and I left the Duke of Middlebottom.

Oliver, *why* did you leave the Duke?

One of his young ladies wished to whip[31] me, sir. The incident aroused the Duke. He forgot himself, sir. May I say good-night, sir?

Good-night, Oliver.

Harold fell back against the pillow, his aching head throbbing with horror. Not that he fully understood all that Drains had intended to imply. Needles baffled him, and pipes. Didn't people *eat* opium and wasn't it a Chinese vice?

---

[30] Side, a colloquial expression, British in origin, meaning 'to put on airs'.
[31] In the expurgated British edition, 'whip' was replaced with 'kiss'.

Obviously, however, Drains had lived with a man of the lowest type, no matter
how many points there were in his coronet. And this was the fellow his father
had chosen to be his servant! A man who began by offering him cocktails and
ended by asking if a young lady would share his breakfast in bed! What were his
father's intentions? What would Aunt Sadi think of all this? What would *Alice*
think? It was a long time before he felt calm enough to press the button at his
side which extinguished the lights; it was very much longer before he was able
to go to sleep.

At a quarter after eight the next morning, Harold stood before the Players'
Club in Gramercy Park.[32] He was amazed to discover that the park itself was
enclosed by a high iron fence, the gates of which were locked, although several
people, principally nursemaids and their charges, were enjoying the warm June
air under the trees within the enclosure.[33] Presently, he observed an elderly lady
open one of the gates with a great brass key. So, it appeared, he must encircle the
iron fence until he found Alice. He walked on past the Players', turning up the
west side of the park; then east, and down the north side. He circled the fence,
indeed, three times. As he was striding up the west side for the fourth time, he
observed a furtive figure hurrying towards him from Lexington Avenue, a trim
little figure in blue serge. He advanced rapidly to meet her.

I've had such a time! She was almost in tears again, but it must be admitted
that tears were becoming to her.

Poor child.

I had to stand in the library near the door until the man arrived with the
summons. Then, this morning I have no lessons and I am not supposed to
go out. I asked papa if I might do some shopping, but there seemed to be no
occasion for it, at least I was too nervous to think of any. Finally, I told him that
I had a dreadful headache and must go for a walk.

Poor child! Harold unquestionably was sympathetic but he could think of
nothing else to say.

We must hasten! The policeman told me to be in court at nine o'clock. We
must find a taxi.

They walked towards Fourth Avenue and Harold hailed a passing cab.

But it isn't a cherry cab.

It's too late to be particular, Harold muttered as he helped her in.

I suppose so ... but papa says ...

Ascending to the court-room at the Jefferson Market Police Court,[34] they

---

[32]   Private club, established 1888 by Shakespearean actor Edwin Booth (1833–1893).
[33]   Gramercy Park is a residents-only gated park.
[34]   One of the busiest courthouses in Manhattan, located in Greenwich Village at Sixth
Avenue and West Tenth Street.

passed, on the stairs, a motley crowd of bondsmen, witnesses, shyster lawyers, friends of prostitutes, and hangers-on. Court, they noted, on entering, had already opened. A frowzy female was telling the judge how a neighbour's child had stuck pins into her little girl. The little girl, according to the testimony of the defence, had begun the sticking. The judge, a slender, elderly man with a great beak like that of a parrot, on which was fastened a pince-nez, did not appear to be listening. He examined papers with one hand while, with the other, he ceaselessly tapped the desk with a silver paper-cutter. A row of dingy witnesses fidgeted on the front benches, waiting for the cases in which they were interested to be called. The clock ticked. Some one whispered. A clerk pounded for order. Case followed case. The heat was stifling and the odour unspeakable. It was nearly twelve o'clock before the driver of the truck, a burly Irishman, was called to the stand. The chauffeur of the taxi in which Alice had been driving began his story in so low a tone that Harold and Alice could not catch a single word. The judge never looked up. He continued to fuss with his papers and to tap the desk with his silver paper-cutter. The policeman was called before the bench and corroborated the testimony of the taxi-driver. He, too, spoke in a low monotone, but it was possible to hear a part of what he said: the truck-driver had turned to the left.

Miss Blake! called the clerk.

Alice, blushing furiously, rose, stumbled, tottered to the witness-stand. She could have felt no worse had she been on trial for murder. Her eyes were shut tight, and she held a handkerchief to her dry lips.

Do you solemnly swear that you will tell the truth, the whole truth, and nothing but the truth, so help you God?

I do.

Name?

Alice Blake, she scarcely whispered.

The judge looked up for the first time; nor, it should be noted, did he look down again.

Address?

56 East Thirty-seventh Street: this in a considerably lower tone.

What do you know about this case?

I was driving in the taxi-cab …

Go on, Miss Blake, put in the judge in a manner which was kindly but certainly not paternal. Tell us your story in your own way.

That man — she pointed to the Irishman — ran into my car…. He turned to the left.

The prisoner was sworn.

Your honour …

Don't lie now! Tell the truth! The judge was stern. His eyes were on Alice.

Your honour, I ... Yer see, it wern't my fault. There wern't no signal at that corner ... I was turnin' ...

To the left, interjected the lawyer for the taxi-driver.

Were you drunk?

No, your honour: with great indignation.

Was he drunk? This to the policeman.

I don't think so, your honour.

I'm tired of these cases. You truck-drivers think you can run the streets. This little girl — he beamed through his pince-nez at the shrinking Miss Blake — has been thoroughly shaken up as a result of your wanton behaviour. I cannot have the little girls on the streets in danger of their lives on account of such men as you. I'm going to make an example of you. One hundred dollars or ten days in the work-house.

The judge smiled at Alice, and Alice began to cry.

The truck-driver stood before the bar. No, he couldn't pay the fine.

Alice turned quickly to Harold.

Have you a hundred dollars?

I don't ... I'll see.

He looked in his pocket-book and to his great astonishment found nearly five hundred. Drains must have put it there while he was asleep.

Yes, I have.

Will you lend it to me?

I'll pay the man's fine.

No, this is my affair. If you will lend it to me, I will pay the fine. I can get the money.

Let me ...

Please ... Alice began to cry again. Harold was certain he had never seen any one so adorable, never imagined that any one so adorable could come into his life. He pressed the money into her little hand, and she rushed to the bar, almost breathless.

I'll pay his fine.

The judge glanced down the extensive length of his nose at her. He said nothing, but his face was more expressive than usual.

The clerk took the money.

The Irishman turned to Alice.

I couldn't bear to think, she stammered, that you had been sentenced because I appeared against you. I couldn't help it. I didn't want to come. They made me. I had to tell the truth. You *will* be more careful, won't you?

Shure, mum. The Irishman scratched his red-thatched head.

The judge leaned over the bar.

Miss Blake, he began.

Alice looked up.

Won't you come and sit beside me and listen to the other cases?

She declined with thanks.

Let's get out of this horrid place, she adjured Harold.

You are adorable, he muttered, as they descended the stairs.

I couldn't bear to think of that man going to jail. He may have children. I'd always feel it was my fault he was there. Oh! if papa hears about this!

I don't think he will.

It might get into the newspapers.

The horror of this idea expanded. Harold was innocent enough to believe that it might, but he kept his opinion to himself.

It's over now anyway, but if papa finds out!

Please, don't cry again. I can't bear it!

I won't if I can help it.... She tried to straighten her lip. We must find another taxi.

Two taxis stood by the kerb but both were silver grey.

We *must* find a cherry cab....

They walked towards Fifth Avenue. Several cabs passed them but all the cherry cabs were occupied. They always were, Alice explained drearily.

We may as well walk home, Alice conceded.

When may I see you again?

Of course, I must pay you the hundred dollars.

I'd forgotten all about that. I don't want the money. I want to see you.

It is a debt. I'll send it to you ... I don't know your address.

Harold wrote it out on a card.

I want to see you, he pleaded. Won't you write me that I may call?

Oh! no, no! She was positive. Papa would question me. He would want to know where I had met you.

What shall we do?

I don't know. I can't meet you again. I can't invite you to the house.... Don't think me ungrateful ... I simply can't. And you mustn't telephone me again. I was so afraid last night. Nobody heard ... but if they had!

Harold's expression was rueful. I must see you, he urged. Don't you want to see me?

You have been very kind to me.

I have done nothing I didn't want to do. I ...

Alice seemed to have an idea: Haven't you any friends?

Friends?

Somebody I know, for instance.... Can't we be introduced properly?

Harold shook his head. I don't know anybody except — I don't know anybody at all in New York.

Nobody! Alice's tone was slightly one of alarm.

Nobody.

Oh! You mustn't walk with me any farther. Somebody might see us. I can go home alone. I'll send you the money. Good-bye.

Harold held out his hand, but Alice was gone, almost running, indeed, ahead of him up the Avenue.

Chapter IV

In a room, the walls of which were lined with pale-green taffeta, a man and a woman were sitting in the late June afternoon. It was a charming room with orange and gold lacquer screens, escritoires and tables of a severe Directoire pattern,[35] needle-point chairs, and a chaste marble fireplace. Stalks of indigo larkspurs and salmon snapdragons emerged from tall crystal vases. A few books bound in gaily coloured boards lay on one of the tables, and the others were cluttered, hugger-mugger, with a variety of picturesque and valuable objects. A bright Manila shawl, embroidered in vermilion and lemon flowers, was thrown over the piano, and was held in place by a blue Canton china pitcher full of magenta roses. A copper bowl, heaped with ripe figs, stood on a console-table. Sanguines by Boucher and Fragonard,[36] with indelicate subjects, hung on the walls. The broad windows looked down on Gramercy Park. This was the living-room of an apartment which included two small bedrooms, and an alcove, which served as a kitchen.

A young man in white flannels, a young man with curly golden hair and blue eyes and a profile that resembled somewhat Sherril Schell's photograph of Rupert Brooke,[37] a young man with slender, graceful hands which he was inclined to wave rather excessively in punctuation of his verbal effects, reclined on a divan upholstered with green taffeta, smoking a cigarette in a jade holder of a green so dark and so nearly translucent that it paraphrased emerald.

In one of the heavier and easier chairs sat a lady, with a face which, perhaps, you would not call beautiful, but which would assuredly awaken your interest. The forehead was almost entirely obscured by a wave of chestnut hair, bobbed at the back. The eyes were grey, the nose retroussé. She had a good artificial colour and her rather sensual lips were enamelled a vivid carmine. Her jaw was square but it was the square jaw of character, by no means detracting from her charm. She, too, wore white, a robe of Chinese brocaded crêpe, with a girdle of

---

[35] Style of decorative arts and furnishing of the late eighteenth and early nineteenth centuries, between the fall of Louis XVI and the reign of Napoleon. It is neoclassical, emphasising clean lines and light, graceful forms.

[36] Red chalk drawings by François Boucher (1703–1770) and Jean-Honoré Fragonard (1732–1806), exponents of a rococo style, characterized by risqué subject matter, frivolity, and hedonism.

[37] Schell (1877–1964) was an architectural and portrait photographer who photographed the British poet Brooke (1887–1915). One of his pictures served as a frontispiece to Brooke's posthumous *1914 and Other Poems*, helping to immortalize the handsome poet, who epitomized the tragic loss of youth during World War One.

uncut chalcedony,[38] into which she had inserted a cluster of scarlet geraniums. These flowers bloomed also on her small white French hat, a creation of Evelyne Varon.[39]

Campaspe Lorillard was about thirty, intensely feminine, intensely feline, in the most seductive sense of the word. She was addicted to chain-smoking, that is she lighted one cigarette from the other as fast as it burned too near the end of her amethyst holder. She was regarding Paul Moody with some intensity and was obviously interested in what he was about to say.

Out with it! she commanded, and her voice, clear and soft and sympathetic, although it contained a suggestion of mockery, was not lacking in force or intention.

Yes, I must tell you…. He'll be here in a few minutes, Paul groaned.

Campaspe remained silent, blowing delicate and wistful rings of smoke into the air.

Do you remember the poet who was too proud to die and who sent his servant out into the street to beg for him?…[40] I had to do something; you will admit that?

Campaspe did not help him.

I couldn't go on. Father won't send me another dollar.

If you are going to give Mrs. Whittaker the honour of keeping you, tell me this instant, Campaspe interpolated.

It's not quite as bad as that. It isn't marriage.

I never had any such idea.

Oh! It isn't that either!

Well, Paulet, what is it?

Campaspe regarded her sheer white stockings with some interest; her eyes followed on down to her trim shoes of white suède, which fastened across the ankles with a curious arrangement of straps with chalcedony buttons.

I may as well tell you…. An unintimate observer would have been puzzled to decide how much of Paul's misery was feigned…. I'm going to become a tutor, 'paspe.

A tutor! She smiled. A tutor! A guide to fast life! How to smoke opium in three lessons?

Not so bad for a guess, Paul grinned. He began to feel more comfortable. You've more or less hit it.

Who wants to learn?

That's the strange part. I answered an advertisement. It's here somewhere….

---

[38]   Quartz gemstone that comes in various forms. The form most used in jewellery and accessories is translucent ranging from bluish to white or grey in colour.

[39]   Fashionable Parisian milliner (sometimes spelled Evelyn), popular in America through the 1910s and 1920s.

[40]   Luís Vaz de Camões (1524–1580), Portuguese lyric poet.

He rose and fumbled about in an escritoire until he found the clipping.

What kind of jest is this? Campaspe's interest was not on the wane.

That's just what I thought. I went to see him ... an old man, in earnest. It's his son, a milksop, I take it. I don't know. I've never seen him. He's coming in today. You've got to help.... Everybody's got to help....

Teach him the vices?

I really don't know. It's all queer. The old fellow didn't tell me much. He asked questions. He seemed particularly pleased when he learned that my wife had supported me. That appeared to settle the matter for him.

But Amy doesn't any more. She even made a quite violent effort to get you to return the compliment.

He liked that too.... He seemed to like everything about me.

Swank!

Perhaps, but my new income begins today. I don't have to do anything for it, so far as I can see, except introduce the — the — the offspring to my friends. The old gentleman stipulated, though, that I should never mention business. He doesn't want ideas of that nature put into the boy's head.

What is the name of this horrid old man?

Prewett, George Prewett.

We don't know him, do we?

God, no! He belongs to one of the 1870–90 families, I should gather from the house. Stained-glass and wainscoting. I'm sure they give turkey dinners on Thanksgiving and Christmas.

And you don't have to teach the boy anything definite?

No. Nothing was said about reading or study.... I rely on you, the old 'un said, to introduce my son to existence. I don't know exactly where it is to be found, but you look as if you do. You know, at least, the things I want my son to know.... The old boy was abrupt and brusque, not at all hesitant or indecisive. He signed a cheque at our last interview yesterday morning and passed it over to me.

Paul removed a leather money-case from his coat-pocket, extracted a pink slip of paper therefrom, and handed it over to Campaspe.

As much as that! Are you feeding the boy?

No, he has his own money.

This is all?

Another cheque in a month.... Sooner, if I want it. There are no limits set to my rapacity. Oh! he's rich!

Well, Paulet, you're in luck again. You're always lucky, she commented, rather pensively.

I don't do anything about it: his answer was not uncomplacent.

Nothing unpleasant ever happens to you, she continued to muse aloud, or if it does, like Amy's divorce, it serves to make something pleasant happen. Even when you were in Ludlow Street Jail you ate hot-house grapes and pickled walnuts and read Turgenieff.[41] I sometimes regret that I didn't marry you myself.

I wish you had.

God forbid! It's better for us to be friends.

Alive to the cozenage, Paulet's face assumed the rather silly but extremely sympathetic expression of a chow puppy having its belly massaged by a friendly hand.

I haven't given you a cocktail, he remembered. Ki!

A diminutive Jap[42] in a white linen uniform appeared from the alcove.

Make some of your best Bacardi cocktails.[43]

Yessir.

Campaspe was thinking. When, exactly, do you expect him? she asked.

Harold? He telephoned, or a man named Drains, *his* man, telephoned that he would come in this afternoon.

So he's named Harold. Prewett — she rolled it over — , no, I don't remember *that*.

The glass that held the cocktail was Venetian. Campaspe regarded its crumpled and gold-flecked convolutions before she began to sip the contents.

Ki makes good cocktails. I'm glad you're not going to lose him, glad you're not going to lose the green taffeta. Oh! I suppose you wouldn't anyway. You are lucky, Paulet. Hundreds of people would give you a dime a week to keep you from going under. You are cheerful and amusing and decorative. I'm glad I didn't marry you. No husband can be cheerful and amusing and decorative to his wife, and a man who is cheerful and amusing and decorative to the world, but who ceases to be so to his wife, soon loses his self-confidence, and fails to interest anybody.

Paul sipped his cocktail. The clock struck five. Ki opened the door for John Armstrong, a young stock-broker, who suggested something of the prizefighter in his good-natured virility.

Hello, Mrs. Lorillard…. Hello, Paul. Drinks?

Just in time. Ki!

Surprised to find you in town, Mrs. Lorillard.

I've been away for two days. I scarcely ever go to the country, never for long. It's dull and lonely and hot; a convention, this going to the country. New York

---

41 Ivan S. Turgenieff (also Turgenev) (1818–1883), Russian poet, playwright, and author who wrote social realist novels about provincial life.
42 Shortened form of Japanese, not considered derogatory at the time, as it is now. Domestic work was a common occupation for Japanese immigrants in this period.
43 Bacardi, a Cuban rum, the first clear white rum. The Bacardi cocktail is a blend of rum, lime juice, and grenadine.

is an ideal summer-resort. I like it better in the summer than I do in the winter. Only one detail I deplore: the straight streets. The cow-paths, the lanes, the byways, and the turnings exist only in quarters I never visit.

But don't you go to Europe?

Europe! Why all this racing over Europe? I did the museums when I was seventeen. Paris is provincial, démodé. Nothing remains but the dressmakers, and they work only for American women. As for the people … people are the same everywhere. If you have imagination, you don't need to travel.

Hadn't thought of it. Guess you're right. I've got to stick. It's a good idea to have reasons. I'll use yours. May I?

I expect you to.

Paul, Campaspe noted, was beginning to look a trifle perturbed. He dreaded, she said to herself, the coming encounter, but Harold's entrance proved a happy surprise for both of them. He was so young, so entirely adequate in appearance. Even with the ideas of an adolescent he would do, would pass. He did resemble a frightened dormouse, but he was very handsome. And Campaspe's instinct told her at once that this boy was the opposite of Paul in everything.

Come over here and sit down, young man, she ordered, although in a kindly enough tone. Ki will give you a cocktail.

Harold said nothing this time about his previous temperate habits, but the size of the drink alarmed him. Ki was not penurious with alcohol.

After Harold had drunk half his cocktail, he even attempted a little sally.

You will pardon me for speaking of it, he said, but I am admiring your flowers. I never saw any one wear geraniums before. I didn't know they were worn. They seem to belong in boxes outside windows, or in pots, or in parks, but they are just right on you.

'paspe always wears geraniums, said Paul, probably because Cupid doesn't like them.

Cupid? queried Harold, more comfortable, a trifle bolder.

Mr. Lorillard. Madame's husband. We always call him that. Cupid and my Campaspe played for kisses; Cupid paid,[44] you know. He pays all right, but he doesn't get the kisses…. Hello, Bunny.

Paul rose to greet the newcomer, Mr. Titus Hugg,[45] a very short man, shorter even than Ki, inclined towards rotundity, but young and rosy and extremely affable.

---

[44] Lines from a song by John Lyly (1553 or 1554–1606) from his play *Campaspe* (1584), based on accounts of the relationship between Alexander the Great, his mistress, and the painter, Apelles, who falls in love with Campaspe when he paints her portrait. Alexander gives up Campaspe to Apelles, seeing in the painter's image a love surpassing his own. The quotation is from Apelles's song in which he wonders what will become of him given that Campaspe has defeated Love himself so roundly.

[45] Titus Hugg's nickname, which makes him Bunny Hugg, plays on the name of a popular ragtime dance of the period, the Bunny Hug, developed as part of a craze for dances with animal themes, most famously the Fox Trot.

I've been composing, Bunny remarked, a wonderful thing, and I was getting along splendidly until the telephone set me off by ringing in the identical key as that in which I was writing. I couldn't think of another dissonance. I quit!

Noises usually inspire you, suggested Campaspe.

Always, until today. I wrote a queer, strange thing, created after a creaking door. The maid broke china. I used the crash. Even the sound of soapy suds, rubbed up and down, up and down, was good for a little piece.

What are you writing now, Bunny, a symphony? queried John Armstrong.

Mr. Titus Hugg looked at the stock-broker with disgust.

A symphony! Say, don't you know this is the twentieth century? A symphony! Does your firm sell spinning-wheel stock? Music has got to be less tenuous; all this going on and going over is finished. Brevity, that's what we want now. All the old stuff is too long. My new pieces are over in five or six bars, one of them in only two. Do you want to hear it?

I could stand two bars, John Armstrong replied.

Bunny disregarded the insult; Paul, Harold, and Campaspe all urged him to play. He sat down before the Steinway grand, looking portentous.

La pavane pour une Infante défunte, he read the title of the piece of music on the rack in front of him. One sees that everywhere now,[46] just as in the eighties, I have been told, it was always La prière d'une vierge.[47]

He did not make a tentative attack on the keyboard, as is the bad habit of amateurs. Instead, he plunged at once into a conglomeration of harsh seconds. After a few raucous but brilliant wrestlings with the keys, he ceased.

What do you call it? Campaspe demanded.

Fourteenth Street.[48] It's part of my Manhattan Suite.

Play Fifteenth Street, suggested Harold.

I haven't written all the streets, only twenty-five of them, and not consecutively.

Sheridan Square![49] was Paul's idea.

Certainly not.... I'll play you Sutton Place[50] if you like.

---

[46] 'Pavane for a Dead Infanta' (1899), solo piano piece by Maurice Ravel (1875–1937) and inspired by a nostalgia for sixteenth- and seventeenth-century Spanish court life. A pavane is a slow processional dance. Ravel, who wanted to bring his music to a wider public, recorded this piece for piano roll in 1922, hence Bunny's reference to its ubiquity.

[47] 'A Maiden's Prayer' (1856), popular sentimental piano piece by Tekla Bądarzewska-Baranowska (1829/1834–1861).

[48] Major crosstown street, marking the divide between upper and lower Manhattan, separating Greenwich Village and the Lower East Side to the south, from Chelsea and Gramercy to the north.

[49] From the mid-1910s, Sheridan Square was the centre of the touristy, faux bohemian section of the radical and avant-garde Greenwich Village.

[50] Beginning in 1920, this formerly working-class industrial area on the East River became a fashionable residential area, popular with socially progressive women.

Not that! cried Campaspe. We must have some reservations.

I'll play you Albéniz's Triana,[51] said the intransigent musician, and he did play a few bars, but he broke off in the middle of one with the cry, J'en ai marre![52]

Play *that*!

J'en ai marre! J'en ai marre!

After a cocktail, Bunny was more complaisant.

I'll play Columbus Circle.[53]

Childs'[54] by moonlight?

The Maine Monument[55] in the late afternoon?

The Columbus statue?[56]

Well, judge for yourselves!

This time, with one finger, Bunny picked out a tune which wandered from the top to the bottom of the piano.

I can't play the accompaniment to that melody until I get the right kind of piano. It's not written for the tempered scale. I must have quarter and sixteenth tones. Moses[57] played it for me on his violin.... You heard it, Paul.

Like a cat singing to the discoverer of America.... You saw him sailing on and you listened to the cat.

In spite of himself, Harold smiled.

Bunny played his Bowery[58] Ballet in two bars.

I'm tired. He wheeled around. 'paspe, sing for us, one of those nice, old-fashioned songs your mother used to sing.

Do! Do! from John Armstrong and Paul. Even Harold caught the infection of their enthusiasm.

Fannie's so adorable when she sings them, Campaspe said, as she went to the piano. She settled herself, preluded with a few bars, and then began:

> Bedelia! Prends garde aux faux pas!
> Bedelia! Ne tombe pas!
> En France, on est connaisseur;

---

[51] Isaac Albéniz (1860–1909), Spanish pianist and composer. 'Triana' is from *Iberia* (1905–1909), an impressionist suite for piano. Triana is the name of the Gypsy quarter of Seville and the song is inspired by the folk songs and dances of the area, notably the flamenco. Van Vechten wrote about Albéniz in his essay collection *In the Garret* (1920).

[52] French for 'I'm fed up'.

[53] Busy traffic circle at the southwest corner of Central Park, marked by a statue of Christopher Columbus.

[54] National restaurant chain providing economical meals in a clean and hygienic environment, with outlets in New York City.

[55] Statue situated at the southwest corner of Central Park, dedicated to the men killed on the USS Maine during the conflict with Spain over Cuba in 1898.

[56] See note 53.

[57] Unidentified reference.

[58] In the 1920s, a seedy area of lower Manhattan, home to cheap housing, entertainments, and illicit bars.

Va z-y donc sans avoir peur!
Soutiens l'honneur national —
Le cak' walk sans égal,
Oh! Bedelia, elia, elia,
Tiens bien haut et ferme le drapeau
Des enfants de Chicago![59]

It's lovely, cried Harold.

It is nice, Campaspe admitted. Time makes tunes classic.

She had a talent for singing popular airs, and the boys were delighted when she attacked another, broken by, harmonized and syncopated with, the shaking of cocktails.

A la Mâtiniqu', Mâtiniqu', Mâtiniqu'!
C'i ça qu'est chic!
C'i ça qu'est chic!
Pas d'veston, de col, de pantalon,
Simplement un tout pitit cal'çon.
Y'en a du plaisir, du plaisir, du plaisir,
Jamais malad', jamais mourir;
On ôt le cal'çon pour diner l'soir,
Et tout le monde est en noir![60]

In spite of the French words they sound so American, was Harold's comment.

They *are* American, affirmed Campaspe, by Stephen Foster, or Edward MacDowell,[61] or one of those dead composers. They are almost folksongs now, and what a quaint old-fashioned air they have, like the names of absinthe frappé, or sherry flip, or pousse café.[62] You should hear Fannie sing them; she's so young, so indecently young. You know my mother, don't you, Bunny?

---

[59]   Based on, but not a translation of, a best-selling 1903 Tin Pan Alley novelty tune, 'Bedelia: The Irish Coon Song Serenade'. The French song (author and date unknown) imagines Bedelia coming to France. The section Campaspe sings is the advice given to Bedalia by her family as she sets sail: 'Bedelia, beware of social blunders | Bedelia, don't fall | In France, they are knowing, sophisticated | So come on, without fear | Uphold the national honour | the unrivalled cake walk [a popular dance of the era] | Oh! Bedelia, elia, elia | Hold high and firm the flag of the children of Chicago'.

[60]   A verse from a popular French song of 1912, 'A la Martinique' (Henri Christiné, lyrics and music), in Antillean Creole dialect that plays on the racism of the period in its representation of Caribbean men: 'In Martinique ... | That's what's chic | ... | No jacket, no collar, no trousers | Just undies | There's lots of fun, fun, fun | Never sick, never die | we take off our undies to eat in the evening | and everyone's in black'.

[61]   Stephen Foster (1826–1864), world-famous American songwriter known for sentimental parlour music and blackface minstrel songs; Edward McDowell (1860–1908), American classical composer and pianist. Ironically, the origin of 'A la Martinique' was, in fact, American. It was based on 'Belle of the Barber's Ball' (1908) by George M. Cohan (1878–1942), a major figure in musical theatre.

[62]   Cocktails popular in the late nineteenth and early twentieth centuries.

Never had the pleasure.

She looks younger than 'paspe, Paul explained. Always going to fortune-tellers. One told her last summer that she would fall in love at the age of thirty-two!

Dear Fannie, I'd like to see her again, Campaspe mused.

Where is your mother? asked Paul.

Fannie's in Paris.

Have you read about the Siamese twins?[63] John Armstrong interpolated.

What? from Bunny.

One of them died!

Oh! from Campaspe.

One of them had a son, put in Paul.

If the public were more imaginative, the newspapers could not print such things, commented Campaspe.

Ki brought in a trayful of cocktails.

Why do Japs always smile? asked John Armstrong, as Ki retired to his little kitchen.

It's their mask, a perfect one, Campaspe replied. You never know what they are really thinking. I have a harder one. Why do Greek bootblacks always have such wonderful hair?

I suppose it's the essential oils, Paul began…. And then, with a swift transition, Let's go junketing; let's go to Coney Island![64]

Just the thing, assented John Armstrong, and Bunny and Campaspe approved. Nobody asked Harold for his opinion of the projected excursion.

Have you got your car? Bunny demanded of Campaspe.

It should be outside.

Ki! Paul shouted.

Flurry and rush began, preparation for excitement and adventure, a swift appraisal of boxes of cigarettes. Ki poured whiskey and gin and rum into tube-containers enclosed in field-glass cases.

Hats! Hats! cried John Armstrong.

The little Jap ran about, smiling, executing commands, bearing hats, ridding the apartment of guests. They walked out into the bright sunglare of Gramercy Park. Inside the railing, a half-dozen children, watched by their nursemaids, were attempting to pretend to enjoy themselves in the little forest of shrubbery under the melancholy statue of Edwin Booth.[65]

---

[63] A reference to Josefa and Rosa Blazek, conjoined twins who died on 30 March 1922.

[64] Between 1880 and 1920 Coney Island was the largest amusement park in America. Originally a leisure site for the wealthy and middle classes, by the 1920s it became more accessible, providing cheap entertainment for working and immigrant classes.

[65] American Shakespearean actor (1833–1893) and one of the Park's most famous residents. The statue at the centre of the Park depicts him as Hamlet.

Have you heard about Amy? asked Paul.

Has Amy married again? Bunny queried.

That I don't know, but she smoked a cigarette in Gramercy Park the other evening and the pious trustees have taken her key away from her.

Poor Amy! Campaspe mused aloud. She doesn't understand how to enjoy her freedom. She doesn't understand her world. She wants to live her own life, as she sees us live ours, and she doesn't know how. She's always having keys taken away from her. Everything will be locked to her soon.

Would you smoke a cigarette in Gramercy Park? asked Harold, as they stepped into the car.

Sit in front with the chauffeur, Harold, she directed. John, you and Paul sit with me. Bunny, take the strapontin.[66]

They followed her instructions, and the Rolls-Royce swung out into the street and turned down Irving Place.[67]

I wouldn't want to: Campaspe at last found time to reply to Harold's question. Amy is trying too hard to fight the world, to soften the world's corners, instead of softening her own. In the end, of course, martyrdom is waiting for her. I have no respect for martyrs. Any one who is strong enough shapes the world to his own purposes, but he doesn't do it roughly; he accomplishes his object in just the way that any woman you know gets anything she wants out of her husband ... by appearing to be in sympathy with those who oppose him. Conform externally with the world's demands and you will get anything you desire in life. By a process of erosion you can dig a hole in two years through public opinion that it would take you two centuries to knock through. It is just as great a mistake to reject violently ideas that do not appeal to us. Rejection implies labour, interest, even fear. Indifference is the purer method. Indifference rids one of cause and effect simultaneously.... The world — she appeared to be in a kind of revery — is a very pleasant place for people who know how to live. We are the few. The rest are fools, and all we have to do to persuade the fools to permit us to live our own lives is to make them believe that we, too, are fools. It's so simple, once you understand. But what does the martyr gain? He has lost the suffrage of public opinion and he has done nothing to advance his own cause, for unless he has made the world believe in it he cannot carry it through. Bah! she repeated, I have no respect for martyrs. Give me an intelligent hypocrite every time!

What an extraordinary woman! thought Harold, and it occurred to him that he was learning more from her than he was from Paul. It was she who was giving him his first lessons in worldliness and he did not sense anything

---

[66]   Foldable seat.
[67]   Street running from East Twentieth to East Fourteenth, between, and parallel to, Park and Third Avenues.

tangible in the manner of these lessons which he could resent. He found himself less aggressive, less inclined to obstinacy, chip more off shoulder, and back more flexible, than he had found himself with Drains. Paul seemed decent enough, he admitted, but he did not feel quite natural with Paul, quite ready to relax in his presence. With Campaspe, on the other hand, he already seemed acquainted; she awakened his sympathy. Part of this readier acceptance was doubtless due to his early environment. He knew women and trusted them. In spite of his college years, perhaps because of them, he never felt quite comfortable with men…. He was left to himself. The four in the back of the car were conversing in an animated manner about matters with which he had no concern. There was, however, he perceived, no rudeness in connection with this exclusion. He did not have the feeling, which had come to him so many times at college, that he was being ignored. It was rather as though these people considered him already enough of a friend so that they might talk freely in his presence without making any mechanical attempt to draw him in. Presently, he discovered that the motor of a Rolls-Royce heats the feet mercilessly. He spoke of this to the chauffeur, who opened an aperture near Harold's ankles, permitting a draught to blow across them.

There is something pathetic about the young, the suffering of a young man trying to adjust himself to circumstances which he does not understand. Harold presently began to miss the compassion assuredly due him, and his mood shifted. In spite of the friendly attitude of his companions, he began to pity himself, as he sat silent and alone on the little seat beside the driver of the Rolls-Royce, which was breaking all the speed laws, as it burst forward down the Long Island turnpike. Houses, farms, trees, Socony signs:[68] a monotonous prospect. Harold, saddened a little, it is presumable, by Bacardi rum, thought of himself as helplessly immeshed in a kind of life which he certainly did not understand and which he felt sure he never could like. Helpless! From his earliest childhood he had been accustomed to accepting, unquestioning, the arrangements others had made for him. He remembered how he had been brought up like a girl, with long curls which had not been clipped until he was nearly seven years old. He recalled, with shame, the day on which he had been permitted to discard his kilts for a boy's proper apparel, and how at the time, he had been ashamed, rather, to make the change. He thought of his college days, one long struggle at hopeless compromise. He had not been a particularly good student, and the external activities of his fellow-students had proved utterly alien to his taste. How many times he had walked alone across the campus! How many nights he had remained alone in his room! His vacations were a repetition of his childhood: Aunt Sadi, *dear* Aunt Sadi, he thought today, Persia Blaine, Miss Perkins; riding, swimming, reading, the quiet, easy security of

---

[68] Major oil company of the era that exploited highway billboard advertising.

farm life, safe but unrevealing…. That extraordinary interview with his father: whatever happened he could never forget that. Then Alice Blake, who reminded him of Persia Blaine and Aunt Sadi, and who was young and beautiful besides, had passed his way, had been swept from his vision, and nothing remained but this new life, this incomprehensible and silly life, compounded of cocktails and chatter and music, which in its dissonances sounded almost obscene to him. In spite of Campaspe, he felt that he would never be able to cope with it. Why didn't he break away and find himself? That seemed to be the most impossible procedure of all.

At last the towers and minarets and wheels and scenic railways of Coney Island came into view in the sonorous light; then, the wide strip of ocean, the beach strewn with refuse and bathers, fat Jewesses, and flashy young clerks from Broadway shops. There was a curious confusion of artificial and natural odours: the fishy, salty smell of the sea; the aroma of cooking-food, steaming clams, sausages, frying pork. A mechanical piano wailed out Say it with music[69] a quarter tone off key. Barkers everywhere: Now, ladies and gentlemen, I have the honour to present this afternoon this little lady here on my right, the Princess Sesame, considered by many to be the GREATEST LIVING EXPONENT of oriental harem dancing. The little lady will perform for you here this afternoon, INSIDE THIS TENT, a feat hitherto unattempted by any of the world's great terpsichorean[70] marvels, NAMELY, the Sicilian shimmy dagger dance!... Balloons, captive and toy, elongated and round, purple, green, and red. Ferris wheels, airplane swings, merry-go-rounds, tinsel and marabou, hula dolls, trap-drummers, giant coasters, gyroplanes, dodge 'ems, maelstroms, frolics, wonderlands, poses plastiques, pig slides, barbecues, captive aeros, witching waves, whirlpools, whips, chute the chutes, Venetian canals, fun houses, targets, shooting galleries, popcorn, cracker-jack, pretzels, soft drinks, eskimo pies, ice-cream cones: all the delights of the greatest of American amusement parks.[71]

Campaspe clapped her hands. It's superb! she cried. Just what I imagined. I'll never have to see anything again. It's all of life and most of death: sordid splendour with a touch of immortality and middle-class ecstasy. This is Ella Wheeler Wilcox, and Thomas Hardy, and Max Beerbohm, and Bret Harte, and even James Joyce.[72] It's a parable; it's an allegory; it's the pagan idea of heaven,

---

[69]   Popular song of 1921 by Irving Berlin.
[70]   Relating to dancing.
[71]   Of the 'delights' listed, most are rides. A trap-drummer is a street musician who plays the drum and other instruments at once. *Poses plastiques* (flexible poses) were an adult entertainment involving nude models.
[72]   Campaspe juxtaposes popular and high or avant-garde artists: Ella Wheeler Wilcox (1850–1919), a widely popular poet, known for poetry of sentiment and uplift; Thomas Hardy (1840–1928), renowned British novelist and poet; Max Beerbohm (1872–1956), British essayist, parodist, and caricaturist, associated with Oscar Wilde; Bret Harte (1836–1902), fiction writer, best known for his tales of the wild West; James Joyce (1882–1941), Irish

and the Christian conception of hell. It burns and it freezes. It is clamour and it is silence. It is both home and the house of prostitution. It is what you want and what you want to escape. It is — she turned to Harold — complete experience. It is your education.

Harold was dazzled by her enthusiasm, but he certainly had no idea what she was talking about.

What shall we do first? asked Paul, rather languidly. They had descended from the motor and were walking along the beach.

I'm hungry, struck up Bunny.

Get Bunny a hot dog, suggested John Armstrong.

I could eat a smoked Pom,[73] was Bunny's riposte.

Presently, they were all munching sausages laid in between two strips of bun, larded with mustard.

Buy me a balloon and a kewpie,[74] John, cried the ravished Campaspe. Can you find me a geranium balloon? ... No, they're all off-colour. I'll take a blue one. Harold, come here! Stay with me and you'll enjoy yourself. John, the other side for you. I find you charming, John. There's something so fresh and wholesome about you Wall Street men after a week-end in the country. The country is so perverse, nothing normal about it at all. The boy who took care of the cows had jaundice.

You're a duck, Cam — Mrs. Lorillard, John laughed. Let's do a scenic railway[75] in the same seat.

Game! This long one. She pointed to a great structure, waving up and down cross country on incredibly tall stilts. They entered the gateway and booked places. As they swung and pitched down the headlong descents, she grasped him first by the arms, then round the shoulders, leaning against him, and, while he was only mildly thrilled by the motion — he had been an ace in the army —,[76] her magnetic propinquity proved more unsettling. At the end of the ride, she removed the withered geraniums from her belt and tossed them away.

I'll get you some more: Harold was beside her again.

No more flowers today, she announced decisively, but thank you, Harold.... She turned to John: With you next to me, I'd like to do that over.

Game! he echoed her earlier refrain.

She laughed. We'll try another sport.

They stood before a small, brightly decorated wooden structure, in front of

---

modernist avant-garde writer.
[73]   Short for a Pomeranian, a kind of dog, classed as a toy dog due to its small size.
[74]   A brand of baby cupid-style dolls, one of the first mass-market toys, based on a popular comic strip.
[75]   Term for a rollercoaster.
[76]   Air Force pilot who destroys five or more enemy aircraft.

which, stretched on ropes, a dozen rudely painted banners informed passers-by of the nature of the attractions to be viewed within. It was a sideshow, a congress of freaks, an assemblage of strange people. There were, the posters promised, a sword-swallower, a tattooed lady, giants and pigmies, a three-legged man, a bearded gentlewoman, a man with an iron tongue, a fellow with a revolving head, a wild man of Borneo, an armless man; in short, an auspicious miscellany. The barker, standing on a low platform, was functioning, waving his hands and shouting to the curious crowd which had assembled.

Within, he declared, we have the greatest collection of abnormal human beings ever exhibited together under one roof. Where else can you see the little lady only two feet high, who is ninety years of age? Where else can you gaze upon a death-defying demon who eats sharp knives and thrives on fire? He swallows the burning flames as you and I swallow our bread and meat. His throat is the wonder of science. See the Rrrrrrrussian cossack who carries thousands of pounds in weights on a hook passed through his tongue! The man with the iron tongue! See the little lady with her snakes. This little lady, a picture of female beauty, is only sixteen years old, and yet she wraps a forty-pound boa constrictor around her waist and defies him to crrrrrush her. The most terrifying spectacle you can observe on the entire island.

That settles it, exclaimed Campaspe. I adore snakes, and so they passed the entrance. A few others followed them in, but the greater part of the crowd lingered outside to stare at the huge, crudely painted banners, and to listen to the gifted barker.

Inside, a series of platforms circled the small room, and on these platforms were ranged the strange people, the midgets, the tall men, the sword-swallowers, and ladies bearded and tattooed. Some of them looked merely bored, but most of them wore a superior expression of conscious pride, considering themselves, indubitably, of some importance in the world, contemptuous of that part of the public which did not share their peculiar perfections. Their costumes ran to red and blue and gold and pink, tricked out with tinsel and machine-made lace. All were retailing photographs of their strange selves, and a few sold booklets. Occasionally, these favoured folk conversed with one another, spoke a few words, casual and solemn at best, for it could be seen that they had nothing of importance to say to one another or to the world, nothing, save: Here I am; look at me; I am a brilliant exception on this sphere where you are conspicuously and defectively normal. You have only two legs, the three-legged man seemed to assert sneeringly, while the lady with The Last Supper tattooed on her back and Rock of Ages[77] on her belly was obviously a trifle impatient with such women as were forced to wear mere clothes by way of decorating their bodies.

Campaspe noted these impressions, while the barker was introducing the

---

[77]   Tattoos of these subjects were popular with circus and dime-museum performers.

little ladies and the wild men. Now he stood before a platform on which was seated a girl who immediately drew the attention of Campaspe's group. She was assuredly an exception, a special jewel. She had the delicate features of a beauty from the Caucasus or an aristocratic Levantine Jewess, her fragile nose, her exquisitely formed lips, her high cheek-bones had been modelled by an artist.[78] She was a girl, evidently, for whom God had determined to do his best. Short and slender, her body was rhythmic and full of grace. Her head was set above her shoulders in a piquant, bird-like way, while a mass of fluffy brown hair surrounded her pale face and her great green eyes with a delicious shadow. She wore a costume of spangled crimson, cut off at the knees, with a low neck and no sleeves, and on her head a skull-cap fashioned entirely of purple sequins, and surmounted by a feather almost as tall as herself. Her stockings were the colour of the blue-jay's feathers.

What a lovely creature! cried Campaspe.

She's beautiful, said Paul.

Even Harold regarded the girl with curiosity, as she stood up to go through with her act without any of the abandon of the other performers. Ill at ease in her costume and out of place in the show, still it could be seen that she was lacking in self-consciousness. There was no rouge on her face, no paint on her lips.

This little lady to the right, announced the barker, is the bravest little lady in the show. Only sixteen years of age, she handles the fiercest and most dangerous rrreptiles with the carelessness of a farmhand petting a tame calf. She has visited the jungle and brought back with her vipers with fangs so deadly that one dart would kill a buffalo, boa constrictors who could fold a full-grown African lion in their coils and crrrush him to death, the deadly poisonous Indian cobra, more dreaded by the natives than the man-eating tiger! And to make her act more dangerous, it is our custom to feed these venomous reptiles only once a month. They are hungry now. They have not been fed for three weeks. Show the ladies and gentlemen what you can do, Zimbule.

As a hurdy-gurdy groaned out a melancholy rendering of I hear you calling me,[79] the little lady stooped over a great chest, painted bright pink and studded with brass-headed nails, and raised the cover. From the gaping box one gathered a confused impression of a nest of lethargic serpents. One, more active than the rest, elevated his great jewelled head, with its staring, beaded eyes, and protruded his forked tongue. With a lack of relish, an active distaste, indeed, which must have been apparent even to the small boys present, the little lady lifted the huge,

---

[78]   Caucasus borders Europe and Asia, while the Levant covers modern-day Palestine, Jordan, and Syria, suggesting the girl is Eurasian or Middle Eastern in appearance.
[79]   Popular British sentimental song of 1908 (Harold Lake, lyrics; Charles Marshall, music).

scaly monster out of the chest and disposed his heavy iridescent folds around
her torso. Up to a certain point, the snake submitted with an easy grace and a
seeming lassitude. Quite suddenly, however, with a quick brilliant movement,
which in its intricacy baffled the beholder, he coiled himself securely three or
four times about her waist in an embrace which constantly grew more perilous,
while, with his head pointing vertically straight upward from her abdomen, he
darted what might be called forked kisses at her chin. The girl's face assumed
a pallor which gave to her beauty an even greater delicacy. Her lips quivered;
immediately, only the whites of her eyes were visible; her body collapsed, and
she fell heavily to the floor. The serpent, alarmed, perhaps, by this new game,
swiftly unrolled himself and glided back into his box.

Quick! Campaspe whispered to John. Quick! Get the child!

Armstrong vaulted to the platform, caught Zimbule in his arms and,
descending, made his way through the group, too astonished to question or
oppose him, out to the open air. Thence Campaspe and the others followed
him.

That's right! the barker approved. Take her out! Give her the air!

It's criminal. She's only a baby … Campaspe exclaimed.

They all have to begin, said the barker. It's her first show here, but she swore
she was on. These kids lie like hell.

To a little plot of grass behind the show-building John had borne her, laying
her gently on the sward, while Campaspe and the others swiftly surrounded her
and kept the crowd from surging too close. Paul had found some water which
he dashed in her face. Presently, she opened her great green eyes.

Who are you? she asked, and Campaspe was relieved to discover that a rather
common voice and accent offered the proper contrast to the refined beauty of
her features.

Don't talk, suggested Campaspe. Wait till you feel better.

The amateur snake-charmer glanced searchingly into the faces of her new
friends; presently, she smiled.

Well, I was game.

What did you do it for? demanded Campaspe.

Coin. You gotta eat.

Hungry?

Ain't had a good feed for a week.

Where do you live?

No place.

Where's your family?

In hell, I guess.

Any friends?

Don't kid me.

Campaspe turned to John again. Carry her to the car, she directed.

He bent over to lift her once more, but the child, now resting her chin on the palm of her left hand, and half sitting up, rejected his offer of assistance.

Say, I can walk.

Come with us. We'll get you something to eat, Campaspe explained. She slipped a five dollar bill into the palm of the barker, with the words, She doesn't belong here.

The barker grinned. Glad to get rid of her, lady, so easy. I couldn't leave her do another show.

The group, pressing close about to protect her from the still curious crowd, made their way slowly to the spot where the motor was parked. Once in the car, Campaspe directed her chauffeur to drive to a hotel further down the beach. The girl slid into the cushions, between John and Campaspe. The others found places.

As the car started, the girl's distrust awakened. Say, she cried, what's the idea?

You're hungry, aren't you?

I sure am.

Want something to eat?

God, yes.

Well, you're going to get it. Keep quiet for a while. You're not strong enough to talk yet.

The child offered no further resistance, but at the entrance to the dining-room of the hotel, Campaspe met with a new form of opposition. It was early, and the room was practically empty, but the costume of the young lady! Campaspe sent for the head-waiter.

You know Mr. Lorillard?

Certainly, madame.

Well, I am Mrs. Lorillard. This is the Duchess of Manchester. She is studying Coney Island for her book on America,[80] and it is her fancy to dress like this.... Shall we go to the ...? She named another hotel nearby.

Certainly not, Mrs. Lorillard. The man became obsequious at once. Come right in here, of course. He led them to a table near the window.

What do you want to eat? asked Paul.

Steak, pork chops, ham and eggs.... Whether from lack of breath or lack of imagination the girl did not make the list longer.

Campaspe turned to the waiter. Bring her a glass of milk and some toast

---

[80]   The real Duchess of Manchester in this period, Helena Zimmerman, was, in fact, American. The idea of a British aristocrat writing a book on America would not have been strange. Margot Asquith, for example, celebrated socialite and wife of a former British Prime Minister, published her impressions of America in 1922.

and be quick about it. The girl is starving. Then to the pseudo-enchantress of serpents: You can't have everything you want now. You're not strong enough to eat it. It would make you ill. Now don't talk any more till you've swallowed some food.

The girl obeyed and remained silent, but her great green eyes wandered curiously from face to face. When, after a very short interval, the waiter returned with the order, she drank the milk at a single gulp, and crunched the toast between her strong young jaws with an intensity which betokened anxiety lest the food should be removed before she could dispatch it. Campaspe and the boys were sipping glasses of orange juice, into which Paul had dexterously inserted drops from the field-glass cases which Ki had prepared.

Feel better now, kid? asked John Armstrong.

I feel all right.

What is your name? Campaspe asked.

Wotschures?

Campaspe Lorillard.

Zimbule O'Grady.

Zimbule O'Grady, exclaimed Paul, with delight.... Zim —

The girl misunderstood his tone. Don't you like it? she flared.

Paul was quick to aver that he adored it.

Bunny, whose mind, as usual, was wandering, accidentally saved the situation. He was sitting with his back to the corner, facing the entrance. Idly watching people coming in, his attention was attracted by a pair just about to sit down at a table across the room.

My God! 'paspe, he cried, look at Cupid!

Campaspe and the others turned to gaze across the long, vine-hung and trellised room, at a short, fat man, slightly bald, who stood beside a massive blonde, wearing a black dress, quivering with jet, an enormous hat, trembling with paradise plumes, and from whose wrists dangled enough gold-bags, vanity-cases, bracelets, chains, gold pencils, and bangles to set a minor Sixth Avenue merchant up in business.[81]

Campaspe smiled. What abominable taste Cupid has in women, she remarked. He looks like an olive on a holiday. Then: I think we'd better start back. We've had our adventure.

What about dinner? asked John Armstrong.

We'll stop somewhere else for that.

Why not go back to the apartment? Paul suggested. Ki can run out for some cold cuts and a salad.

---

[81]   Sixth Avenue was the centre of the developing 'ready to wear' trade and was, hence, less exclusive than the high-end shopping of Fifth Avenue.

Kalter Aufschnitt![82] Just the thing! cried Campaspe, delighted, and no danger of seeing vulgar people!

Can he get some ham? Zimbule demanded hopefully.

Yes, and you will be ready to eat it then.

For the drive back, certain rearrangements of position were effected. Bunny attempted to slip into the back seat beside Zimbule, but, with some dexterity, Campaspe pushed John Armstrong between herself and the girl, and, as Harold and Paul already occupied the strapontins, Bunny was forced to take the seat by the chauffeur. He sulked. Harold was feeling altogether confused and uncomfortable. Paul was highly amused.

Zimbule now seemed as strong as a young ox, as alert as a wren searching for worms. She had completely forgone her momentary distrust, and was behaving as only a young animal, bereft of self-consciousness, can behave. In the restaurant, she and Bunny, from their positions of propinquity, had indulged in quaint plays of words and hands. They had even been a little rough at times. Now she called out to him, and occasionally reached over to poke him in the back or to pull his hair. Campaspe, for some curious and secret reason, was concentrating her attention on John Armstrong, flattering the handsome stock-broker with overt suavities until he responded with some of the clumsy intuition of a Newfoundland dog. Bunny, too, found that his feet were getting hot. These Rolls-Royces! But what a burrrrrrrrrrrrrrr for a tone-poem! Inns and trees flew past. Farmhouses and fields, aqueducts, railroad embankments. At last (it was late twilight), the illuminated city, the tall gloomy towers, their pinnacles gleaming, the serrated silhouette of Manhattan. John Armstrong ventured to take Campaspe's hand in his. She made no objection.

Ki opened the door with his habitual enigmatic smile, and when bidden to seek refreshments, he smiled more blandly than ever. While Ki laid the table, Paul was shaking cocktails, assisted by Harold, who cracked the ice and squeezed the oranges. Zimbule was sitting on Bunny's lap.

Oh, Ki! cried Campaspe, I forgot to tell Ambrose I wouldn't need him any more. Run down and tell him not to wait. I'll walk home. Well — she turned to the spread table — here we are again. As for you, young lady, you go home with me, of course.

What will Cupid say? from Bunny.

Whatever he likes.

A dubious expression lurked between Zimbule's eyebrows, and Bunny crossed his fingers. The girl seemed as comfortable as if she had been accustomed to pass every evening in Paul's apartment, showing no curiosity. She was, Campaspe noted, oblivious to surroundings. Things, in themselves, meant nothing to her. Harold, she saw, was too self-conscious and embarrassed to eat.

---

[82] German, meaning 'cold cuts'.

After supper, Campaspe settled herself on a couch, with John Armstrong on the floor beneath her.

Lucky I came today, 'paspe. I thought I should never see you again. It's been six months since we met for the first time.

You really like me?

I adore you, 'paspe.

That's right ... You Wall Street men! So substantial! No jaundice.

Paul turned to Harold: There won't be many days like this.

It doesn't matter. Father said ...

Oh! I know. Strange bird, your father. I don't mind telling you I'm not wise.

What kind of women do you like? Campaspe was hailing Harold.

I like you. He was very much in earnest.

Very good for an amateur. You shall have your day, but this is John's night.

John squeezed her hand. You're making fun of me, 'paspe.

She regarded him quizzically.

Towards two o'clock, Campaspe glanced at her wrist watch.

I must take the child home, she said. She must be tired.

Where is your child? Paul set down his cocktail glass. Both noted for the first time that Zimbule was no longer in the room.

Where is Bunny? demanded John Armstrong.

Paul rose and strode across the floor to the closed bedroom door. Opening it softly, he emitted a low chuckle. The others joined him.

The bed-lamp, shedding a soft amber glow, was still lighted. The floor was strewn with spangled crimson skirts, stockings the shade of blue-jay feathers, sequined caps, boots, trousers, shirts, chemises.... Under the sheet in Paul's superb bed, with a crest-emblazoned head-board shaped like the facade of a Dutch house and with its posts terminating in bleeding pomegranates, in this bed, which had once been the property of some Iberian grandee, lay Bunny and Zimbule, their bare arms entwined round each other's throats, their lips slightly parted, their eyes closed. They were asleep.

C'est Venus toute entière à sa proie attachée![83] whispered Paul.

Don't disturb them, said Campaspe quietly. They look too cunning like that. Zimbule passes the night here. John can take me home.

Harold's expression was one of the wildest horror.

---

[83] French, meaning 'Venus herself fastened to her prey!'. Paul quotes from Jean Racine's (1639–1699) neoclassical tragedy, *Phèdre* (1677), about a woman's doomed passion for her stepson.

Chapter V

Campaspe lived on East Nineteenth Street,[84] just around the corner from Paul's apartment in Gramercy Park. In the cool, June night air, John Armstrong walked home with her. Directly they were alone her manner changed almost imperceptibly; not that she seemed more dignified — Campaspe, even in her most apparently careless moments, always had dignity — ; rather, she appeared to be preoccupied. As they strolled down Irving Place John made an effort to arouse her from her presumed lassitude. He started to speak and, indeed, did form sentences, but her replies were abstract and distant, if not entirely formal. Once or twice his hand edged nervously towards her arm, and even touched it, but she gave no sign that she was aware of this contact: she made no effort to move away, nor did she respond to it. Her mood was exacerbating, and it roused in John a kind of dumb anger and childlike helplessness. In a few brief moments, however, they stood before her door. After the fashion of the houses on this street, a short flight of steps descended to the entrance. He followed her, without a plan, largely without hope, but with a blind animal instinct, into the darkened vestibule and, as she was fitting her key in the lock, drew her quickly to him and kissed her, perforce, on the throat, as she had turned her head away.

Good-night, John, she said in an even voice, as she swung the door open.

Good God, Campaspe!

She slipped through the open doorway and shut the door behind her, not ostentatiously slamming it in his face, but closing it softly. Nevertheless, she noted, to John the effect wore the same air of finality. Through the eyes in the back of her head she was aware that he hesitated for a moment, dazed, before he walked away.

Campaspe, meanwhile, ascended the stairs, entered her chamber, and pressed a button, flooding the pleasant room with light. The soft toile de Jouy[85] hangings at the windows blew gently back and forth with the refreshing breeze. The bed with its delicate linen was spread open, waiting for her. Frederika, her maid, following instructions, had long since retired, and Campaspe did not awaken her. It was with rather a sensuous feeling that she slipped off her clothes,

---

[84] East Nineteenth was the jewel of Gramercy Park in this period. Known as the 'Walk Beautiful' and the 'Pomander Walk', it featured artistically redesigned rowhouses. Van Vechten lived here from 1915 to 1924.

[85] Decorating pattern for fabric or wallpaper, usually with a pastoral theme in one colour, set against a white or off-white background.

and stood before a long mirror, regarding herself. At length, she donned a night-gown of French hand-manufacture and the colour of champagne, as filmy as it is possible for such a garment to be made. Over her shoulders she drew a négligé of the shade of the green orchid, as she sat down before her dressing-table, an elaborate altar, laid with rose-jade cists for cosmetics and crystal vials of French holy waters, blessed by Houbigant and Coty.[86] She combed out her short hair until it bristled on either side of her face. Now she rubbed cold cream into her flesh, wiping away the discarded artificial complexion with a towel. Then she carefully made up again, applying fresh carmine to her lips, new rouge to her cheeks, and outlining her eyelids with a blue pencil. This was her invariable custom before retiring, and she often said to herself that she looked at least as well in bed as she did at the opera. Presently, still sitting before her dressing-table, she lighted a cigarette and began to reflect, one knee resting lightly on the other, swinging her leg backwards and forwards, from the foot of which a satin mule, the toe sparkling with an infinity of tiny mirrors, depended.

John Armstrong: she really never could accustom herself to men who smoked cigars. The manly American. Why, she wondered, was it deemed manly in America to drink coffee and effeminate to drink tea?.... A strangely reluctant boy, Harold. It would be interesting to know why he was so reluctant. She hoped, however, that he always would be. In his reluctance lay his claim to charm.... Lucky Paul! And lucky Bunny! Would he ever write fine music? she asked herself. Could a woman help him do this? Could this woman? A fine animal. The finest animal she had ever seen. Delicate and exquisite, and yet like an animal. She considered: not like a doe, more like a tiger; graceful and exquisite ... and hungry! Campaspe smiled.

She recalled a phrase from A. E., which she had run across a day or so earlier: I could not desire what was not my own, and what is our own we cannot lose.... Desire is hidden identity....[87] Was life, she queried of the alert face in her mirror, a straight or a zigzag line? Do we, perhaps, live backwards and forwards, with memories of the past and mystic visions of the future? She remembered how some one had said of her that she was like a pleasant pool ... exposing a dormant silvery surface ... or rippling placidly ... with shadows, which portended hidden depths. No one, she reflected, save herself, knew how deep the pool was, or what might lie concealed at the bottom.... Shadows! There must be a philosophy of shadows! Shadows were the only realities.[88] And there

---

[86]   Parisian perfume makers, the first founded in Paris in 1775, the second in 1904.

[87]   A. E., the pseudonym of George William Russell (1867–1935), Irish writer, nationalist, and theosophist. Campaspe quotes from his spiritual autobiography, *The Candle of Vision* (1918), in which he recounts divine visions.

[88]   Campaspe's idealization of shadows as reality counters Plato's classical philosophical view from 'The Allegory of the Cave' in *The Republic*. Her views correspond with the Celtic mysticism of A. E. in which shadows function as a metaphor for the spirit.

were always shadows, but most people overlooked the shadow in their search for the object which cast it. It was, she assured herself, like searching for Richard Wagner, instead of listening to Tristan.[89] She smiled again as a phrase of Paul's recurred to her: Campaspe does not know the vices, she invents them! Invents them! Imagination, that was the shadow of personality, assuredly the deepest enchantment! Savoir n'est rien, imaginer est tout. Rien n'existe que ce qu'on imagine, the sagacious fairy had remarked to Sylvestre Bonnard....[90] Campaspe sprayed herself with Guerlain's l'Heure Bleue.[91]

She put out her cigarette and, casting aside her négligé and her mules, got into bed. Pressing a button in the jewelled head of an enamelled tortoise on her bed-table, she extinguished the lights, save that of her reading lamp, a great iridescent dragonfly, suspended over her bed. Propping herself up against the pillows, she examined the books on her bed-table: plays by Luigi Pirandello, tales by Doppo Kunikida, poems by the Welsh poet, Ab Gwilym, Jésus-la-Caille by Francis Carco, Las Sonatas by Del Valle Inclán, and Aldous Huxley's Mortal Coils....[92] She swept these from the table, leaving one or two at the bottom of the pile. Choosing Rachilde's l'Animale,[93] she read a few lines, and then put it aside. She opened a slight volume by Norman Douglas,[94] and that met a similar fate. Two paragraphs in Ronald Firbank's Vainglory[95] satisfied her. She was not

---

[89] German composer and theatre director (1813–1883), famed for his operas, including *Tristan und Isolde* (1865).

[90] French, meaning 'To know is nothing; to imagine is everything. Nothing exists but that which is imagined'. Campaspe cites Anatole France's (1844–1924) *Crime de Sylvestre Bonnard* (1881), in which the protagonist has a vision of a fairy who denounces his pedantic empiricism.

[91] French, meaning 'the blue hour'. A perfume, first issued in 1912, by Parisian perfume manufacturer Guerlain, meant to evoke dusk in Paris and inspired by impressionist painting.

[92] Pirandello (1867–1936), Italian avant-garde playwright, noted for existential, psychologically-driven dramas; Kunikida (1871–1908), Japanese author, who wrote in a romantic and, latterly, naturalist style; Dafydd ab Gwilym (also Dafydd ap Gwilym) (fourteenth century), medieval Welsh poet whose love and nature poems bore the influence of the European courtly love tradition and Provençal troubadour poetry; Carco (1886–1958), French author, known for his works about the Parisian underworld, written in the vernacular, including *Jésus-la-Caille* (1914; 1920), whose protagonist is a transvestite; Ramón María del Valle-Inclán y de la Peña (1866–1936), modernist author, often styled a Spanish James Joyce, whose *Las Sonatas* (1902–1905) are the fictional memoirs of a Don Juan figure's romantic adventures; Huxley (1894–1963), British writer of social satire, including *Mortal Coils* (1922), a short story collection.

[93] Pen name of Marguerite Vallette-Eymery (1860–1953), French decadent and symbolist writer, whose *L'Animale* (1893) centres on the perverse sexuality of its female protagonist.

[94] George Norman Douglas (1868–1952), British writer, known for travel writing.

[95] Firbank (1886–1926), British writer, whose mannered prose style, eccentric characterization, and sharp wit owed much to the decadents of the 1890s and are a feature of *Vainglory* (1915). Van Vechten promoted Firbank in an article in the *Double Dealer* (1922), reissued in his essay collection *Excavations* (1926).

criticizing the authors of these works, but it was her habit to insist that a book should satisfy a mood. With a sigh, again she stretched her arm towards her bed-table, and her fingers closed on a little volume bound in black leather: The Book of Common Prayer.[96]

Opening at random, she happened on the service for St. Mark's Day: I am the true vine, and my Father is the husbandman. Every branch in me that beareth not fruit he taketh away: and every branch that beareth fruit, he purgeth it, that it may bring forth more fruit.... I am the vine, ye are the branches....[97] She flipped the pages: Whither shall I go then from thy Spirit: or whither shall I go then from thy presence? If I take the wings of the morning: and remain in the uttermost parts of the sea ...[98] A veil of silver betraying violet shut the page from her eyes. Instead, rose a vision of the sufficing peacocks designed by Gaston Lachaise.[99] She must have an avenue of these, carved from semi-precious stones: chalcedony, sardonyx, malachite, onyx, pink and black, brown and carnation jade, crystal, and chrysoprase.... The veil lifted and exposed a brilliant flight of butterflies: the White-letter Hairstreak, the Dingy Skipper, the Camberwell Beauty, and the Pearl-bordered Fritillary, sapphire and emerald butterflies, and one of pale silver.... And the book was open at the Veni Creator Spiritus:

Come, Holy Ghost, our souls inspire,
And lighten with celestial fire.
Thou the anointing spirit art,
Who dost the sevenfold gifts impart....[100]

Campaspe fell asleep.

About three o'clock in the afternoon she awakened feeling refreshed. She was one of those who awaken from the deepest sleep to immediate consciousness, and she was at once aware that it was raining. The room was gloomy, the curtains at the windows still drawn, but from the bathroom came the sound of water pouring into her tub. Frederika, with a curiously exact intuition, invariably anticipated the rising of her mistress by two or three minutes. The maid entered.

---

[96]   Official service book for the Anglican Communion, including the forms of service for daily and Sunday worship.
[97]   St Mark's Day is April 25. From *John* 15. 1–5.
[98]   *Book of Common Prayer*, Day 29 morning prayer, *Psalm* 139, lines 6 and 8.
[99]   Gaston Lachaise (1882–1935), French-born American sculptor. His Art Deco sculpture 'Peacocks' was first exhibited as a plaster model in New York in 1918. In 1922, Lachaise created fourteen bronze casts of the work which he sold to a wealthy gallery owner.
[100]   From 'The Form of Ordaining or Consecrating a Bishop', *Book of Common Prayer*.

Good afternoon, madame.

Good afternoon, Frederika. Campaspe smiled. She was in the best of
humours....

Frederika brought the Times[101] and the morning mail on a tray, and then
retired to prepare Campaspe's breakfast. Campaspe picked up the Times and
rapidly glanced over the headlines.... The Kaiser's state carriages bought by
a funeral director caught her eye.[102] How splendid, she turned it over, to be
borne to the tomb in such a manner, and she wondered if these royal vehicles
resembled the state coaches of Ludwig of Bavaria,[103] rococo, with Cupids and
gilt.... She read of a blind man at Peekskill who had attended an execution at
Sing Sing so that he might sense *the feeling of it*....[104] She fingered the envelopes
on the tray. One of them, in a strange handwriting, she opened. It was a bill
from a hat-shop on Fifty-seventh Street.[105] She tore this up slowly. The other
letters she tossed unopened on her bed-table. Frederika had returned, and
Campaspe sipped her coffee.

Paul had promised to come in at five. Would he bring Harold? She laughed
to herself as she recalled the precipitate romance of Bunny and Zimbule. Two
babes in the woods, she mused aloud.... There were a few orders for the cook,
which Campaspe delivered through Frederika. She never had trouble with
servants. She had a system, which was to give each of them a certain part of the
work to do. When they had completed their allotted tasks they could come or go
as they liked. She put no restrictions on their time. As for Frederika, a middle-
aged Alsatian woman, with a sad face, which reminded Campaspe irresistibly
of Duse's,[106] she adored her mistress, and was inventive in contriving ways to
please her.

After her bath, Campaspe dressed carefully but comfortably. She liked to feel
the stiff brush moving through her hair, and the pressure of Frederika's arm.
She took quite as much pleasure in her body as she did in her mind. Was not
her body, indeed, her chief mental pleasure?... An hour later she descended to
the salon in a frock designed by Erté,[107] of cornflower-blue batiste, with soft
butter-colour linen collar and cuffs. The drawing-room was spacious and cool.
Campaspe did not like crowded rooms. There were few rugs, few pictures, few
pieces of furniture. The chairs and the couches were covered with toile de Jouy,

---

[101]   The *New York Times*.
[102]   This article appeared in the *Times*, 30 June 1922, p. 20.
[103]   Ludwig II (1845–1886), King of Bavaria, renowned for his extravagance.
[104]   This article appeared in the *Times*, 21 July 1922, p. 2.
[105]   Fashionable high-end shopping destination in the 1920s.
[106]   Eleanora Duse (1858–1924), Italian actress, celebrated in Europe and America.
[107]   Pseudonym of Romain de Tirtoff (1892–1990), famed Art Deco artist and designer who
worked in fashion, costume and set design, jewellery design, and graphic and decorative
arts.

with a design printed in mauve, a design in which Cupid and Psyche embraced in the company of nightingales and camellias.[108] The pictures on the walls were by Monticelli, Derain, Jennie Vanvleet Cowdery, and Matisse.[109] Near the high windows, looking down on the street below, stood great jars of lustre ware in which were growing forced geranium trees, nearly three feet tall, the stalks bare, bursting, at the top, into clusters of scarlet blossoms framed in velvet-green. She moved to the piano and touched the keys. On the rack was a jumble of sheets, in great disorder, pages of this laid between pages of that, fox-trots and jazz tunes, music by Manuel de Falla and Darius Milhaud.[110] She mentally noted her intention of purchasing some American Indian and Spanish gipsy records for her victrola. She rang the bell. Are there brioches, Frederika? Mr. Moody likes brioches. Yes, madame. Again it occurred to her to wonder if Paul would bring Harold.

When at last he was announced, he had come alone. Sensitive to impressions, he was immediately aware of her disappointment and of the occasion for it.

You wanted me to bring Harold, he said. Of course, I intended to bring him, but he has not been near me today. I'm afraid last night was more than he expected.

I hope the poor boy is not too alarmed. He is reluctant, Paulet....

Frederika bore in the tea in a miniature alabaster pot, set, together with three alabaster cups without handles, on an engraved and filigreed alabaster tray. Campaspe was standing by the mantel. Raising an ancient burnished copper mirror with a phoenix picked in the back to a level with her face, she contemplated her reflection.

I've just finished my breakfast, Paulet ... I can't drink any tea. Pour some for yourself. She handled the mirror in a reverent, even an affectionate, manner.

I had breakfast at ten, Paul groaned. The snake-charmer was hungry and she began to prowl about for food!

Are they there still? Campaspe smiled at the memory of the pretty picture.

No. After breakfast — Zimbule ate seven eggs — Bunny telephoned for a taxi,

---

[108]   Cupid, the Roman god of love, and Psyche, a mortal loved by Cupid, are famed lovers of the classical tradition who undergo a series of trials before being reunited.

[109]   Adolph Monticelli (1824–1886), French painter whose subject matter included rococo revival Watteau-style court scenes and whose textured painting style is said to have influenced Vincent Van Gogh; André Derain (1880–1954), French artist and founder of Fauvism, a movement renowned for the use of vibrant, unnatural colours; Jennie Vanvleet Cowdery (1855–1941), also spelled Jennie Van Fleet Cowdery, was an amateur artist who experienced a vogue after being featured in a 1921 New York exhibition of French and American artists; Henri Matisse (1869–1954), leading figure in the development of modern art and Fauvism.

[110]   De Falla (1876–1946), major Spanish composer, who combined Spanish folk influences with French avant-garde musical trends; Milhaud (1892–1974), French avant-garde composer, whose work was indebted to Brazilian popular music.

and they departed together, after kissing me. They have sworn eternal affection and they have begun housekeeping in Bunny's apartment.

I'd like to have them here, Campaspe threw in, *almost*....

Almost ... is what I felt. It's the way we both feel about so many things.

It's my philosophy ... almost. Campaspe replaced the mirror on the mantelshelf.

Paul had walked to the window and was looking down on the rain-swept street. Suddenly he exclaimed, How strange! A sailor with an umbrella.

Why? What? How strange? Campaspe joined him.

Sailors don't carry umbrellas. Never. It's an unwritten law in the navy.[111]

The sailor was now passing the house. The wind was high and as he walked abreast of the window the umbrella tilted far back, exposing the young man's face.

The rule remains unbroken, Campaspe cried. It isn't a sailor at all. It's the Duke!

The Duke?

The Duke of Middlebottom.[112] I thought he was in Capri,[113] but he's always travelling about in some disguise or other. How delightful of him to come here. He will assist in Harold's education.

Is he the man you told me about ... the man who gave those parties in London?

Yes.

God help Harold!

Oh! We'll look out for Harold. What a splendid prank. I wonder what can he be up to?

A little later, after Paul had gone and it had grown quite dark, Campaspe still lingered in the drawing-room. Frederika came in to light the lamps, but Campaspe requested the maid to leave the room dark. It was still drizzling outside and the drops of rain rattled against the window-panes. The rain fell interminably this summer. Campaspe sat quietly in a high-backed chair, resting her chin on her palm, thinking ... Presently she heard a step in the hall.

Is that you, Cupid? she called.

Campaspe! He came in; slunk would be a better word.

She rang the bell, and asked Frederika to light the lamps. As the room became brighter she looked at her husband; he was so small, so tired, so worried, so

---

[111] There are, in fact, navy regulations prohibiting the use of umbrellas.

[112] Van Vechten playfully signals the Duke's homosexual inclinations through his name and in having him appear first in sailor garb. Sailors, as George Chauncey argues, 'epitomized the bachelor subculture in the gay cultural imagination [...] serv[ing ...] as the central masculine icon in gay pornography' (*Gay New York*, 78).

[113] Italian island in the Tyrrhenian Sea and popular gay tourist destination in this era.

generally insignificant. She also noted, with some alarm, that he wore an air of conscious guilt, which betokened an effort at explanation.

He began, indeed, at once: Campaspe, can you forgive me?

Forgive you? Her tone was gentle. For what?

For what I did last night.

She was very languid, very uninterested, very kind, a trifle impatient, perhaps, with his stupidity.

There is, of course, nothing for which I need forgive you.

Campaspe!

What have I to forgive you?

You saw me with ...

That! She laughed. Cupid, why will you always be so romantic? Will you never believe me when I tell you that I don't care in the least what you do? I should never have married you if I had planned to worry about you. I married you because I knew I should never have to worry about you. You understand my views perfectly. Do just as you please, but I will not have you making these scenes over nothing.

Campaspe ... Couldn't things be different between us? Couldn't you?...

She rose with a look of determination. It's quite impossible.... Her tone was firmer now.... It's no good going over it. You must understand that it is quite impossible. We have our children, and it is very comfortable living this way. So long as you are satisfied, I am content, but anything else is quite impossible.

Campaspe!

She was leaving the room, but she turned back to face him. In her face now there was an expression of definite displeasure. Her square jaw was set hard.

Do, please, she said, stop pronouncing my name like a moonstruck savage.

Where are you going? His look was haunting, intense, pitiful, helpless.

I am going to change my dress.

Are you dining at home tonight? He was *almost* pathetic.

I had intended to ... but now, I don't know. I can't bear you when you're sentimental.

I'll promise ... he choked ... not to be.

And you'll stop apologizing?

Yes.

And you'll talk about something else than me?

Ye-es.

And do get over looking moonstruck, Cupid, and, for God's sake, don't call me Campaspe again tonight!

She passed on through the open door, and ascended the stairs. Cupid stared after her with the rapt, hopeless expression of a dog who has howled in vain for two hours, and has at last lost faith in his power to open doors.

Chapter VI

The morning after his first lesson with Paul Moody, Harold's mail contained an envelope which he tore open in febrile haste. Within the envelope he found a sheet of folded note-paper, but there was no writing thereon. The paper merely served as a garment for a crisp new one hundred dollar bill. Not a word! She had already thanked him, he recalled, but she might have found the heart to say something more. His life, begun so pleasantly on his first day in New York, now seemed to be caught in a perilous and inextricable tangle. The matchless Alice Blake had vanished, while a more motley crew than he had imagined could exist outside of literature had taken official possession of him. These wasters, apparently, incessantly staggered about seeking sensation. They had, it would appear, no other consistent aim. Sensation, in itself, was at the farthest pole from Harold's true desire. What he thought he wanted was a little grey home in the east with Alice Blake. Instead, he had been delivered, uncompromisingly, by an eccentric father, whom he was beginning to hate, into the hands of Paul Moody, a strange, cynical fellow. Worse even than Paul was his entourage, Bunny Hugg, John Armstrong, and now, this beastly little animal, Zimbule O'Grady. Would she and Bunny go on living together frankly at Paul's, or was that simply a lodging for the night? He could not answer this question from his limited experience. He realized that the conventions of this new existence, if there were any, were entirely unknown to him. What — he summed up his distrust in one vague, generalizing query — what did people do who lived as these people lived? What, indeed, did they not do? Had they any beliefs or faiths? Had they any responsibilities or duties or consciences? Were their days compounded of visits to Coney Island and the discovery of snake-charmers? The prey of such meditations — phantoms to which his tranquil past had not accustomed him — , Harold felt terribly alone. There was, to be sure, the horrible Drains, more horrible than ever in his massive attempts to be sympathetic. And there was … Mrs. Lorillard. But was she laughing at him? At moments, in her frankness, her ease, her buoyant assertion of personality, she had reminded him irresistibly of his aunt. Could he, however, he wondered, count on her as an ally in this thicket of foes? Were they, definitely, foes? In his ignorance he was unable to decide. He only was aware of how uncomfortable they made him feel, and he fortified himself with the assurance that the more they advanced, the more he would retreat.

He determined, as the day wore on, to write to Alice. Sitting down before his desk, he tried to compose a letter. It was a difficult matter, he soon discovered, to compose a letter — the first — to a girl with whom he was in love, a girl whom, at the same time, he scarcely knew. Dear Miss Blake, he began; after a moment of perturbed reflection he drew his pen through these words. Dear lady; too formal. Dear friend; how absurd! She might even deny this. Dear stranger; more absurd still. Finally, he decided to begin his letter without any address at all, and now he found that he could write it quite easily.

> You have frightened me, his pen traced. I know nobody in New York. Absolutely nobody. I haven't had time to tell you my story, and so you will not understand, but I cannot hope ever to be formally introduced to you. Couldn't you, in some way, explain to your father? I do so want to see you, to know you. We have met under such strange circumstances that there has been no opportunity for a quiet talk. Can't you arrange something? *Please do.* I *must* see you. I eagerly await your reply.

He gave the letter to Drains to post, but immediately after Drains had departed on this mission, he felt the need of going out himself. A novel restlessness had besieged him. Drawing on his rain-coat, he left the house. Without being particularly conscious of where he was walking, without any desire to walk to any definite place, he directed his steps towards Gramercy Park. The rain-drops pelted his face with a welcome freshness. He did not want to go to Paul's but he craved the opportunity of talking to somebody, and to whom else could he talk? Ki, at the door, informed him that Paul had gone out. Would he come in and wait? He declined. Too nervous to sit still, he preferred to walk around the iron-grating enclosing the park. The benches in the enclosure were deserted. The trees, drenched by the windy rain, shook drops of water on the vivid green grass…. Harold walked round and round the iron fence. A policeman in a rubber-coat stood on the corner of Lexington Avenue. On the other side of the park, Harold passed a sailor under an umbrella…. What would Alice say? Would she answer his letter at all? He felt completely miserable. Why couldn't his father give him a position in his own home where he could meet people? He was, he assured himself, to all intents and purposes an outcast. He returned to Paul's. Paul had not yet come in. Ki smiled. Would the gentleman wait? Harold again declined. Round and round the grating. The rain continued to fall. It was twilight.

Drains, too, was smiling, as he opened the door for Harold. How could everybody smile? And they all smiled cynically, as if they knew some secret of which he was not aware. Did they all understand why life was so cruel? Did they all comprehend the jest of the cruelty? The evening was almost a replica of his first evening in his own apartment. Drains asked what he would have for dinner … and gave him chops, etc. Again he went early to bed with books and magazines which he did not read. He could not tolerate this waiting. He, who had been patient all his life, was becoming impatient. He lifted the receiver from the hook … and put it back again. She had asked him, he forced himself to remember, not to telephone. Drains departed for the night. The driving rain was still beating against the window-panes. The lightning flashed occasionally and there were heavy crashes of thunder. Harold shuddered. How lonely he was! He who had been alone so much formerly, now could not suffer being alone. His circumstances had been so different then. Now he felt that the world was against him, had separated him from the one person he wanted to see. His heart almost stopped beating when the telephone bell tinkled. It was Paul. Harold's voice registered his disappointment. Yes, he had called. No, nothing in particular. Yes, he would drop in tomorrow.

What are we going to do? Harold asked desperately.

Anything you like. We'll decide when you arrive.

Then, quite suddenly, after the naive manner of youth, Harold cried out for sympathy: Can I come over tonight?

Sorry, old man, Paul answered; it's quite impossible. I have a rendezvous in a doss-house with my aged grandmother.

Realizing that he had made a mistake, Harold mumbled a good-bye. Tears streamed out of the corners of his eyes. He felt more alone, more miserable than ever. At this moment, he would have been glad to see even Drains. He tried to read, but nothing held his interest. At last, he got up and walked about, his restlessness increasing as he fed it. Suddenly his eye fell on a carafe, half-full of brandy, standing on the side-board. Grasping it, he poured out enough to fill a wineglass, and, with much gulping, he contrived to swallow the burning fluid. Then and then only was he able to fall asleep.

The answer to his letter was delivered by messenger in the afternoon. The envelope, he noted, was addressed in a different hand from that which had penned the envelope containing the hundred dollar bill. Still it must be … He tore it open. His own note, the top of the envelope neatly slit, tumbled out first. Then a letter:

Sir: —
My daughter has informed me of the manner in which you have become implicated in her affairs. I take this occasion to thank you for your assistance, if you have given assistance, but I must ask you not to pursue my daughter further. If you seek more than gratitude for what you have done, I shall be glad to send you a check. Under no circumstances, however, are you to address another letter to my daughter. Any such I shall be obliged to open and, if you persist in making her the butt of your unwelcome attentions, I shall be obliged to pay a visit to the police court myself.
very truly yours,
BECKFORD BLAKE.

What an insult! The hideous mortification of receiving such a letter burned

Harold's cheeks with shame. And poor Alice. How must she feel? What had her father done to her? Then he suddenly remembered that he had been on the verge of telling the whole story to Paul. If he had seen Paul last evening he certainly would have told him, and Paul would have laughed. Paul surely would laugh at this story; so would Drains. With a sort of furtive intuition he began to believe that no women were innocent in the eyes of Paul and Drains. Harold felt more than ever a martyr. His life, which, it seemed, began with a mistake on the day he was born, would, he was convinced, never shape itself. All his existence, apparently, would continue to be one long mistake. Again, quite spontaneously, the idea recurred to him that he hated his father for, however unconsciously, shaping it for him. It wasn't, he began to realize, his college years which had proved his present undoing, but his early bringing up, the inadequate and unworldly supervision of Aunt Sadi and Persia Blaine. And this was his father's doing! To be sure, his aunt and Persia had meant well; they had loved him … but they had not been capable of preparing him for the perils he had to face.

Paul, that day, and for several days following, was rather inclined to be distrait, and Harold, silent concerning the only matter which really interested him, on his part found comparatively little to say. He encountered Campaspe on several occasions, and once or twice, he fancied, he saw her looking at him with sympathy, but they were never alone, and mainly she was preoccupied with gossip about the Duke of Middlebottom, who had arrived, unaccountably, in New York *in June*.

June, he had remarked to Campaspe, is the London season; why not make it the New York season as well? I told him, Campaspe repeated in her narrative to Paul, that all he would need was an impresario to produce an opera or two, three or four ladies of society, and a climate. His answer was direct. He said, and it is perfectly true, that New York is cooler than London in the summer, that wherever I was there was sure to be society, and that he would give the opera himself. He is committed to some such plan.

Bunny and Zimbule, also, offered matter for discussion. They were much talked about and, when one wasn't talking about them, they ran in to talk about themselves. They were settled in Bunny's small apartment in Greenwich Village[114] and were living a life in which love and ambition played equal parts. Bunny was composing his two bar songs and piano pieces, and he had succeeded, without much difficulty, in securing Zimbule a situation on the stage for, after a day's reflection, she had decided that she would rather go on the stage than do anything else.

She spent days in Campaspe's motor, and out of it in smart shops, outfitting

---

[114]   Area of lower New York that served as an enclave for avant-garde and bohemian artists and political radicals in the late nineteenth and early twentieth centuries.

herself at Campaspe's expense. She was aware of her beauty and not without taste, it was discovered, when it came to adorning it, withal this taste was somewhat bizarre. She had begun by assuming such ready-made dresses as could be easily summoned from the backs of models at Bendel's, Tappé's and Gilbert Clark's,[115] but very soon, under the spell of the compliments which her really exquisite loveliness won from the lips of the attendants in these shops, she was encouraged by Campaspe, whose desire in life was to amuse herself, and whose purse was sufficiently heavy to make the carrying out of this desire facile, to go a little further along the route of self-expression. Campaspe's philosophy was as sure at this point as at another. It was only, she frequently said, those who expected to find amusement in themselves who wandered about disconsolate and bored. Amusement was to be derived from watching others, when one permitted them to be entirely themselves. One was born with oneself and, if one were intelligent, one got to know oneself thoroughly at the age of four. Thereafter, a life of boredom intervened until the grave yawned, unless one surrounded oneself with people who were individual enough to comport themselves with some eccentricity, not to say perversity. Zimbule was not cut to any conventional pattern. She filled Campaspe's bill.

Soon the child began to notice the difference between stuffs, the difference between patterns and colours. Warm as it was, she affected an interest in kinkob[116] and camel's-hair shawls, and she became aware of the sacred names of Reboux, Premet, Chéruit, and Maria Guy.[117]

I adore her! Campaspe ejaculated one day. I can never cease to thank God that we captured her from those embracing snakes. She is the most amusing person we've ever discovered. She's wholly natural, wholly an animal. I've never met a woman like her. When she's hungry she eats; when she's sleepy, she sleeps; and when she's amorous, she loves.[118] She's imitative like an animal too. Having observed that I wear geraniums, she's clever enough to realize that geraniums are not her flower. When I called for her the other day she was sporting a great bouquet of orchids. Bunny, of course, can never pay for them and so I have taken to sending her orchids every morning, developing an expensive taste.

---

[115] High-end American fashion designers and importers. Bendel's (est'd 1895), the first American outlet to sell Chanel, and Tappé's (est'd 1910) were on fashionable West Fifty-Seventh Street in the 1920s, while Gilbert Clark's was on Fifth Avenue.

[116] Indian brocade of silk or silk/cotton weaved through with gold and/or silver thread.

[117] Reboux, Premet, and Chéruit were preeminent Parisian fashion houses that defined the modern look for women. Reboux, for example, was the reputed inventor of the iconic flapper cloche hat, while Premet was noted for gamine fashions and the little black dress. Guy was a Parisian milliner.

[118] This description of Zimbule echoes Charles Baudelaire's (1821–1867) musings in 'Mon coeur mis à nu' (published posthumously in 1887), in which he contrasts what he regards as the primitive, animalistic qualities of woman with the cultivated refinement of the dandy. While these animalistic qualities disgust Baudelaire, Campaspe finds them admirable.

Her next lover may be rich enough to afford them. But you can never tell with Zimbule. Animals are not interested in money. If she falls in love with a rich man it will be an accident.

Bunny, it was certain, was deeply in love with Zimbule. He had no eyes for her eccentricities, but he was delighted that Campaspe had dressed her up. The practical side of these attentions dawned on him more fully when she was engaged, solely on her looks, for a good part in support of a female star. Zimbule took this engagement entirely as a matter of course. Everything with Zimbule was a matter of course. She ate, slept, lived, loved as a matter of course. And, quite naturally, like the little animal she was, she never thought at all.

One afternoon, the Duke of Middlebottom appeared at Paul's apartment, and Harold was astonished by the grace and charm of Drains's former master. The Duke immediately manifested an interest in Harold which appeared to be sincere. As for Harold, the Duke appealed to him from the beginning, without giving him the sense, which the others made him feel so constantly, that he was being made game of. The Duke was younger than Harold had expected to find him. Somehow, Harold had thought of all Dukes as middle-aged men, and this particular Duke was but scantily past thirty. He was a tall, blond Englishman; his hair, of course, was curly; his cheeks were rosy, and his eyes were blue. He was always dressed to perfection, wore a monocle, and had the habit of flaunting three cornflowers as a boutonnière. His trousers flared at the bottom and his small feet were encased in round-toed French boots with cloth tops. He had very ugly hands, thick across, with short, stubby fingers with spatulate terminations, and nails which seemed never to have permitted the attentions of a manicure. Not only were they unevenly clipped; often, they were actually dirty. Another peculiarity of the Duke was that he stammered, but this apparent defect actually added to his attractiveness. His name was eponymous for a certain group that frequented the Café Royal in London[119] and with his crest on his stationery was the motto: A thing of beauty is a boy for ever.[120] The Duke made it a point to live by the Julian Calendar, thirteen days behind the Gregorian.[121] In this wise he contrived to evade all unsatisfactory engagements,

---

[119] From the 1890s on, the Café Royal on Regent Street attracted artists and sophisticates, most famously Oscar Wilde and his circle. Due to this association, it became a popular gay hangout in the early twentieth century.

[120] A play on the opening line of John Keats's *Endymion* (1818), 'A thing of beauty is a joy forever'. In one of his notebooks (Carl Van Vechten Papers, New York Public Library, Box 122), Van Vechten attributes this pun to his friend, Allen Norton, and reports that Frank Harris responded, 'How Oscar will regret not having said that'. This sentence (beginning from 'His name') was expurgated from the British edition of the novel.

[121] The Julian calendar was a reform of the Roman calendar brought about by Julius Caesar in 45 BC. It was gradually replaced by the Gregorian calendar from 1582.

especially if they were complicated in any way by daylight-saving time,[122] an American refinement of which he was utterly ignorant.

Harold found him very delightful and wondered if Drains's strictures were part of that valet's demoniacal cynicism. He judges everybody, thought Harold, in terms of himself and his own rotten life. It was plainly to be seen that the Duke of Middlebottom never entertained an evil thought.

Campaspe and the Duke were old friends, and they talked of Capri, from whence the Duke had recently emerged, the new English plays, the best of which, the Duke appeared to believe, were by Beaumont and Fletcher, Poiret's inventions for the grues at Auteuil, Cocteau's café, Le Bœuf sur le Toit, and kindred subjects.[123] He was a charming and engaging conversationalist, and the most winning quality of his manner was its utter frankness and apparent absence of guile. Harold had been fully prepared, by advance reports, to meet an ironic epigrammatist, who perhaps removed his coat in public to inject a shot of morphia into his arm. The Duke seemed free from a mania for exhibitionism. Not only was he delightful to Harold, he was equally at his ease with Paul, and he had bestowed upon Zimbule, whom he playfully described as a sciurine oread,[124] the accolade of his particular interest. He had made her his friend at once by promising to present her with a long string of coral beads of the valuable and rare colour of the berries of wintergreen.

At their first meeting, she had challenged his monocle.

What'd you do if it dropped and broke? she asked.

For answer, the Duke relaxed the muscles around his eye, and the glass fell to the floor, shivering into fragments. Immediately, he took another glass from his waistcoat pocket, and adjusted it.

The Duke questioned Harold regarding his tastes, and told him long stories of harmless adventures among the Italian peasantry, in which shepherd boys and bersaglieri[125] figured in sympathetic guises. Sheep were saved, and ladies

---

[122] The Duke is mistaken in his view of daylight saving time as an American innovation. It was first implemented by Germany and Austria Hungary and both the UK and America practiced daylight saving in the 1920s.

[123] Francis Beaumont (1584–1616) and John Fletcher (1579–1625), Jacobean dramatists who wrote collaboratively and whose work experienced a revival in the 1920s; Paul Poiret (1879–1944), leading French fashion designer, who revolutionized women's clothing by controversially launching his influential oriental style, an uncorseted look with harem pants, at the Auteuil horseracing course in Paris; Grue is French slang for a prostitute, the implication being that Poiret's models were prostitutes, such was the effect of his designs on the general public; Jean Cocteau (1889–1963), a member of the early twentieth-century Parisian literary avant-garde. Parisian cafés were a major venue for meetings of the avant-garde, but it is unclear what 'Cocteau's café' refers to, though it may refer to *Le Bœuf sur le toit* (Ox on the Roof), an avant-garde cabaret-bar opened in 1921 and frequented by Cocteau and his coterie. The cabaret itself was named after a 1920 surrealist ballet by Cocteau (scenario) and Darius Milhaud (music).

[124] Squirrel-like mountain nymph.

[125] Italian term for army sharpshooters or riflemen.

escorted through perilous mountain-passes, while banditi rained down shot from convenient posts above. There was also a harrowing, but amusing, account of the birth of a child in the compartment of a railway carriage during the prolonged passage through the Simplon Tunnel.[126] Only once did Harold betray what he thought was a trace of affectation in the Duke when that one, being questioned, declared that he had never seen the Blue Grotto.[127]

But you have just come from Capri!

The boy does not believe you, Campaspe interposed. Ronald never lies, Harold. Think a moment. How long have you been in New York?

Nearly three weeks.

Have you seen the Statue of Liberty?

No.

Or Grant's Tomb?

No.

Or the Metropolitan Museum of Art?

No-o.

Or Poe's house?

No.

Or the Bronx Zoo?

No.

Or Fraunces' Tavern?

No.

Or the Aquarium?[128]

No.

And you have been here three weeks. The Duke spent two or three weeks in Capri and yet you expect him to have seen the Blue Grotto!

During the progress of this dialogue there was a crescendo in Harold's abashment, but the Duke only smiled and did not seem to be at all put out.

Youth, he remarked, is always incredulous. The Firebird, however, hasn't t-t-t-told you the whole truth. I pass t-t-two or three weeks in Capri every year, and yet I have never seen the B-B-B-Blue Grotto.

I believe you, said Harold fervently.

I would never see Mount Ætna at T-T-Taor- mina, or Vesuvius at Naples if it were possible to escape them.[129] But they see me first and then they insist that I look.

Why, asked Harold, quite ready to let this subject drop, do you call Campaspe the Firebird?

---

[126]   Railway tunnel through the Alps connecting Switzerland and Italy.

[127]   Sea cave characterized by the beautiful azure colour of the water when lit by sunlight. In ancient Roman times, it was used as a place of worship.

[128]   Then, as today, the places Campaspe mentions were New York tourist sites.

[129]   Ætna (Etna) and Vesuvius are volcanoes in Italy.

It seems natural, even inevitable, to do so. Her p-p-plumage is so brilliant. It glistens and d-d-dazzles.

Oh!

Wait. There is more. I am not thinking of the Zhar-Ptitsa of Russian legend.[130] Rather I am making an impious in-t-t-terpretation of certain passages in the Comte de Gabalis.[131] Probably you have not yet read that fascinating seventeenth century satirical romance in which the author, the Abbé de Montfaucon de Villars, was undoubtedly poking fun at the occultists. Ironically enough, the modern Rosicrucians have taken the b-b-b-book seriously and use it as their B-B-Bible. In this delicious capolavoro,[132] the Comte discourses with the author, somewhat after the fashion of … Well, certainly such works as W. H. Mallock's New Republic and Aldous Huxley's Crome Yellow stem from this book.[133]

The Comte recommends marriage with one of the immortal beings who people the elements rather than with a human; he advises cohabitation with the nymphs who swim in the water, the gnomes who inhabit the earth, the sylphs who fly in the air, or the salamanders who thrive in the fire. Campaspe, I am convinced, has married a salamander and has embraced his element. She b-b-b-burns like a clear white flame, using our emotions for fuel. Wherever there is passion, Campaspe's incandescence increases, but she remains faithful, under all circumstances, to her salamander. Occasionally, in one of her soaring flights, she drops a fiery feather, and some poor mortal mistakes it for the living bird.[134]

But I have married a mortal, Campaspe objected.

Your children are salamanders, was the Duke's final word.

Harold was uncertain whether to tell Drains that he had met the Duke, but Drains saved him the trouble. As he brought in Harold's coffee one morning, the man remarked:

---

[130]   In Russian folklore, the firebird is a magical bird that represents a blessing and a curse to its capturer.

[131]   Published in 1670 and written by Henri de Montfaucon de Villars (1635–1673), the book is a series of philosophical and symbolic discourses between an occultist and his disciple professing to explain the mysteries of the universe. It was influential across Europe, notably for its depiction of elemental beings that interact with humans. As the Duke suggests, it was viewed by some as a satire, by others as a serious work of mysticism.

[132]   Italian, meaning 'masterpiece'.

[133]   New Republic (1877), a satire of the British Aesthetic movement; Crome Yellow (1921), a critique of fashionable British artistic and aristocratic circles of the 1910s. While vastly different in subject matter to Comte de Gabalis, they are similarly characterized by lengthy discursive passages.

[134]   The Duke's explanation follows that of Discourse II of Comte de Gabalis, which tells of a mortal who marries an elemental creature and becomes immortal.

I saw my old master yesterday, sir.

The Duke … Yes, I know. I've met him. He isn't a bit the sort you described.

Drains raised his eyebrows.

I described the Duke! he exclaimed. I told you that I had been in his employ, sir, but I scarcely permitted myself to go further.

You told me why you had left him, dared Harold.

Drains's face had regained its customary imperturbability.

I cannot, of course, contradict you, sir, but I assure you, sir, that you are labouring under some misapprehension. I could never have discussed the affairs of the Duke. He is a fine gentleman, sir.

Well, for once we agree, said Harold, and he began to wonder if he had misjudged Drains.

Chapter VII

Ronald, Duke of Middlebottom, had taken a furnished house on West Twelfth Street for the summer,[135] against the advice of friends who had urged the advantages of Sutton Place.[136] The owner of this property, a woman, had individual taste, somewhat influenced by the Italian of various epochs and styles, and the Duke had added his own touches here and there. The drawing-room, a vast chamber on a level with the street-door, approached by a flight of steps, extended the full depth of the house. The walls of this room were stained a curious olive-green, and the windows were curtained with stiff draped silver-grey taffeta, bound with narrow bands of turquoise-blue. Silver and crystal candelabra were placed at convenient intervals along the walls, but no central chandelier depended from the ceiling. On the marble mantelshelf stood two Venetian glass Ethiopians, clad in white, clasping baskets of multi-coloured crisp glass flowers, from the midst of which emerged white wax candles.[137] On a long, polished walnut table there were more glass figures, capricious examples of the art of the verrier,[138] a Spanish Infanta of rosso Murano and black,[139] a white-spotted black deer, a saucy red-lipped Columbine. The chairs and divans, possibly of Italian renaissance design, were covered for the season with a gay Derryvale linen.[140] A few pictures hung on the walls: a bowl of zinnias by Florine Stettheimer, orchids by Charles Demuth, and magnified, scarlet cannas by Georgia O'Keeffe.[141] The hallway, painted a bright Italian blue, sprinkled

---

[135]   In the late 1910s and early 1920s this area of Greenwich Village was being regentrified to attract affluent tenants.

[136]   See note 50.

[137]   Venetian glass is a highly elaborate, decorative, and colourful form of glassware, much of it made on the island of Murano. It usually takes the form of glass jewellery, chandeliers, art glass, and, in the case of this collection, figurines. African subjects were a popular motif in Venetian glass and in the decorative arts more broadly from the seventeenth through the twentieth centuries. Van Vechten's inspiration for the Ethiopian figurines and other pieces described on this mantelshelf and walnut table are the designs of American artist Clare Avery (dates unknown), as depicted in an April 1922 *Vogue* article, 'Venetian Glass from American Designs' (84, 122). All but the Columbine figure, which, in Avery's design, was a Pierrot, are as described in this article.

[138]   French, meaning 'glassblower'.

[139]   Infanta, a Spanish term for a King's daughter. Popular depictions show infantas in exaggeratedly wide side-hooped dresses after the fashion of seventeenth-century Spanish court dress. Rosso Murano is a red colour distinctive to Murano glass.

[140]   Manufacturer of table linens and textiles for interior decoration.

[141]   Stettheimer (1871–1944), eccentric wealthy artist, salon hostess, and friend of Van

with tiny gold stars,[142] ran parallel with the drawing-room from the front to the back of the house, leading down a flight of steps into the garden in the rear, where a shell-walk wandered in and out between tiny beds of azure flowers, planted under symmetrical chestnut-trees and catalpas with their heart-shaped leaves and ridiculously long and slender seed-pods, to a fountain in the middle of the back wall, a fountain inspired by Nijinsky's interpretation of Mallarmé's faun.[143] A huge umbrella, striped orange and black, almost like the canopy of a pavilion, protected a black table and chairs from the sunglare. The dining-room was in the basement and it had been the happy fancy of its mistress to hang the walls with an old-fashioned paper, printed in pink and white stripes after the manner of stick candy. On these walls she had fastened by means of pins a few ribald covers torn off Le Rire and La Vie Parisienne.[144] The prim little black marble mantelshelf held half a dozen painted sugar statuettes, ravished from a Houston Street pasticceria,[145] representing Sicilian banditi, not unmenacing, and bland shepherdesses with thick ankles, guarding shapeless sheep. The table, at dinner, was usually a confusion of fragile, opaque Bristol Glass,[146] with decorations of birds and flowers, old Staffordshire china,[147] and ornaments of artificial grapes and crystal, laid on the bare walnut board. Sometimes a great bronze Buddha panted on his back in a bowl of nasturtiums, his hexagonal belly looming high above the posies.

The second floor was divided into two bedrooms, the walls of one of which were hung with an old eighteenth century paper, depicting rather fanciful South Sea Islanders enjoying themselves in the shade of great palm-trees, while other cannibals with formidable spears navigated the sea in extravagant canoes.[148] This was the back chamber, and because it overlooked the garden and was free

---

Vechten's, who rarely exhibited her work. *Zinnias* was exhibited in March 1922 at the Salon des Indépendents and was purchased by Van Vechten. Demuth (1883–1935) and O'Keeffe (1887–1986), modernist American artists, whose depictions of flowers combine fidelity to detail with an emphasis on the sensuality of their subjects.

[142] In the fourth printing of the novel, 'gold stars' corrects what appeared previously as 'blue stars'.

[143] Vaslav Nijinsky (1889–1950), dancer and choreographer for the Ballets Russes, who, in 1912, famously and controversially adapted Debussy's *Prélude à l'après-midi d'un faune*, based on the 1876 symbolist poem by Stephane Mallarmé, into a modernist ballet. The choreography was highly stylized and eroticized, drawing on the art of Greek vases. Images of Nijinsky as the faun by artists and photographers circulated widely in the period.

[144] French satirical magazines, known for their racy covers.

[145] Houston Street is in New York's Little Italy. A pasticceria is an Italian pastry shop.

[146] Blue, green, and amethyst decanters and drinking glasses, often decorated with flower motifs.

[147] Staffordshire was a major centre for the production of ceramics from the seventeenth century.

[148] The South Seas was a popular motif for scenic wallpapers of the eighteenth and early nineteenth centuries. A feature on this topic appeared in a December 1922 article in *Arts and Decoration* ('New Acquisitions in American Museums', pp. 136, 140).

from the noises of the street, the Duke had chosen it for his own. When the Duke moved into a hotel room, the decorations of which were distasteful to him, he frequently sent for a paper-hanger and ordered the room repapered. He did not go so far in this instance, but he had contrived to conceal a good part of the pseudo-Marquesan landscape with shungwa, a special class of Japanese prints, erotic and often obscene. The room was always in the uttermost disorder, as most of his personal belongings and the books and pictures and knick-knacks which he was constantly picking up were littered within its four walls. A gate-legged table in the corner served as an uneasy resting place for a bronze torso by Dujam Penic, the Serbian sculptor, a pair of yellow-green glass candlesticks in the shape of inverted dolphins, De Berg van Licht by Louis Couperus, boxes of cravats from Charvet, consignments of pleasant odours from Bichara,[149] and a hand-illuminated quotation from Goethe:

> Hätte Gott mich anders gewollt,
> Er hätte mich anders gebaut;[150]

neatly framed in gold. As the Duke had a fancy for frequently changing his clothes, it was well-nigh impossible for the Ceylonese servants, tall, brown fellows with combs in their straight ebony hair, to put away the procession of trousers, coats, boots, and stockings which marched over the floor and the chairs. The front chamber was a serene little Louis XIV room, and always gave the appearance of never having been occupied, even after some one had been living in it for several days. These apartments were connected by the bath, panelled in alternating squares of malachite and lapis lazuli, with a tub of rose-jade with golden faucets. The floor was paved with diamond-shaped bloodstone flags. Two full-length mirrors, set in the wall, were backed with black instead of quicksilver. The long dressing-table, gilded, and surmounted by an oval, black mirror, held a mysterious array of luxurious objects and a profusion of crystal bottles with gold tops. The Duke admitted frankly that he had taken the house for the sake of this bathroom, and confessed that he passed most of his time there when he had no guests. It may be added, however, that the Duke was seldom alone. The third floor the owner had transformed — old New York

---

[149]   The art deco work of Penić (1889–1946) was exhibited in New York in this period and featured in *Vanity Fair* in June 1919 and April 1920; dolphin candlesticks were part of an American tradition of glass design dating to the Colonial period; Couperus (1863–1923), Dutch novelist and poet, whose 1905 novel *De berg van licht* (*The Mountain of Light*) about the decadent Roman Emperor Heliogabalus dealt controversially with homosexuality; Charvet, high-end designer of shirts and neckties; Bichara, Paris-based Syrian perfumer renowned for exotic, heavily-scented perfumes.

[150]   German, translating as, 'If God had wanted me otherwise, | He would have created me otherwise;'. From *Zahme Xenien* (*Tame Invectives*), a series of satirical epigrams by German philosophers Johann Wolfgang von Goethe (1749–1832) and Friedrich Schiller (1759–1805).

houses are as capable of countless metamorphoses as Ovidian gods[151] — into a miniature theatre, the walls of which had been decorated by Paul Thévenaz with dying stags, agile monkeys, wriggling serpents, gorgeous macaws, iridescent humming-birds, mad huntsmen, bayaderes, odalisques, and Hindu Rajahs.[152] The drop-curtain was of silver cloth into which had been woven an infinity of semi-precious stones, in a conventional Persian design. It was in this theatre that the Duke proposed to give New York its season of summer opera.

On a sultry day, late in July, Campaspe, in a clinging garment of chartreuse swiss,[153] with a Lucie Hamar[154] hat of geranium-red, flesh-coloured stockings, and ivory kid shoes with vermilion heels, sat with the Duke and Paul under the great umbrella in the garden, discussing plans for the opera. Out of Jacobite ale-glasses with air-twist stems they were sipping that pleasant hot-weather mixture, gin and ginger beer, cooled with ice and flavoured with limes. A bowl of chopped ice, several unopened stone bottles of Idris, and a blue pitcher half-full of Gordon gin stood on the table between them.[155] The Duke's suit, too, was of blue, the coolest of colours, he explained, exactly the colour to compete with the sirocco. And, he went on, as was his wont, exactly the wrong colour for a theatre. A theatre should never be blue, for a theatre must be warm; even in summer, the effect of a theatre should be warm.

Ronald dear, I agree with you, said Campaspe. We cannot discuss that. Anyway *your* theatre isn't blue, so there would be nothing to discuss even if I felt argumentative. But the opera …

Well, of course, the Duke began tentatively, I don't mean exactly an opera. Rather a p-p-p-play, b-b-b-but the kind of play you don't see in New York. Not modern either. Whenever I hear the word I think of Cocteau's phrase, a nigger prostrate before the telephone.[156] Everything one called modern a year or two ago is old-fashioned: Freud, Mary Garden, Einstein, Wyndham Lewis, Dada, glands, the Six, vers libres, Sem Benelli, Clive Bell, radio, the Ziegfeld

---

[151] Ovid (43 BC–17/18 AD), Roman poet of the Augustan age, whose influential epic *Metamorphoses* chronicles the history of the world through myth.
[152] Thévenaz (1891–1921), modernist portrait painter, muralist, costume designer, and dancer, who drew inspiration from the Ballets Russes and whose work included commissions for wealthy New Yorkers.
[153] Swiss muslin, a fine thin cotton, plain or dotted.
[154] Fashionable Parisian milliner. Along with Reboux (see note 117), Hamar is often credited with the invention of the famous 1920s cloche hat.
[155] Idris, a brand of ginger beer; Gordon's gin, one of the leading gins in America and Britain since the nineteenth century.
[156] From Cocteau's article 'Jazz-Band' (*Paris-Midi*, 4 August 1919), in which he says, 'the word "modern" always sounds naïve to me. It makes me think of a negro prostrate before the telephone'. In the essay, Cocteau argues that high art is rendered more virile through contact with the popular, where the latter is largely associated with modern American art forms. The Duke uses the term 'nigger', controversial even in this period, and a term Van Vechten would employ for deliberately provocative effect for the title of his 1926 novel *Nigger Heaven*.

Follies, cubism, Sacha Guitry, Ezra Pound, The Little Review, vorticism, Marcel Proust, The Dial, uranians, Gordon Craig, prohibition, the young intellectuals, Sherwood Anderson, normalcy, Guillaume Apollinaire, Charlie Chaplin, screens in stage d-d-d-d-decoration, Aleister Crowley, the Russian Ballet, fireless cookers, The Chauve Souris, Margot Asquith, ectoplasm, Eugène Goossens, the tango, Jacques Copeau, Negro dancing![157] Let's not be modern.

---

[157] Sigmund Freud (1856–1939), founder of psychoanalysis, whose ideas became popular in America in the 1920s; Garden (1874–1967), Scottish-American operatic soprano, whose performances included modern operas, famously Richard Strauss's (1864–1949) controversial *Salomé*, about which Van Vechten wrote in *Interpreters and Interpretations* (New York: Knopf, 1917), pp. 78–83; Albert Einstein (1879–1955), Nobel-winning physicist for 1921 whose theory of relativity earned him celebrity; Lewis (1882–1957), English writer, painter, and critic, associated with the modernist Vorticist movement of 1914, favouring abstraction in art; Dada, an avant-garde art movement characterized by nonsense, irrationality, and anti-bourgeois sentiment; glands, a reference to the vogue for the monkey gland treatment for male sexual and mental regeneration first performed in 1920; The Six (Les Six), a group of Parisian avant-garde musicians founded in 1920 comprised of Georges Auric (1899–1983), Louis Durey (1888–1979), Arthur Honegger (1892–1955), Darius Milhaud (1892–1974), Francis Poulenc (1899–1963), and Germaine Tailleferre (1892–1983); vers libres, a free form of poetry eschewing consistent rhyme and metre originating in late nineteenth-century France and popular with Anglo-American poets in the 1910s; Benelli (1877–1949), Italian playwright who had Broadway success in 1919; Bell (1881–1964), British literary and art critic and member of the Bloomsbury Group, whose *Since Cézanne* (1922) represented an important celebration of post-impressionist art; radio was first publicly broadcast in America in 1920, developing mass appeal through the decade; the Ziegfeld Follies, lavish theatrical revues, famed for beautiful chorus girls; Cubism, an influential abstract modernist artistic style associated with Pablo Picasso (1881–1973); Guitry (1885–1957), French playwright, director, and actor, popular also in the English-speaking world; Pound (1885–1972), American poet and critic, who exerted influence in the transatlantic modernist literary movement; *The Little Review*, avant-garde magazine, famous for serialising James Joyce's *Ulysses* from 1918 to 1921; Vorticism, see comments on Lewis, above; Proust (1871–1922), French author of the monumental *A la recherche du temps perdu*, much admired by the modernist avant-garde and first issued in an English translation from 1922; *The Dial*, an important organ for modernist arts in the 1920s, famous for the publication of T. S. Eliot's (1888–1965) *The Waste Land* in 1922; Uranians, a term used in the period to denote homosexuals, as popularized by socialist and homosexual activist Edward Carpenter (1844–1929) and sexologist Havelock Ellis (1859–1939); Edward Gordon Craig (1872–1966), experimental actor, director, and scene designer, whose ideas were influential for modernist theatre; 'young intellectuals', a term used to describe the rebellious, iconoclastic figures associated with new American artistic and literary movements in this period, most notably in critic Harold Stearns's (1891–1943) *America and the Young Intellectual* (1921); Anderson (1876–1941), American modernist writer who achieved fame in 1919 with *Winesburg, Ohio*, a psychological analysis of small-town life; normalcy was a popular neologism of 1920 and 1921 coined by presidential candidate Warren Harding (1865–1923), who called for a 'return to normalcy' after the upheaval of the First World War; Apollinaire (1880–1918), French avant-garde writer and art critic who coined the terms Cubism and Surrealism and helped define the movements; Chaplin (1889–1977), world-famous actor and director whose 1921 *The Kid* was a smash hit; 'screens in stage decoration' likely refers to the avant-garde experiments of Gordon Craig (see comments above) with moveable screens in the theatre; Crowley (1875–1947), British

Let's turn back to the great period around 1910 — even a trifle earlier.

The Frogs?[158] suggested Campaspe.

Oh! No croaking.

Lysistrata?[159]

That's an idea. You are warmer.

Less blue.

Redder. Oranger. Lysistrata! Perhaps. But I should prefer something more curious. I like B-B-B-Bacon's phrase: There is no excellent beauty that hath not some strangeness in the p-p-p-proportion....[160] He appeared to ponder ... I have it! Rachilde's l'Araignée de Cristal.[161]

The Crystal Spider.

Firebird! You understand French.

I seem to foresee this play: cold and perverse.

Blood.

Cold blood.

There's a mother and a boy who is afraid of mirrors. I will play the b-b-boy and you will p-p-p-play the mother.

Frozen blood. No mother for me! Out! What else?

---

occultist who spent the war years in America and published his controversial *Diary of a Drug Fiend* in 1922; Russian Ballet (*Ballets Russes*), experimental ballet troupe (1920–1929) headed by Sergei Diaghilev (1872–1929) that commissioned work from avant-garde composers, artists, and costume designers; fireless cookers, labour-saving stoves that enable cooking with retained heat and were popular in early twentieth century America; *Chauve Souris*, a popular Russian touring revue of the early twentieth century that came to America in 1922; Asquith (1864–1945), socialite, author, and wife of a British Prime Minister, whose *Autobiography* (1920) contributed to her celebrity; ectoplasm, a supernatural substance that exudes from the body of a medium, was the subject of numerous controversial studies in the 1910s and 1920s; Goossens (1893–1962), British modernist conductor and composer, who exploited the potential of gramophone recording from the early 1920s; the tango had mass appeal in the 1920s, prompted by silent film star Rudolph Valentino's (1895–1926) performance in *Four Horsemen of the Apocalypse* (1921); Copeau (1879–1949), French director and actor who innovated stage practices in France and America; 'negro dancing' achieved mainstream attention as jazz music, Harlem nightclubs, and Broadway shows featuring black performers (such as 1921's *Shuffle Along*) introduced white Americans to dances such as the Charleston and the Lindy Hop. In this period, the term 'negro' was not considered offensive.

[158]   Ancient Greek comedy by Aristophanes (405 BC), taking the form of a debate between playwrights Euripides and Aeschylus presided over by the god Dionysus to determine who is the better artist.

[159]   Ancient Greek comedy by Aristophanes (411 BC) in which the women of Greece stage a sex strike in order to bring an end to war.

[160]   English philosopher Francis Bacon (1561–1626), from his essay 'Of Beauty', from *Essays, or Counsels Civil and Moral* (1625).

[161]   Rachilde (Marguerite Vallette-Eymery, 1860–1953), French decadent author. *L'Araignée de cristal* (1892), a one-act avant-garde symbolist Oedipal tragedy involving a tyrannical mother and her troubled son.

Ronald Firbank's Princess Zoubaroff[162] is perhaps more colorado.[163]

Oh! Firbank.

I hear, hopefully put in Paul, who did not understand Spanish, that he is an indecent writer.

Every alternate line is decent, exclaimed the Duke. A master of wordcraft! He's writing something new — I forget the name — : Mackerel Fishing in the Bois de Boulogne; perhaps that's it — or Cocktails.

Is it about America? asked Paul.

Possibly. Le vit est dur partout.[164]

Campaspe ended this: The Princess Zoubaroff is an idea. If we give that we must ask all New York.

And cable Ronald to come over to make bows.

Ronald cables Ronald.

The Duke grinned at the possibility as he lifted his glass automatically to search for the rough pontil mark.[165] The group was now disturbed by a sudden raucous tumult at the other end of the garden. The white dachshund and the golden Pomeranian were engaged in a noisy dispute. Presently two Ceylonese servitors appeared and, separating the combatants, bore them yelping into the house.

Terrible d-d-d-dogs! remarked the Duke. I call them Dédé and Eskal Vigor.[166] Ils ont de mauvaises mœurs.[167] He returned to the subject under discussion: I've really made up my mind.

I was sure of it, Campaspe declared. What is it?

Nozière's l'Après-midi Byzantine.[168]

I don't know it.

Certainly, you don't. It's in one act and no costumes: cool for the actors, and hot for the spectators. Grues[169] and a charioteer and a boy. La scene est à

---

[162]   On Firbank, see note 95. *Princess Zoubaroff* (published 1920 but not publicly staged until 1975) treats homosexuality and lesbianism and includes characters based on Oscar Wilde and his lover Lord Alfred Douglas.

[163]   Spanish, with the literal meaning of 'red', but also used, as here, to mean 'off-colour' or 'indecent'.

[164]   French, meaning 'life is hard everywhere'.

[165]   Scar on a piece of hand-blown glass indicating where the iron was broken from the base.

[166]   The Duke's dogs are named after two tragic turn-of-the-century homosexual romances: Achille Bécasse's (1868–1936) *Dédé* (1901, written under the name Achille Essebac) and Georges Eekhoud's (1854–1927) *Escal-Vigor* (1899).

[167]   French, meaning 'they have bad manners'.

[168]   Fernand Nozière was the pseudonym of Fernand Weyl (1874–1931). *L'Après-midi byzantine* (*A Byzantine Afternoon*) of 1908 is a short play about infidelity centred on two courtesans and their lovers.

[169]   The Duke uses the French slang term for prostitute, referencing the livelihood of the play's two central female characters.

Byzance. Le principal meuble est un siège bas qui ressemble à un lit.[170]

You will play the boy.

I will play the charioteer. In Paris a girl played the b-b-b-boy: Madeleine Carlier. It is b-b-better so. It makes the piece more perverse.[171]

And what am I to play?

Xantippe or Myrrha…. Zimbule must play the boy, Clinias.[172]

You seem more interested in casting Zimbule than in arranging a part for me, Campaspe bantered.

You shall play Myrrha. It is the b-b-b-best rôle.

Do I have scenes with you?

With me, with Zimbule, with everybody. There are two servants, but their parts present no difficulty, and a dancer. I can arrange that. A Byzantine Afternoon! What an opera for New York! July is already the season.

If you can get an audience, put in Paul.

Ah! They will come in f-f-from the mountains. They will rush over from London. The Aquitania[173] will b-b-bulge.

There's no part for me, I take it, Paul remarked.

You can be a stage-hand; Harold, an electrician.

He will have to join the union, said Campaspe. Then, more seriously, There's something there. None of you understands Harold. I like the boy.

So do I, said Paul.

Firebird, we all d-d-do, protested the Duke. And I understand him. He is like a silver flamingo.

A silver flamingo?

Yes, glowing, glamourous, shining — like Galahad in armour[174] — and strange, aloof; he d-d-does mate with the rose flamingos.

Campaspe smiled and smoothed out her frock. You are describing yourself, Ronald, she said.

You, Firebird, he went on, paying no heed to her interruption as he was in the mood for similizing, you are the crystal spider. You draw them all into your net: these Harolds and Bunnies and Zimbules. What a crew! Where do you find them?

It's my life to find them, but I never hunt.

---

[170] French, meaning 'The scene is Byzantium. The main set piece is a low couch that resembles a bed'.
[171] Carlier (dates unknown), French actress and cabaret singer. Having a woman play the boy makes the play more 'perverse' because the sexually suggestive dialogues between the boy and the female courtesans would lend a homoerotic element to the drama.
[172] Xantippe and Myrrah are the courtesans and Clinias is a young artist.
[173] A Cunard ship, one of the most popular transatlantic ocean liners of the 1920s.
[174] Legendary gallant knight of King Arthur's Court involved in the quest for the Holy Grail.

He was, apparently, bent on comparison, for he continued, ponderingly, A catalyst, perhaps ... Yes, certainly, a catalyst.

What, asked Paul, is a catalyst?

An agent which effects a chemical reaction while appearing to take no part in it, the Duke replied.

Campaspe enjoyed talking nonsense with the Duke. She wondered if they all were aware how different she was with each of them, how she reflected their respective temperaments. It was one of her purposes in life to act the part of mirror. Was it a black mirror today? she questioned herself.

Plans for the play progressed. The Duke thought of Drains, who, it appeared, had a talent for light magic. He could make rabbits appear from hats, and balance an eel on his left ear. Zimbule was delighted to assist. Her initial adventure in the theatre had proved sufficiently diverting. She had been rehearsing with a brown-haired star who objected that Zimbule's hair was too near her own colour. At the next rehearsal Zimbule appeared in a yellow wig. The star now developed a decided aversion to wigs. Zimbule dyed her hair. The star discharged her. I don't blame the dame, the girl said. She's forty-five and she looked ninety 'side o' me. I showed her up. At any rate, Zimbule was now free to appear in the Duke's opera.

The Duke began to exhibit a lively interest in the composition of the audience. There should be an audience of tired business men, he announced, American business men. It will amuse them; it will wake them up, he explained.

You have such romantic ideas about America, Campaspe expostulated. Is there such a thing as a business man in America? I suppose so. Cupid, even, does something down town. But we try to keep that sort of thing in the background. We try not to be aware of it. It is the smart thing to do nothing, or, at any rate, to appear to do nothing. It is even a trifle démodé to write or paint. Of course, she observed in conclusion, there are people from Chicago who might do.

Oh! those furtive people from Chicago! Paul exclaimed. Those wicked, rich Chicagoans, who come to New York to be naughty, like American sophomores in Paris. Once here, you would imagine that they devote their whole lives to libidinous adventures. But if you see them back in Chicago, I am told, they are respectable fathers of families who dine at home every night, and eat breakfast across the table from their wives. Those middle-western group breakfasts! And if a word is used that the very children speak in the streets of Vienna, these Chicago business men blush.

Why, Paul! Campaspe cried, you must feel about Chicago business men the way Laura feels about Jews. When did you meet these monsters?

Meet them! Paul shrieked, waving his jade cigarette-holder about in the air. Meet them! How did you get such an idea? Meet them, indeed!

The Duke, slightly bewildered by this discourse, attempted to pull the conversation back into its proper channel.

You know perfectly well what I mean, he said. I want a reaction. I don't want a lot of b-b-b-b-bored lollers[175] out in front.

You'd better ask the Brooklyn Elks,[176] Paul suggested.

Or the Campfire Girls,[177] put in Campaspe.

Or the Academy of Arts and Letters,[178] alternated Paul.

I don't think, the Duke asseverated solemnly, that you and Paul appreciate your great country. The Hackensack meadows always remind me of the Roman Campagna, and yet I find that no one drives about in them.

What are you going to have to eat? Campaspe asked by way of creating a diversion.

Pickled walnuts, p-p-p-p-potted b-b-blackbirds, plovers' eggs....

Paul began, unreasonably, to grin. I don't know what reminds me, he said, but have you heard about Bunny? He's had Zimbule's name tattooed on his person so cunningly that it can only be deciphered under certain conditions.

The rehearsals were very strange. A friend of Paul's had been called in to play Xantippe. After the cast was arranged the Duke remembered that he had not yet translated the play. He began to do so, and then he conceived the idea of leaving his own part in French.

I will play the charioteer in French, while the other characters play in English, he announced. It will add a fillip!

But Zimbule objected to this proposal, refusing point-blank to play her scene with him in any such manner.

The Duke began to enjoy directing the piece.

Firebird, please say that line again; a little more emphasis on the word love.... Miss O'Grady, please stand down centre d-d-during this scene.

But this was unnecessary. Zimbule was always standing down centre. It was difficult, if not impossible, to persuade her to stand anywhere else. She took the best position as naturally as an old stock star would have taken it.

When the Duke, enamoured of directing, dropped out of the cast, Harold was drafted to fill his place. Never having acted before, the boy was appallingly self-conscious, all arms and legs, nor can it be said that he was an ideal choice for the role of a debauched athlete of the arena, bent on persuading his mistress

---

[175]   The Duke is using this obsolete word in the sense that it was used in the fourteenth century in the context of British religious controversy, when it was a derogatory term for those without an academic background and often lacking education.

[176]   Fraternal order and benevolent society.

[177]   Sister organization of the Boy Scouts (founded 1912).

[178]   Founded in 1904, modelled after the French Academy, and comprised of leading figures in American literature, music, and art.

to deceive him. He was serious, however, and came to his second rehearsal letter-perfect. A new phenomenon caught the eye of the observant Mrs. Lorillard: Zimbule, seemingly having exhausted Bunny's attractions, appeared to be developing an interest in Harold. Campaspe took her on another shopping tour.

Never, she was explaining, wear clothes with designs in the cloth. You are much too beautiful for that. Wear the plainest, simplest things. Give your face a chance.

But you ... began Zimbule.

I am not beautiful, Campaspe replied. I can wear what I please. Even so, I am careful. I once owned a watch, the case of which was cut from a single sapphire. I christened it at a dinner in Rome, but I never wore it again thereafter. It was too marvellous. I could not compete with it.

Zimbule gazed at her with admiration. The girl was extremely adaptable, took everything in. In a month she had learned more about dressing, walking, standing than some women ever know. Even her speech was improving.

Never keep your rooms too dark, Campaspe continued. Bright rooms are best. Bright lights. Always sit facing the window. Then there will be no shadows and shadows across the face make even the youngest of us look old. So few women know this.

Zimbule drove away from Bendel's in a new Lanvin frock,[179] black and severely plain. With her yellow hair and green eyes, she was sufficiently striking but she instinctively knew how to wear clothes, and was not even lacking in a certain kind of distinction. Campaspe, on the whole, was proud of her.

In the motor Campaspe ventured a question, What is Bunny doing?

Oh! Bunny! I don't know. Writing music, I suppose. There was a touch of petulance in the reply.

Nice boy.

Is he? Zimbule, obviously, was uninterested. There was a short pause before she said, Mrs. Lor — Campaspe, do you know Harold very well?

I've known him such a short time, Campaspe parried.

But what a kid!

I applaud you.

I like him.

Campaspe veiled her curiosity. So do I, was all she said.

At rehearsal that evening she observed that Zimbule had begun her siege. Bunny, brought thither to arrange or compose the music for the Duke's opera, sulked in a corner. The Duke had evolved the idea of reviving music by Salvatore Viganò,[180] music entirely antipathetic to the mood of the piece. Bunny, on the

---

179   Bendel's, see note 115; Lanvin, one of the most influential Parisian haute couture houses of the 1920s.
180   Romantic-era Italian choreographer, dancer, and composer (1769–1821), who composed

contrary, wanted to fit the play with music by Arthur Honegger,[181] or possibly something by himself.

The Duke shrugged his shoulders. Zimbule was whispering to the embarrassed Harold in a corner.

I think, growled Bunny, I'd like to write some modern jazz for this show.

The Duke began to brighten. That, he remarked, would be as good as music by Viganò. Jazz for a B-B-B-Byzantine play! He urged Bunny to carry out his idea.

Bunny scowled. He had no idea. His temper was one of opposition, and he had given voice to the first contradiction that had surged into his brain. His mind, on the whole, was not on jazz. Zimbule was wearing a gown of rose charmeuse,[182] without a single decoration or ornament. Her movements and gestures were all quick and abandoned. She buzzed about Harold like a brilliant hummingbird hovering over a tropical flower. The tropical flower, it was perceivable, belonged to the vegetable kingdom. It made no false effort to enter into the movement. It sat quietly awaiting the attack, perhaps even unconscious that there would be an attack, but dimly aware that some unnatural phenomenon was in process of accomplishment. Quite suddenly, casting off the semblance of the radiant bird, Zimbule became as colubrine as one of her ex-serpents, and coiled as if to strike. Campaspe watched her, fascinated; Bunny watched her, glowering.

The great night arrived. There had been more discussion about the spectator-guests.

Ask your friends, Campaspe had suggested, mocking despair.

I have no f-f-f-friends, retorted the Duke, only people that amuse me, and people I sleep with.

Well … ask them.

The people that amuse me are all in the p-p-p-play…. The theatre isn't b-b-b-b-b-big enough to hold the others.

Still, from somewhere, he had gathered an audience, a splendid, showy throng. Campaspe, through the folds of the curtain, watched them file into the theatre. Some of the faces she recognized; others were unknown to her; but the assembling of such a representative collection on a hot night in July was a feat which she appreciated. As she looked out over the house, a fluttering, fragrant acervation of luminous colour, like the flowerbeds at Hampton Court,[183] she was irresistibly reminded of an opera night at Covent Garden,[184] and this, she recalled, had been the Duke's idea, to give New York an unseasonable opera.

---

music for his own ballets.

[181]   Swiss modernist composer (1892–1955) and member of Les Six (see note 157).
[182]   Lightweight silk fabric suited to dresses that cling to the body.
[183]   Royal palace in London, renowned for its gardens.
[184]   Famed London opera house.

Ronald had a faculty for arranging things, and Campaspe loved efficiency. Whatever he put his mind to, she began to believe, happened. It was seldom enough, however, that one could be altogether certain what he was putting his mind to. Even now ...

In the little balcony reserved for it, the orchestra was tuning up, discordantly. Presently, the leader lifted his baton, and the men began to perform Bunny's overture. It was a new kind of music, she told herself at once, contrapuntal jazz, in which saxophones whistled and shrieked and groaned like hysterical school-girls telling lewd experiences, while the violins and double-basses vamped rhythmically. Flutes cried out in the tones of insane criminals. There was an indescribable clatter of tambourines, bones, triangles, castanets, gongs, drums, tomtoms, cow-bells, cymbals, wood-blocks, and rooster-crows. Listening behind the folds of the silver curtain, Campaspe realized that at last she was hearing the music of the future. Ornstein, Prokofieff, Schönberg would sound, in comparison, like a minuet by Luigi Boccherini.[185] There was a rush, a push, an extravagant primitive quality in this music. If I listen to this music, I shall forget my role, she confessed to herself, and it occurred to her to wonder if Bunny was, after all, a genius. Anybody must be a genius who could stir her as this music was stirring her. She was drenched, nay submerged, in merciless floods of clang-tints: unnamable sins obsessed her consciousness. She exerted her will, and peeping between the folds of the curtain, gazed at the assemblage. The ladies' faces were drawn taut and pale; some of them were contorted by strange grimaces. Bosoms rose and fell in a shuddering, broken rhythm. The men looked hard and cold, like men who had just had their toes chopped off, but who were too stoical to scream. Suddenly, with one shrill blast from the saxophones, one crisp screech from the flutes, the band saw purple and cavorted into obsolete keys, neglecting its duties towards the tempered scale. Then, swiftly, with a tortured snatch of parody of I'll build a stairway to paradise,[186] the overture ended. The men were now flushed and restless, seemingly ashamed to look at their companions. The ladies, as if to recover their poise, began to chatter affectedly. There was no applause.

A triumph! A complete triumph! Campaspe turned to the Duke.

Rather! he admitted. And I wanted this man to arrange some of Viganò's p-p-p-paltry tunes. He's better than Stravinsky![187]

---

[185]   Leo Ornstein (1895–2002), Sergei Prokofiev (1891–1953), and Arnold Schönberg (1874–1951), avant-garde experimental composers, notable for their use of atonality and dissonance. Van Vechten wrote about Ornstein in his essay collection *Music and Bad Manners* (1916) and about Schönberg in *Music After the Great War* (1915). Luigi Boccherini (1743–1805), Italian classical composer.

[186]   Gershwin tune, written for the Broadway revue *George White's Scandals* (1922).

[187]   Igor Stravinsky (1882–1971), Russian composer who gained fame in the 1910s for his avant-garde experimentation with folk forms. Van Vechten wrote about him in *Music and Bad Manners* (1916).

Campaspe was reflective. He never wrote like this before. I wonder if it is Zimbule who has inspired him?

He has seen something. It is the last wail of a d-d-discarded mule in hell.

Zimbule, in her boy's costume, approached.

Say, what is it?

Bunny's overture, Campaspe muttered.

Sounded like a stale calliope[188] at Coney. Where's Harold?

Clear the stage, shouted Paul in his capacity as stage-manager.

They obeyed him and, as the silver folds parted, out into the void before a yellow satin drop walked Oliver Drains in a suit of purple tights which terminated only in a white-ruffed collar. For some time Drains had fancied himself arrayed à la John Barrymore in The Jest.[189] He had seized his opportunity. The orchestra played Some sunny day.[190] There was a ripple of applause for the performer. Drains bowed. He began by tossing gold balls in the air. He continued the ritual. White mice were discovered harboured in the kinky wool of a recalcitrant coon. Artificial mango bushes bloomed from empty jars. An otiose table suddenly offered support to a bowl of swimming goldfish, which, apparently, had come out of the air. The orchestra played Dear old southland.[191] The spectators seemed to have regained their equilibrium. Only one woman, far in the back, gazed about furtively in an attempt to discover if any one recalled what her condition had been but a few brief moments earlier.

May I borrow a hat? Drains called out.

The hats were piled in the Louis XIV bedroom. One of the Duke's Ceylonese servants descended in search of the demanded article. There was a flutter of fans through the heated chamber. An old gentleman already suffered from a sad and correct drunkenness. Two young men strolled out, feeling their hips. This recognition scene became more general.

After Drains's number absinthe was served in goblets.

Next came the acrobats, four brothers from the halls, professionals in pink fleshings, with spangled ruching about their middles. The orchestra played I'm just wild about Harry.[192] The fans pursued their endless game. After this turn the Ceylonese servants served arrack[193] in crystal bowls, and passed cigarettes with lighters on beaten copper trays.

---

[188]   Steam organ used for circuses and fairs that is loud and difficult to tune accurately.

[189]   Barrymore (1882–1942), popular stage and screen actor who created a sensation in his form-fitting tights playing a sensitive young artist in a 1919 Broadway production of Sem Benelli's *Jest*, a historical revenge drama set in the time of the de Medicis.

[190]   Popular hit of 1922 by Irving Berlin.

[191]   Popular jazz hit of 1921 by Turner Layton (music) and Henry Creamer (lyrics).

[192]   Hit by Eubie Blake (music) and Sissie Noble (lyrics) from the African-American Broadway production *Shuffle Along* (1921).

[193]   South Asian rum-like liquor made of coconut flowers, sugarcane, and grain or fruit.

Now the glow in the auditorium was extinguished. The Ceylonese boys set fire to braziers and the odour of Narcisse Noir[194] permeated the atmosphere. Again, the orchestra played Bunny's music, the incidental music he had composed for Nozière's baroque comedy, l'Après-midi Byzantine, music which began with a faint roll of drums, which grew louder and louder and then died away. Now a clarinet, solo, played a plaintive, incestuous melody in a scale much higher than that which is usually associated with this instrument. The saxophone took up the thread, playing a few bars, and when the saxophone had finished, the double-bass had something indelible to say. Then, quite unreasonably, the piano held a soliloquy. Campaspe was glad that she was not looking at the audience. She could imagine the faces. Her hands, she felt, were as cold as fresh spring water.

The silver curtains parted anew and the play proceeded. The first great moment was the appearance of the Cambodian dancer, a slender, full-bosomed bayadere, clad, like Moreau's Salome,[195] only in jewels. Sparkling with light, her face as expressionless as a Noh mask,[196] she stood on a small round platform in a miniature circle of illumination. Her movements were slow and insinuating; there was no abandon, no swift grace, in this dance. But she contrived to invest her slightest gesture with a leste[197] significance, and when, seated, cross-legged, she bent her long fingers back until they touched her forearms, her face remaining the face of an unwrapped mummy, she suggested, irrevocably, the expiatory pain of a supreme sin.

Zimbule, too, tossed by the intricate intrigue of the play into the arms of one character after another, exhibited a nonchalance and rare perversity which lifted her performance into the realm of something rich and strange. In her scene with Harold, the scene of the charioteer with the boy-sculptor, a scene written in a mocking, cynical spirit, she far transcended anything, however curious, that the author had imagined. To this episode, in which Clinias, betrayed with the mistress of Hippolyte, attempts to conciliate the burly athlete, she gave a touch of mystic sensuality, aided by Bunny's music, which, in its definite contradictions, its wholly inappropriate rightness, wailed on. Harold, naturally, was lamentably bad. The curtain fell in silence, but, almost immediately, there rose a great storm of applause.

It belongs to Zimbule and Bunny, said Campaspe. Let them take the calls. Bunny, morbid with grief and chlorosis, and yet transfigured with excitement, was discovered hovering in a corner. As the curtains parted again, Paul pushed him on to the stage. Zimbule strolled on unconcernedly from the other side,

---

[194]   Exotic rich jasmine and orange scented perfume by Caron, popular in the 1920s.
[195]   French Symbolist painter Gustave Moreau (1826–1898) depicted Salomé in two 1876 paintings: L'Apparition and Salomé dansant devant Hérode (Salome Dancing Before Herod).
[196]   Stylized masks used in traditional Japanese musical drama.
[197]   French, meaning 'nimble'.

dragging the reluctant Harold in her wake. Bunny groaned and buried his face in his hands. There were cries of Bravo! and Brava!

There has never been anything like it, Ronald, Campaspe exclaimed. I don't feel as if I had been part of it at all. I was so occupied looking and listening. Did I remember my lines?

You were perfect, Firebird. The Duke was distrait.[198]

Strange. I don't remember having spoken a single word.

Drains had departed. The acrobats were dressing. The actors in their costumes mingled with the throng. Many of the guests, like sharks after a slain leviathan, crowded into the dining-room for supper, chaud-froid, truffle salad, spumoni…. Others lingered in the theatre. In the garden a little group of lanky, pale youths, demi-puceaux,[199] congregated. The silent Ceylonese passed, expertly, up and down, through and about, with cigarettes and trays laden with minuscule glasses and fat bottles of Danziger Goldwasser.[200]

Little by little, the excitement dwindled, and there were signs that the New York season would soon come to an end. One of these was the demeanour of the Duke who, from time to time, frankly yawned, making no effort to conceal his dehiscent jaw. Bunny had disappeared shortly after his tragic curtain call. Zimbule accepted her encomiums as if she found them exceedingly tiresome. She seemed exalted, disembodied. Campaspe, conscious of impending drama, hovered in her wake.

With a fiercer intensity Harold felt that a fatality assembled the elements which made up his life. He had begun to think of himself as an automaton, set up and wound to give pleasure … to whom? Not to himself. Not too much, apparently, to these others. Was he giving, then, some form of pleasure to his father. Was his father taking a perverse joy in watching him struggle in these nets of silk and gilt. At least, and at last, he was free of Zimbule. Once the curtains had fallen she had released his hand and left his side.

Campaspe, in her clinging blue robe, followed Zimbule down the stairs, listening to the re-echoing Remarkable! Marvellous! Divine! Extraordinary! Kolossal! Epatante![201] The crowd had seen something, heard something, tasted something, touched something, smelled something. And Campaspe, as always, had experienced the reflex of the crowd. That was about all there was left, she admitted to herself, but it was wonderful when it happened. Zimbule seemed tired and listless, petulant even. She shook hands and received compliments languidly, without any interest, Campaspe thought, and yet she still sensed a

---

[198]   French, meaning 'distracted', 'absent-minded'.
[199]   French, meaning 'semi-virgins'.
[200]   Strong herbal liqueur with flecks of gold.
[201]   Kolossal, German, meaning 'tremendous'; épatante, French, meaning 'amazing'.

strange vibrancy in the girl, a curious electrical quality, preserved for future transmission. Where, and to whom? Campaspe looked about for Harold. He was nowhere to be seen. The Duke, too, had disappeared, and several escaping guests shook hands with Campaspe, mistaking her for the hostess. She asked Zimbule if she would like to change, and the girl assented, almost eagerly, Campaspe noted. They installed themselves in the magnificent bathroom and Campaspe dispatched Frederika to the top floor for their dresses. Meanwhile, she watched Zimbule, as the child quickly divested herself of her ivory tunic and the single protective piece she wore beneath this, and soon stood in her sandals, rose and perspiring in her nudity, before the black mirrors. How wonderful it was that this girl, who had never taken any care of her body, should possess such a perfect body, perfect in its proportions, perfect in its details. Women with beautiful bodies never suffer from modesty or a sense of shame, Campaspe said to herself, and she remembered that some man had told her recently that he had been married for five years but had never seen his wife's feet. He had been certain that her feet were ugly or deformed or that they suffered from one of the diseases that feet suffer from. Looking at this child, exquisite in her lack of shame, her natural ignorance of an occasion for it, Campaspe assured herself that the man had judged his wife justly.

You are lovely, she said.

Zimbule, already silent for some time, said nothing now, but her face brightened with an appreciative smile, and there was something interrogative also in her expression.

I wonder if he will think so, she breathed at last.

Frederika had returned with their white evening gowns, and she helped them to don them. Campaspe, dressed first, directed her maid to draw on Zimbule's stockings and her little satin shoes.

Shall I ask you both to my house tomorrow? was her suggestion.

Zimbule threw her a swift glance of gratitude. I shan't wait till tomorrow, she said, the colour mounting to her cheeks. She had rubbed off the last vestige of make-up, but she was still as rosy as a country milk-maid.

Tomorrow, too, if you like, Campaspe encouraged.

Oh! well! We'll be in bed, I hope.

Some one was pounding on the door.

Who's there? Campaspe demanded.

Ronald, came the reply. They've all g-g-g-gone, and I want to go to b-b-b-bed.

Campaspe opened the door.

We're dressed, she said. Ronald, the opera was a success. New York has had a summer season. I can pass the autumn in Sicily with perfect safety.

Did you like it? was his indifferent query. It bored me. It was fun to plan, but stupid to do....

Where's Harold? Zimbule asked.

Harold? repeated the Duke, alarmed by the idea that there might be still others who had not departed.

Mr. Prewett, he dress upstairs, volunteered one of the Ceylonese servants.

Good God! Not gone yet, groaned the Duke.

We're going now, said Campaspe.

Good-night, Firebird, and thank you.... He kissed her.... Good-night, little O'Grady. You shone.

Thanks. Good-night, Mr. Ronald. Zimbule could never be persuaded to call the Duke anything else.

They went on down the stairs, Frederika following with their bags.

Can I drive you home? asked Campaspe.

No, thank you. I have a taxi waiting. I ordered it some time ago.

At the foot of the stairs an obstruction appeared: Bunny.

Zimbule was direct: I'm not going home with you, Bunny.

You can't do that to me! His tone was appealing rather than threatening.

I'm not going home with you. Don't make a row. It won't do any good. I'm roosting with Campaspe.

Oh! God! Zimbule, What have I done? What's the matter? The boy began to weep.

Cut that! You haven't done anything.... I'm going home with Mrs. Lorillard.

She was determined: this much was apparent even to a vision obscured by tears. Bunny stepped back, splashing himself like an ugly blot against the blue wall, and the three women made their way out.

Good-night, Campaspe, whispered Zimbule, as she kissed her friend.

Good-night.

She slipped into the waiting taxi, after a direction to the chauffeur, uttered in too low a voice for Campaspe to catch it, and the vehicle shot away into the black night.

Harold was the last to leave, for Bunny had slunk out as soon as he caught the sound of departing wheels. Harold did not even meet the Duke in the corridor and, as the door of his bedroom was closed, he refrained from knocking. After hesitating a moment in the deserted street, he decided to walk home; it was so hot and so quiet. Turning into Fifth Avenue, brilliantly lighted in spite of the late hour, he walked north until he touched Eighteenth Street.

Soon he was home. Ascending to his floor, he took out his key and prepared to open the door. To his amazement, he found a key already in the lock. Oliver? But Oliver did not stay here nights. Thieves, assuredly, would never leave a key in the door. Still, for a second or two he hesitated, pondering as to whether he should go back for Pedro, the hall-boy. Then he turned the key and entered.

The apartment was perfectly dark. He pressed a button which illuminated the living-room. Nobody there. Passing into the bedroom he pressed another button. His eye fell first on a chair on which was heaped a congeries of feminine apparel. Then he turned to his bed. Curled up, quite uncovered in the heat, sound asleep, in much the same attitude that he had seen her assume with Bunny, lay Zimbule.

Harold stared at her for a moment. Then, his heart beating violently with rage and fear, he pressed the button extinguishing the light. He tiptoed to the hall, pressed the other button, and passed out, closing the door softly behind him.

As he descended in the elevator, Pedro blinked and eyed him curiously, and as Harold rushed out the front entrance, slamming the door violently, the boy whistled softly to himself. Then, with a smile, Pedro lit a cigarette and, like Madama Butterfly,[202] sat down to wait for the dawn.

---

[202] Eponymous heroine of Giacomo Puccini's (1858–1924) opera (1904), who is made to wait years for the return of her American husband.

Chapter VIII

The next day began for Campaspe about one o'clock in the afternoon. The sun was high and bright, but the atmosphere was refreshingly cool; it was one of those charming days with a gentle sea breeze which alternate with sultry, humid weather in any New York summer. Campaspe sipped her coffee in bed, and glanced over her mail. There were letters from her two boys who were passing the summer with their grandfather at Southampton.[203] These she opened first. Esmé had caught a blue-fish and Basil wanted a cowboy's suit with chaps,[204] a red-flannel shirt, a sombrero, and a lariat. Both of them desired to see their mother. Wasn't she coming down? She tapped an envelope against her open lips as she thought of her sons. Campaspe loved her children, and occasionally she had them with her. It was constitutional of her, however, to believe that she was only doing her best for others when she entirely pleased herself. She had decided, quite wisely, events had proved, not to leave New York again this summer. In the fall she would see the boys before she went to Europe and they were sent to boarding-school. It was better so. Boys, she felt, developed more rapidly and more individually if they did not live too much with their parents. Their grandfather, she knew, would permit them to do anything they wanted to do, and she was satisfied that this was the only way to bring children up successfully. Cupid, to be sure, went down to Southampton about twice a month. He was romantically attached to his sons and cherished a father's conventional ideas, but he, as much as their grandfather, could be depended upon not to interfere with their wishes. He wanted them to love him, and Campaspe felt certain that he would never thwart their desires for fear of sacrificing that love. Ironically enough, the boys loved their mother more than they did their father. This, in a way, justified her course of action; not that Campaspe ever sought justification for her acts, but sometimes it gave her a certain human amount of pleasure to realize that she was right…. Later, in boarding-school, there would be interference, of course, but that was external interference of the kind the boys might afterwards expect in life and consequently good for them; it had nothing to do with the family.

---

[203]   One of a group of Long Island villages serving as summer resorts for the wealthy.

[204]   The names of Campaspe's sons allude to Oscar Wilde, another mechanism through which Van Vechten registers queerness in the novel. Esmé was the name of a character modelled on Wilde in Robert Hichens's (1864–1950) *roman-à-clef The Green Carnation* (1894), while Basil was the name of the painter obsessed with the titular hero of *The Picture of Dorian Gray*.

The next letter she opened was from Laura, who was spending the summer in the Berkshires.[205] She, too, wanted Campaspe to join her. All the world, it would seem, was calling for Campaspe, but this was invariably true, she realized, when one was enjoying oneself. It was only when one felt lonely and bored that nobody asked one to do anything or to go anywhere. The thought came to Campaspe that she was seldom lonely, seldom bored nowadays. Only in her extreme youth had she experienced these and kindred unpleasant emotions. She had a practical nature; she hated the ineffectual. She had conquered fear; she conquered any feeling that annoyed or troubled her. She had mastered a formula for handling life, made life her slave, and this formula infrequently failed her.

After her bath, she donned a dressing-gown of pale green crêpe de chine, purfled in silver frogs, their legs extended in queer swimming postures, and sat down before her little writing-desk.

Dear Laura, she wrote:

You are bored in the Berkshires. I am amused in New York. Why should I go to you. Return, rather, to me. I know, of course, you can't or won't. You always consider the feelings of your children or your husband and, as a consequence, always keep them unhappy or uncomfortable. If you lived your own life, they would adjust their lives to yours. I suppose, as a matter of fact, that you are living your own life, doing what you really want to do, just as much as I am. People who suffer usually like to suffer and talk about it. There is Wilson Goodward, for instance, always complaining about his hard knocks, his consistently bad luck, always insisting that nothing ever comes out right for him. He likes to suffer and he likes to talk about his suffering. It is his way of making himself important. He cannot impose his personality on others in any positive way, he cannot work his will with life, and so he employs negative tools. Naturally, I don't mean all this for you. What I really think about you is that you are domestic, that you love your family, and that you adore excursions into the country with them, but before your more sophisticated friends, Laura, you feel ashamed of your true emotions and you believe it is necessary to apologize for your natural feelings. In time, probably, you will cease to do this and begin to lecture me as, perhaps, I seem to be lecturing you now! But I am not, really. I am merely chattering, as I would chatter if you were here. I am too happy to give advice to any one…. I am deliriously happy!

Such a summer! Ronald is here — you know, the Duke of Middlebottom; at least, you have heard me speak of him. He's done such an amusing thing: taken a town house in New York in July to transfer the London season here. At least that's what he says he has been doing; I think he may have other reasons for being here. At any rate, he has carried his masked purpose far enough to give New York a July "opera season." Only one night, but what

---

[205]   Area stretching from Connecticut to Vermont that was a summer resort for the wealthy in this period.

an opera! It really wasn't an opera at all, but there was music, which Bunny
wrote, thereby convincing me that he is a genius. There was one moment
when all veils were rent. You should have seen Mrs. Pollanger![206] But *all*
of them sat naked, just as they will again in hell. That was *my* moment: I
felt that Bunny, unconsciously, had done that for me. Certainly, nobody
else appreciated it. It made no impression whatsoever on the person he
thought he had done it for. She is a snake-charmer, or was for a day or so,
really the most unusual and nicest child — she is nearly seventeen — I have
ever met. She follows her instincts, actually follows them; not the way I do,
consciously and scrupulously, after years of trying to do something else,
but involuntarily, automatically, and she has done so from birth, I should
imagine.... I have had great fun teaching her how to dress, how to walk,
how to speak, not too apparently; just a hint here and a hint there, which
she accepts and takes advantage of, makes her own, so to speak, only too
greedily. She is a born duchess, *natural* like a duchess — never alarmed lest
she be doing something that others will consider wrong or in bad taste —
and, consequently, an aristocrat, entirely free from vulgarity. For you know
it is my belief that only those are vulgar who make pretensions to be what
they are not. Perhaps you would consider her vulgar. Some day, it is entirely
possible, I may consider her vulgar myself. I can see her in the future,
driving past me without bowing, when she reaches a social station in life
which she regards as higher than mine. At present, she is only concerned
with love, but she will doubtless go beyond that. She will be disappointed
and disillusioned by love, as all of us are some time or other, and she will
probably marry a rich man and live unhappily ever after, because, au fond,
she is an animal, and she will only be happy so long as she lives like an
animal, naturally and a little libidinously. She is just through with Bunny,
who adores her.

And that brings me to Paul, who is the only person I never really worry
about. Paul is so good and kind and amusing and helpless and *lucky*. At
present, he is being taken care of by a rich and eccentric old gentleman,
who has put his son in Paul's charge, for a new kind of education. Harold
Prewett — that is the boy's awful name — is, I should imagine, undergoing
a course in worldliness. His father must believe that he is a prig. Harold is
by no means a prig. He is a boy with fine instincts, who has been compelled
by circumstances, as I see it, to lead a secluded life. Paul's way of living, and
mine, do not suit him at all, and I think he must be very unhappy. He is not,
however, as dependent upon fate as Paul. Harold is still young; some day
he will assert himself. Indeed, even while I am writing these words, it has
occurred to me that it may be his father's grim intention to develop the boy's
character in this ruthless fashion so that he will assert himself the sooner.
How, where, or when, I have no idea. But this is one of the reasons I have no
wish to leave New York. I cannot afford to miss the scène à faire.

There are, I have discovered, and I insert the discovery parenthetically

---

[206]   Isabel Pollanger, fictional character who appears in two of Van Vechten's later novels:
Firecrackers (1925) and *Parties* (1930).

for what it may be worth, two kinds of people in this world, those who long to be understood, and those who long to be misunderstood. It is the irony of life that neither is gratified.

I am perfectly frank with you, dear Laura, always; there seems to be no other reason for writing long letters. You know that I seek my thrills in a curious, vicarious way. You know that what befalls others is of more interest to me than what befalls myself. Indeed, you must be aware by now that I do not care to have anything happen to me at all. If I can prevent it, things never do happen to me, and *I can prevent it*. I have even arranged it so that I do not suffer physical pain when it is inconvenient for me.

This is a very long letter about matters in which you will, conceivably, take only a vague interest, but I am clearing my mind for the day, revealing myself to myself, revolving my ideas so that I may the more fully enjoy them.

Now that I have written this letter, indeed, there seems no real occasion for sending it, but I will not deprive you of such small amusement as you may derive from a perusal of its pages.

love from your,

CAMPASPE.

Having finished the letter and addressed the envelope, Campaspe dipped her fingers into a shallow bowl of water-lilies that stood on the desk and with the moistened tips wet the gum of the envelope and pressed the flap closed. Leaving the letter for Frederika to post, she rose and descended to the garden.

Campaspe's garden, at the rear of the house, was enclosed in high brick walls on which were trained espaliered fruit-trees. Dwarf shrubs forced their miniature trunks between the mossy crevices of the flagstones of various sizes and colours that paved the ground. Over these a quaint tortoise of considerable size and incredible age, named Aglaë, wandered in a disconsolate manner. There were a few comfortable chairs and, in one corner, under the shade of a spreading crab-apple tree, a table. In the opposite corner rose a rococo fountain which Campaspe, entranced at first sight, had purchased in an antiquary's shop in Dresden. This fountain gave the atmosphere to the whole place. On a low pedestal, in the midst of a semi-circular pool, a marble Eros, blindfold, knelt.[207] His bow drawn taut, the god was about to discharge an arrow at random. Beneath him, prone on the marble sward, a young nymph wept. The figures were surrounded by a curving row of stiff straight marble narcissi, the water dripping from their cups into the pool below, in which silver-fish played.

Charmed by the sun and the contradictory coolness of the day — nature, she

---

[207] Greek counterpart to the Roman Cupid, god of love. According to mythology, the god of love has the power to make a person fall in love simply by striking him/her with an arrow. Cupid and Eros are often depicted blindfolded, symbolism Van Vechten exploits in the novel's title. The symbolism of the blindfold indicates the randomness with which Love discharges its bow and that, as the cliché goes, 'love is blind'. Campaspe's fountain served as the inspiration for the original dust jacket and frontispiece illustration by Robert Locher.

had noted, could be as contradictory and perverse as life itself — , Campaspe, propped up against cushions, lay back in a comfortable chaise-longue. Frederika had followed her with a pile of books, which she placed on a table by the side of her mistress, but, for the moment, Campaspe did not disturb these. She closed her eyes and half-dreamed in the bliss of her security. She hoped that no one would call. She had too much to think about. Campaspe enjoyed being alone. In fact, it was essential to her happiness that she be alone for at least a part of every day, occasionally for the whole day, and sometimes for a period of two or three days. It was during these self-imposed isolations that she most thoroughly enjoyed the hours in which she was not alone. Retrospection, revery, was her pleasure, her desire, her vice. She had no other. Yet, today, she did not give orders that she was not receiving.

She picked up one of the books, a novel by Waldo Frank,[208] of which she conned the title with some dismay. She had bought it under the impression that it was called Darkey Mothers. She was not interested in the true title. Nevertheless, she opened the book and read a sentence or two. Then, with some impatience, she tossed the volume aside. Why, she wondered, did authors write in this uncivilized and unsophisticated manner? How was it possible to read an author who never laughed? For it was only behind laughter that true tragedy could lie concealed, only the ironic author who could awaken the deeper emotions. The tragedies of life, she reflected, were either ridiculous or sordid. The only way to get the sense of this absurd, contradictory, and perverse existence into a book was to withdraw entirely from the reality. The artist who feels the most poignantly the bitterness of life wears a persistent and sardonic smile. She remembered the salubrious remark of a character in André Salmon's La Négresse du Sacré-Cœur: There is only one truth, steadfast, healing, salutary, and that is the absurd.[209] This book was mush, as sentimental, she felt, as a book by Gene Stratton-Porter[210] — she chose a name at random, realizing that she did not know much about Gene Stratton-Porter except what she had read in the newspapers. This extremely heavy attempt on the part of Waldo Frank to take life seriously was just as sentimental as the attempt of Gene Stratton-Porter to take life, well as *she* found it. She recalled Georg Kaiser's sardonic play, From Morn to Midnight.[211] How much higher it loomed in her consciousness, how

---

[208] Frank (1889–1967), American novelist who favoured a psychoanalytic approach. The novel in question is *Dark Mother* (1920). See the introduction to this edition, p. xv, for more context.

[209] Salmon (1881–1969), French writer and art critic, proponent of Cubism. *La Négresse du Sacré-Cœur* is a fantastical tale of an eccentric who establishes a rubber plantation in bohemian Montmartre which also functions as a *roman-à-clef* for the Parisian artistic avant-garde of Picasso and his contemporaries. The line quoted represents the thoughts of Florimond Daubelle, a poet character based on Salmon.

[210] Gene Stratton-Porter (1863–1924), global bestselling writer.

[211] Kaiser (1878–1945), German playwright and proponent of Expressionism, an anti-

much more lingering the sting, than plays which, on the surface, appeared to be more bitter, plays such as Dreiser's The Hand of the Potter,[212] for Kaiser had laughed at his puppets. On n'apprend qu'en s'amusant, according to Sylvestre Bonnard,[213] and she remembered Nietzsche's defence of the music of Carmen: It approaches lightly, nimbly, and with courtesy. It is amiable. It does not produce sweat. What is good is easy; everything divine runs with light feet: the first proposition of my Æsthetics....[214] How delightful the scene in Kaiser's play in which the German grandmother dies because her son leaves the house before eating his dinner! It had never happened before. What a comment on German character! And ten times as powerful as if the scene had been presented as something to cry over. One could shed tears to be sure, but not in behalf of the grandmother. One wept for her nation. She mentally decided that Hilaire Belloc's The Mercy of Allah gave a much better picture of a modern millionaire, because the book was good-humoured, satirical, and allegorical,[215] than the more solemn performances of W. L. George in Caliban and Theodore Dreiser in The Financier.[216] It was this same lack of humour, this sentimental adherence to a rigid point of view which in her eyes spoiled Three Soldiers.[217] There was something to be said for such a book, undoubtedly, but you could not say that it was written for a sophisticated audience. No, in a different sense, it was written for the stupid, unsophisticated crowd, just as Rupert Hughes's books were written for that crowd.[218] Only Hughes wrote to please the crowd and Dos Passos to annoy it. And such sophisticated souls as were delighted with Three Soldiers were delighted merely because the crowd was annoyed. An artist, she said to herself, would leave this crowd indifferent.

She closed her eyes again ... and lighted a fresh cigarette. As she exhaled

---

naturalist mode in which complex characterization is eschewed in favour of archetypal representation. From Morn to Midnight (1916) concerns the corruption of a bank cashier and was performed in New York in 1922.

[212]   Theodore Dreiser (1871–1945), American writer associated with Naturalism. The Hand of the Potter (1918) was a controversial tragedy exploring the biological basis of criminal behaviour in its treatment of a man's rape of a young girl. It was first performed in 1921 by avant-garde theatre troupe The Provincetown Players.

[213]   French, meaning 'It is only by amusing oneself that one learns'. Bonnard is the idealistic protagonist of Anatole France's novel Le Crime de Sylvestre Bonnard (1881).

[214]   From The Case of Wagner (1888) in which Nietzsche (1844–1900) professes to turn his back on Wagner's decadence to embrace the antithetical popular and populist aesthetics represented by Georges Bizet (1838–1875) and his opera Carmen (1875).

[215]   Belloc (1870–1953), Anglo-French writer, whose Mercy of Allah (1922) employs an Arabian Nights story-cycle frame to satirize modern capitalism.

[216]   George (1882–1926), British writer whose Caliban (1920) is loosely based on the life of newspaper magnate Lord Northcliffe. Dreiser's Financier (1912) charts the rise and fall of an American business tycoon as an allegory of American life of the era.

[217]   Three Soldiers (1921), by John Dos Passos (1896–1970), a controversial anti-war story documenting the psychological effects of war.

[218]   Hughes (1872–1956), writer of popular fiction, drama, biography, and screenplays.

the first ring of smoke a fable related by Babbalanja in Herman Melville's marvellous Mardi came into her mind:[219] Midni was of opinion that daylight was vulgar; good enough for taro-planting and travelling, but wholly unadapted to the sublime ends of study. He toiled by night; from sunset to sunrise poring over the works of the old logicians. Like most philosophers, Midni was an amiable man; but one thing invariably put him out. He read in the woods by glow-worm light; insect in hand, tracing over his pages, line by line. But glow-worms burn not long: and in the midst of some calm intricate thought, at some imminent comma, the insect often expired, and Midni groped for a meaning. Upon such an occasion, Ho, Ho, he cried; but for one instant of sunlight to see my way to a period! But sunlight there was none; so Midni sprang to his feet, and parchment under arm, raced about among the sloughs and bogs for another glow-worm. Often, making a rapid descent with his turban, he thought he had caged a prize; but nay. Again he tried; yet with no better success. Nevertheless, at last he secured one, but hardly had he read three lines by its light, when out it went. Again and again this occurred. And thus he for ever went halting and stumbling through his studies and plunging through his quagmires after a glim.[220]

A book, Campaspe considered, should have the swiftness of melodrama, the lightness of farce, to be a real contribution to thought. Every time, had said the Rabbi Moses Maimonides, you find in our books a tale, the reality of which seems impossible, a story which is repugnant both to reason and common sense, then be sure that tale contains a profound allegory, veiling a deeply mysterious truth; and the greater the absurdity of the letter the deeper the wisdom of the spirit.[221] How could anything serious be hidden more successfully than in a book which pretended to be light and gay? Plot was certainly unimportant in the novel; character drawing a silly device. Anybody could do it. It was like character acting: give a man a beard and a few trick phrases and gestures and you have created a masterpiece. How easy it would be, for example, to put the Duke in a book: his stuttering, his neglected finger nails, and the man would rise before the reader's eyes. Justification? Preparation? In life we never know anything about the families and early lives of the people we meet; why should we have to learn all about them in books? Growth of character in a novel was

---

[219]   Melville (1819–1891), writer of the American Renaissance period, whose *Mardi* (1849) is a fictional travel narrative, philosophical and satirical, featuring Babbalanja, a philosopher who offers lengthy disquisitions on many topics. Largely neglected after his death, Melville was the subject of renewed interest and recuperation in the 1920s. Van Vechten, for example, extolled Melville in a critical essay in *Excavations* (1926).

[220]   From 'Midni was of opinion' to the end of the paragraph is a direct quotation from chapter 51 of *Mardi*.

[221]   Maimonides was a twelfth-century Sephardic Jewish philosopher and Torah scholar. This quotation, from *Guide to the Perplexed*, encapsulates the text's aim, which is to encourage readers to avoid literal interpretation of sacred texts.

nonsense. People never change. Psychology: the supreme imbecility. The long and complicated analyses that serious writers give us merely define the mental limitations of these writers. The Bible, The Thousand and One Nights, and Don Quixote certainly were not psychological novels....[222] As for Ulysses ...[223] Works like Ulysses are always out of date. At first too modern, they soon grow old-fashioned. The very group that is most enthusiastic about Ulysses today will be the first to spurn it tomorrow.

She lit another cigarette, reflecting on the words of Clive Bell, who had said that in the best work of Nicolas Poussin the human figure is treated as a shape cut out of coloured paper to be pinned on as the composition directs.[224] That was the right way to treat the human figure; the mistake lay in making these shapes retain the characteristic gestures of classical rhetoric. She glanced towards the pile of books again. There were, she noted with a new regret, if no surprise, no books by Ouida in the pile,[225] and she suddenly became aware of the fact that only a book by Ouida would satisfy her present mood. Ouida, who had not written for posterity, realizing, no doubt, that the public of fifty years hence would be no keener intellectually than her coeval public. Ouida was entertaining. Her approach was satisfactorily unpretentious. She wrote about high life, the very rich — and who wanted to read about any other kind of life? Certainly not the rich, or the middle classes, or the poor ... Neither the rich nor the poor were interested in reading about the poor except in the form of the Cinderella legend and that had been done too often.... Ouida's characters had amusing adventures; they were cut out of coloured paper to be pinned on as the composition directed. I think, Campaspe began to reason, that Waldo Frank should read Ouida. I wonder if he ever has. But she apprehended that Waldo Frank would not understand or appreciate the work of Louise de la Ramé, and so a reading would have no effect on his own future writing. It was characteristic of Campaspe that she began to feel a little sorry for Waldo Frank.

Two white doves floated down from the blue and settled on the fountain, one on the curly head of Eros, the other on a stiff narcissus stem. She listened to their soft cooing and watched their graceful movements. She recalled the case of the prisoner in the death-house at Sing Sing, who had undergone an

---

[222]   *The Thousand and One Nights* is a collection of ancient Middle Eastern and South Asian folk tales compiled in Arabic over the course of the eighth to the thirteenth centuries; *Don Quixote*, by Cervantes (1547–1616), a Spanish novel about the peripatetic adventures of its romantic and idealistic hero.

[223]   *Ulysses* (1922), by James Joyce (1882–1941), was highly controversial in the period, influential within the modernist avant-garde, but banned in America. It was noted for its psychological realism.

[224]   Clive Bell, see notes 157 and 282. Poussin served for Bell as an exemplar of his theory of significant form, which idealized abstraction, promoting an experience of art derived purely from formal qualities.

[225]   On Ouida, see note 13.

operation for appendicitis two days before the hour set for his execution. Skilled surgeons had been rushed from New York to save his life so that he would not die and "cheat the chair," as the New York Times put it.[226] There also lingered in her hospitable memory the story of the derelict who had been fed by the Y. M. C. A. The secretary of a branch of that organization had offered the fellow regular meals and employment if ... IF he would put himself completely in the hands of the Y. M. C. A. and profess a belief in God. The man had refused, she recalled with delight. Nothing remained to him but his free will, and he proposed to keep that. But the Y. M. C. A. secretary, instead of regarding this stand as an indication of character, wept over this wolf lost to God.[227] These anecdotes, typical press-cuttings from the news of the day, were, in their essence, comic arraignments of our civilization, or so Campaspe considered them. An attempt to trump up tears for the victims would always fail with a sophisticated audience, but when ridicule was aimed at the real offender, modern democracy or the church, a sense of tragic irony ensued. Something might even happen, although she was extremely dubious about this. It could hardly be expected that the best surgeons would be rushed to Sullivan Street[228] to save the life of a poor Italian baby who had no intention of cheating the chair. Campaspe had a savage hatred of cruelty. She watched animal acts at the circus with the constant, but still ungratified, hope that the beasts would kill their trainers.

She lighted another cigarette. The doves had long since flown away. Aglaë, the tortoise, was reposing, the weight of his years weighing down his shell. Soft purple shadows in lacework fell athwart the flagstones.... Considering the heroines of modern fiction, reviewing their qualifications, Campaspe decided that Savina Grove and Mrs. Hurstpierpoint[229] were the only two she would invite to call on her. They had lived their lives, not very amusing lives, perhaps, but at least their own. She remembered Idalia[230] with pleasure. Idalia, though of another age, might come too. She must send to Brentano's[231] for the book and reread it. Did Brentano's still keep the works of Ouida in stock? she wondered. Beyond question the serious books of Ouida were the best antidote she could think of for the serious books of this generation. At least, they were written in

---

[226] This story appeared in the *New York Times*, 20 May 1922, p. 6.
[227] Unidentified reference.
[228] Street running south from Washington Square, which, at this time, had a notable Italian population.
[229] In *Cytherea* (1922), by Joseph Hergesheimer (1880–1954), Savina Grove, the human embodiment of the eponymous goddess, has an affair with a married man that ends tragically for her, while he returns, repentant, to his family; Mrs. Hurstpierpoint is an eccentric character with a penchant for flagellation in Ronald Firbank's (see note 95) *Valmouth*.
[230] Heroine of Ouida's (see note 13) 1867 novel of that name, a spirited adventuress and political revolutionary.
[231] Independent New York bookstore (established 1853).

the grand manner…. Campaspe was enjoying her revery and her face changed expression for the worse as she saw Frederika emerging from the house. Her approach portended callers.

Mr. Moody is in the salon.

Oh! Paul. Campaspe was relieved. Bring tea, Frederika, and send him out.

Iced tea?

No, hot today…. And wait! Take these books in.

She pushed the rejected pile towards Frederika, who gathered them into her arms and retreated. Leaning back in her chair, almost recumbent, gazing at the azure sky through the rent canopy of leaves, Campaspe blew smoke rings lazily upwards. Glancing down, as Paul came through the door, she was aware at once that something had happened. His face wore a harassed expression and there were deep circles underneath his eyes. These, however, might be after-effects due to the Duke's opera.

'paspe, have you seen Harold? Paul was breathless.

Harold? No. What's happened to Harold?

She was interested to discover that she felt a vague alarm.

Gone. Disappeared.

What do you mean?

I called him up this afternoon. Drains told me. The hall-boy reports that he came in last night, but went out again immediately. I questioned Drains further. He knew the reason for Harold's departure. When he got home he found Zimbule occupying his bed.

Campaspe smiled. The girl is not without guile, but I hadn't thought she would do that … Yet, she said she would.

She did. Drains gave her the key. His father …

That horrible father! Campaspe exclaimed in a tone of disgust. What is he trying to do to the boy?

I am beginning to wonder myself. Even Drains feels a little contrite. You see, he likes Harold.

You can't help liking him…. Have you been to Ronald's?

Yes. One of the Ceylonese sent me up to the bathroom. Ronald was immured there, lustily singing Old black Joe….[232] I interviewed him through the door. He knew nothing about Harold.

What has Drains done?

Nothing. He has strict orders not to appeal to Mr. Prewett for help in emergencies. Besides, it is obvious that the boy has merely run away to escape Zimbule…. I thought he might be here.

He'd sooner go to you, she mused, still blowing rings of grey smoke.

---

[232] Parlour song by Stephen Foster (see note 61) in the minstrel tradition, about a former slave nostalgic for his days on the plantation.

No, in some way he connects me with this plot. Of course, I don't know the first thing about it, but *he* doesn't know that…. He trusts *you*.

I'm fond of him, Campaspe remarked simply.

Frederika came back into the garden with the tea-tray which she deposited on the table, and Campaspe filled two cups, offering one to Paul, with a napoléon.[233]

You don't suppose … he burst out suddenly, and then hesitated, appalled by the thought.

No, I don't, Paulet, she replied. He will turn up. I am not really disturbed when I consider his reason for leaving. Zimbule terrified him; that's all. He's probably gone to a hotel. He has plenty of money?

Heaps.

They talked a little longer. Paul, much too nervous to remain seated, walked up and down the narrow enclosure, finally taking his departure with the suddenness of his arrival.

The sun was sinking; the shadows on the flagstones had turned to deep indigo. Campaspe drank in the warm-cool air with delight. The scene was about to be played, the scene for which she had waited. The rebellion had broken out. Instinctively, she had felt the truth when she wrote Laura. Frederika came back into the garden.

Mr. Prewett came some time ago, madame. He has been waiting in the salon until Mr. Moody went away.

Harold! Send him out, Frederika, and bring another cup.

If harassed described Paul's appearance, Harold looked absolutely haggard. His hair was awry; his cheeks were ashen; his eyes bloodshot. He still wore his evening clothes and it was apparent that he had not been to bed.

I hope you'll excuse my appearance, he began. I shouldn't have come, but I had to…. He was almost fierce … I had to.

I'm glad, Harold, she said.

I asked Frederika if you were alone; I've been waiting…. You are the only person I can talk to, Mrs. Lorillard. I haven't any friends.

Campaspe, *please*.

Campaspe, he repeated after her. I'm through, he began again with renewed, withal somewhat shrill, determination. My father can go to hell. I don't give a damn about his money. I'll live the way I want to from now on. I'll … Do you know what's happened?

I can guess.

Some one has …?

Zimbule told Bunny that she was spending the night with me, but she wouldn't let me drive her home.

---

[233]   Also called a *mille-feuille*, a French pastry with custard filling and icing glaze.

What *are* they trying to do to me, Campaspe: Drains and my father? They have some plan.... I am to do whatever I please, but constantly they are *suggesting*....

But, Harold, as you have your father's word that you can do what you like, why don't you take advantage of it?

What I like is impossible. Campaspe, I must tell you! I must tell some one! Then, incoherently, he poured out the story of his meeting with Alice, and what had happened subsequently, but he refrained from mentioning her name.

Campaspe listened, enraptured, masking her too eager interest behind the smoke of her cigarette. It seemed too impossibly romantic to be real. It had happened, however. Of that the boy's manner left no loophole for doubt. When he had concluded his narrative, she paused for a moment before she said:

Obviously, the thing to do is to find some one who knows the girl, and who will introduce you properly.

But who? he asked desperately. Who? Whom do I know that would know people like that, conventional, respectable people? He flushed. I beg your pardon. I ...

Enjoying his discomfiture, she was at the same time amused by his point of view.

I understand, she said, but perhaps *you* don't. It is barely possible, she began and then broke off. Presently, looking at him intently and sympathetically, she suggested, Suppose you tell me the girl's name.

There was another pause, during which Campaspe had time to perceive how altogether miserable the boy was. He appeared to be almost ready to cry. Was he trying to make up his mind whether he could trust her? Would she, she knew he was asking himself, prove to be another illusion? At last he spoke, almost in a whisper and in a tone which bestowed an accolade upon the name.

Alice Blake.

Campaspe, sitting bolt upright, pouring tea, dropped the pot crashing into the delicate Sèvres²³⁴ cup beneath. The scalding water flooded the table, unnoticed by her. Falling back against the cushions, she began to laugh, a loud, pealing mirthless laugh, a more than terrifying laugh. Harold bent over her.

What is it, Campaspe? What is the matter?

She stopped laughing as suddenly as she had begun.

I think, Harold, she said very quietly, that I am acquainted with the lady. The name, however, may not be uncommon. Do you know where she lives?

56 East Thirty-seventh Street.

She is my sister, Campaspe announced.

Not altogether without sympathy, she watched the blood mount to the boy's face, but her sympathy was mingled with another emotion. She could

---

²³⁴   Notable manufacturer of fine porcelain since the eighteenth century.

understand how horrible the idea seemed to him. This news apparently struck him as the direst blow that had yet fallen. Some moments elapsed before he was able to speak, and she made no effort to hurry him. Rather, by her manner, by her poise, by her ease, she indicated an opportunity for the pause.

Your *sister*! With varying emphasis, he repeated her words again almost in a whisper: *Your* sister!

How can that be? you are asking yourself. How can her father be mine? It is very simple. My father has no control whatever over me. When I came of age I inherited money left in trust for me by my grandmother, but even before that I was free, because I married when I was sixteen. I see very little of Alice now, but I can see her when I wish to. As a matter of fact, my sons are visiting their grandfather at Southampton, and Alice is with him too. I can send for her....

Send for her! Would he never be able again to think out a sentence of his own?

Yes, if you want her sent for. Certainly. Her voice was dead in quality.

Would you?... His manner was eager, yet almost tearful.

How tragic, she thought again, is youth. How much youth suffers unnecessarily.

Whenever you like. She spoke calmly, evenly.

He rose to this: Now!

Now? She appeared to ponder. Today? I could telephone, she mused, but, on the whole, I think it's better to write. You must give me three days. In three days I'll bring you and Alice together in this garden.

Three days! He was crestfallen again.

After all, dear boy, you've already waited weeks. What are three days more?

You know best, my dear, dear friend.

She regarded him curiously, weighing him.

Are you ... She began, and then shifting her phrase, went on, Do you want to marry her?

If she will ... at once!

Oh! she will.

You think ...

I am certain of it.

How can I thank you?

Don't thank me, Harold.

Another problem had arisen in his mind.

Where shall I wait the three days?

Go home, of course. It's absurd for you to wander about in those clothes. Now that you know what you are going to do you can handle Drains. Besides, after last night, I have an idea Drains won't bother you any more.

Campaspe had awakened to some show of enthusiasm again. She was making plans. Get some money together, she went on. You will need it. Alice is accustomed to spending all she wants to spend. You must go somewhere and we — you and I — must decide where. Alice has no initiative. I have it — Campaspe's eyes glowed with a ruddy fire — ; I own a tiny cottage at Provincetown on Cape Cod.[235] I've never been there myself. I bought it as an investment for an adventure. This, I fancy, is the adventure. Take it. After you are through with it, I'll sell it.

To us?

If *you* want it, I'll give it to you. I can't use it twice. The bloom will be off.

I love her! Harold cried. If you knew how much I love her, Campaspe!

I'm sure you do, my boy, and in three days you shall see her. Come back to this garden and you will find her here.

He rose, kissed her hand quite spontaneously, although it was the first time in his life he had ever done such a thing, and took his departure. Seized with a new nervousness, Campaspe got up and walked about. Her whole body was glowing and vibrating with joy, and her smile rippled into laughter. The situation was too perfect. Only one more scene was required to end the act and bring down the curtain. That scene, she was now aware, was about to be played, and, consequently, she was in no way astonished when Frederika presently informed her that Zimbule was waiting in the salon. Nor was she unprepared for the black garb, the wholly woebegone appearance of the snake-child, as she slowly emerged from the house and descended the flagstones to meet Campaspe, who was standing near the fountain.

Campaspe clasped her hand. I know, dear Zimbule, she said. Harold has just been here.

The girl threw her arms about Campaspe's neck, her yellow head drooping, and gave way to a passionate fit of sobbing.

I'm too late! she cried.

Rather, too early, corrected Campaspe. He will want you later when you don't want him.

He told you …

He told me nothing. Paul was here before him, and Paul had seen Drains.

Where's Harold now?

He went home.

Zimbule made a movement towards the door. I'll follow him!

Campaspe gently caught the girl's arm.

No, dear Zimbule, you won't do that. It would do no good. The boy is in love.

Zimbule stared hard at Campaspe.

With you?

No, with my sister.

Zimbule, looking straight into Campaspe's eyes, could not doubt that she told the truth.

---

[235] In the early decades of the twentieth century, Provincetown became established as a residence for writers and artists, serving also as a tourist destination.

Did you know this last night? she demanded.

I learned it for the first time five minutes ago.

Are you going to help them?

Yes.

Against me?

It's no good, Zimbule. You know what happened last night. Harold means it.

The girl sank into a chair and began to sob again, making a good deal of superfluous noise, Campaspe thought, and yet she was sorry for the child, and considered Harold a fool for not perceiving how infinitely superior was this lithe, little animal to her silly sister. He had made a stupid choice, but it was not her habit to interfere with other people's choices. Under the circumstances, however, she decided at once that she must keep the girl by her. Such tempestuous natures were capable of suicide. Campaspe was so entirely contented with life in general and her own participation in it in particular that it also occurred to her that she might go so far as to do something for Cupid. She infrequently dined at a public restaurant, more seldom still did she attend the theatre. It pleased Cupid to do these things, which to her were merely dull. Her imagination supplied her with so much better material than such casual experiences could give her. More and more she was finding it futile to leave her garden. In time, she began to believe, all the external life she needed would come to her. But tonight she might make an exception. Rapidly, she planned a dinner at the Claremont,[236] and an evening at some musical show. She rang for Frederika.

Is Mr. Lorillard in the house?

He came in half an hour ago, madame. He is in his room dressing.

Ask him to come out here, Frederika. She turned to the snake-child again. Zimbule, do stop crying. You don't want to go back to Bunny?

The child vigorously shook her head.

Then stay to dinner with us, and spend the night here.

She put her hand tenderly on the girl's head, and she knew that Zimbule would stay.

Presently Cupid appeared, a little alarmed, obviously wondering what was up. He looked rather pompous in his fat, small way. Campaspe noted that he was losing his hair.

Hello, 'paspe, do you want to see me?

Yes, Cupid, I do. This is Miss O'Grady. Zimbule bowed her head but did not offer her hand. She's dining with us, and going to the theatre.

To the theatre! Cupid was very much astonished.

---

[236] Formerly a private home built in the Colonial period, the Claremont, located near Grant's Tomb on Riverside Drive in West Harlem was, from the 1890s, a restaurant and roadhouse frequented by the rich and famous.

Certainly. Why not?

But you usually … I have an engagement, but I'll break it. Whenever you want me, you know I'm here.

Why was every one so pathetic today? She remembered that Paul had once asked her why she had married, and she had answered that everybody should marry at least once, and he had insisted. But why Cupid? and she had replied, He's the very man I should have married. How true! she thought now with a smile.

The dinner, on the verandah of the Claremont, was rather solemn. Zimbule ate little and did not talk at all. Cupid made a determined effort to entertain his wife. He had, she could see, caught a false strand of hope, and had woven dreams for himself out of it; she did not disillusion him. She was kind and gracious and even amusing. She did not try to draw Zimbule into the conversation. The girl, she was sure, would be happier quiet. Occasionally, even while she chattered, she gazed across to the lights on the black river and thought her own thoughts.

It was late when they had finished dinner, too late, she decided, to use their seats for the Follies,[237] and she suggested that they drop into a Negro revue at the Forty-eighth Street Theatre for a half-hour or so.[238] An amazing mulatto woman, Edith Wilson, who sang a song entitled, He may be your man but he comes to see me sometimes,[239] held her attention for a few moments. Presently, she became aware that Cupid was finally awake to Zimbule's beauty. He was the last to observe just what was most obvious to others, she reflected. They drove home.

Escorted by Frederika, Zimbule slipped off at once to her room. Cupid, rather awkwardly, attempted to seize Campaspe's hand.

No, Cupid, don't misunderstand….

The poor little man was ridiculous in his dejection.

I like you, you know, she added…. Good-night.

At the first landing, she peeped over the banisters for a glimpse of the pitiful figure standing alone below, and then she continued on her way upstairs. Before her desk she wrote a short note to her father, and sent Frederika with it to the nearest post-box on Irving Place. Then she went to Zimbule's room and tapped gently on the door.

Come in!

The child was lying nude on the bed, lovely in her despair as she had been the night before in her joy.

---

237 See note 157.

238 *The Plantation Revue*, an all-black revue, was featuring at this theatre in the summer of 1922.

239 Edith Wilson (1896–1981), star of *The Plantation Revue*, rose to fame as a jazz and blues singer in 1921, appealing to black and white audiences; 'He may be your man' is a 1922 blues song by African-American composer and songwriter Lemeul Fowler (c. 1900–1963).

Are you feeling better, dear Zimbule?

Worse.

Do you want anything?

You know damn well what I want.

The girl began to cry again and Campaspe, sitting on the edge of the bed, bending over her, found it difficult to quiet her. She began to stroke the girl's head. Silently, her hand glided back and forth. Quite suddenly, a strange thing happened. Zimbule, Campaspe observed, had fallen into a deep sleep. She stole back on tiptoe to her own chamber. Frederika was waiting for her and, with her maid's assistance, she prepared for bed.

I shall not read tonight, Frederika. Put out the lights … and good-night.

Good-night, madame.

That night Campaspe dreamed a curious dream. She found herself walking in her bare feet on a bed of oyster-shells, but the sharp edges made no impression on her tender soles. Presently, and inexplicably, she seemed to be lying in a nest of silken cushions, which stung her soft flesh like a thicket of nettles. Now a butterfly flew past her, and appeared to be beckoning her to follow. Rising, she ran after the butterfly through a great open doorway into a wide Moorish court, in the centre of which a blindfold, curly-headed Eros, carved in marble, appeared about to discharge an arrow aimed at no target. Her senses swerved in a curious state of transition: she touched Burgundy; she smelled purple; she heard vervain; she tasted space; she saw the chord of B flat minor.[240]

A thick cloud settled down over the court, but through its veils she caught glimpses of shadows, approaching and receding. When she followed them, they glided back, and when they followed her, she ran away from them. The shadows were nude and wore masks. One of them, a woman, lifted her mask and Campaspe recognized Zimbule, Zimbule with a great green letter flaming on her breast. Campaspe raised her hand, her palm towards the vision, and it disappeared.

---

[240] In her dream, Campaspe is experiencing synaesthesia, a condition of sensory intermingling or confusion. Synaesthesia fascinated artists and writers of the late nineteenth and early twentieth centuries and was most famously exploited by decadents and symbolists.

Chapter IX

Greyness was the characteristic tone of Provincetown. The houses were grey; the sky and the sand and the sea often seemed grey. Even the trees, the leaves powdered with dust, assumed a greyish sage-green tinge. One long curving street, fringed with tiny wooden cottages, ran along the shore. These little houses, many of which were surrounded by hedges of untrimmed privet, sprinkled untidily with white blossoms, indifferently faced the road or the ocean. Tods of ivy and clematis, blue and white, draped the painted boards, and in the gardens dahlias, cosmos, zinnias, petunias, verbenas, portulaca, asters, and golden-glow grew in great irregular clumps. The street culminated in two landmarks, a church-spire, that might or might not have been designed by Sir Christopher Wren,[241] and a tall Italian tower of brick, the Pilgrim Monument.[242] In the harbour a warship rode at anchor, and there were fleets of rude fishing-smacks, among which the smug white sails of pleasure sloops looked as uncomfortable and awkward as a Londoner with morning coat and top hat would look in the midst of Shoreditch.[243] The shore was lined with quaint, dilapidated boat-houses, rotting piers, and great nets, their edges bound with bobbins of cork, hung out to dry. As in all fishing-villages, there was a prevailing odour of dead fish. In this grey, gloomy town, the only colour, save that of the flowers, was supplied by the tawny, smiling faces of the Portuguese settlers,[244] who mingled, somewhat aloof, to be sure, somewhat derisively, with the visiting artists from Greenwich Village.[245]

Campaspe's cottage was not on the main street. It was situated about a mile and a half northwest across the cape, facing the open sea, near the lifesaving station. For a time, the rough road leading thither wended its uncertain way through a scattering of scrub-oaks, scrub-pines, and maples, with patches of tiger-lilies, golden rod, purple asters, old maid's pinks, and Queen Anne's lace, on either side, then straggled on across a mile of sand-dunes, rolling down and up, like great stationary waves, some as high as twenty feet, on which the only

---

[241]   Wren (1632–1723), British architect, best known for churches, especially St Paul's Cathedral in London. Wren did not design a church in America, but Provincetown's First Universalist Church (1847) features a 'Christopher Wren' tower inspired by his work.
[242]   Monument commemorating the 1620 landing of the Pilgrims.
[243]   In the early twentieth century Shoreditch was a working-class area in East London.
[244]   Portuguese sailors and fishermen began settling in Provincetown from the 1840s and, by the 1920s, represented a significant proportion of the population.
[245]   See note 114.

vegetation was beach-grass, beach-plums, and bay-berry shrubs. The beach was low and here the sand was packed hard and smooth. Higher up, back a little from the beach near the life-saving station, solitary but for its gaunt, uncordial companion in the midst of the grey dunes, stood the little white cottage with its slanting roof of unpainted shingles, and its great chimney, fashioned of huge boulders by some local builder. From afar, of course, as she had never visited Provincetown, it had amused Campaspe to plan this house somewhat in the spirit (certainly not the style!) of the farms of the Trianon.[246] It had been her intention to arrange an opportunity for a rustic, aquatic villeggiatura,[247] where she might conceivably disguise herself as a sailor's bride and entertain thought of adventures with sea-faring men. Having arranged for this house, actually ordering it built and furnished, indeed, the necessity for further action did not seem to present itself. To all intents and purposes, Campaspe had lived in it, enjoyed the imagined experience, and forgotten the episode.

On the grey, rough plaster walls of the interior hung madonnas, photographs of celebrated paintings, madonnas as placid as though they had never suffered the pangs of childbirth. The furniture was of white maple, polished to a state in which tables might have been used as mirrors, had occasion for such a compromise arisen. The hexagonal dining-table, the ancient chairs and beds and highboys and bureaux, had been bought from nearby farmers, who were glad to dispose of this junk at a low figure so that they might make their homes more modern with show-pieces from the Grand Rapids emporiums[248] and beds of shiny brass from Boston. Bayberry dips stood in the stately Colonial candlesticks.[249] The coverlets on the beds were masterpieces of nineteenth century provincial ingenuity and the rugs on the waxed floors had been woven by tired and patient grandmothers, who had spent their dead living years at work on them. The service was composed of Brittany china, Spanish peasant porcelain, and a gay Hungarian pottery, painted with brilliant flowers. It had been Campaspe's satisfied desire that no two cups or plates should be identical. On the wall a brass ship's-clock ticked out the time, sounding bells in lieu of hours, and lanterns, burning sperm oil, which had formerly served to illuminate

---

[246]   In the late eighteenth century, Marie Antoinette had a small hamlet and working farm built near Versailles palace that served as a private retreat. Here, she would dress up as a peasant and engage in simple pleasures, a form of entertainment popular with aristocrats of the day.
[247]   A holiday spent in the country.
[248]   In this period, Grand Rapids, Michigan, was the hub of American furniture manufacturing.
[249]   Fragrant candles made from wax derived from the berries of a bayberry bush. Van Vechten may have been inspired by a March 1921 article in *House and Garden*, 'The Quality of Candlelight'. This article advised housewives to 'exercise care' in matching candles to candlesticks and candelabras, noting that the bayberry dip was particularly suited to the Colonial candlestick (36).

the cabins of old whaling vessels, hung from the ceilings. The doors, with their oval tops, together with the rest of the woodwork, like the shingles on the roof, were oiled but unpolished.

To Harold, satiated with what he regarded as an exotic and artificial atmosphere, this pseudo-communion with a more natural environment, which, in a sense, reminded him of his boyhood, his Aunt Sadi and Persia Blaine, seemed heavenly. He took long walks on the spar-strewn dunes and, clad in tarpaulins, went fishing for flounders in a decaying boat, rowed to a suitable depth by a weather-beaten tar, who told him venerable yarns of the old leviathan hunts, and more recent scandals of the New England village. Occasionally, with Alice, he went for a sail, the veteran mariner guiding the helm and calling out to Harold incomprehensible nautical directions (subsequently translated) for handling the canvas of the sloop, a sorry affair smelling of dead fish. The sickly aroma of dead fish, indeed, haunted the nostrils and never entirely passed away, just as the dampness penetrated even the heavy cedar clothes-presses, and covered the books, ranged on shelves behind glass doors, with a film of mildew.

Alice, who had come to this retreat straight from Southampton, found this setting for a honeymoon a little primitive, a little abnormally primitive. Her pale blond beauty was curious in this regard, that in the city she seemed decidedly a rural type, while in the country one could only think of her as belonging to the city. She found the old sailor vulgar, and once or twice nearly lost her temper with Emma, a taciturn and sardonic Portuguese woman, of middle-age, who had acted as care-taker of the place and now lingered on in an ancillary capacity. Campaspe's taste in plates also annoyed Alice. Why were they all different? she asked herself. In this prospect only Harold pleased her. The two had had been here nearly a month now, idling together, and it may be reported that they had discovered some measure of happiness. Alice was bored rather than unhappy. She had no leanings towards domesticity, towards keeping house; she gave Emma few orders. It was characteristic of her to complain instead because her unuttered desires were not carried out. She was not interested in reading, resembling Harold in this respect. She sewed a little, finding occupation in the construction of a beaded bag, but time, on the whole, passed slowly for her. She liked best to sit on the dunes with Harold, holding his hand, making plans for the future. She talked quite easily of children, so easily, indeed, that occasionally Harold caught himself wondering if he really wanted children. Somewhat self-consciously, Alice was prone to regard this excursion, this singular honeymoon, in the light of a temporary lark, a lark from which she was not deriving any excruciating amount of pleasure. In the foreground of her mind rose a picture of a somewhat more solid life in New York, with a great house and servants, friends to dinner, dinners which would be returned in due course by these friends, a box at the opera, theatres and shops to visit, calls to pay, the conventional life of a respectable matron, and, in time, her daughters....

She gave voice to some of her ideals, and Harold loved to hear her talk about them. He, too, would be glad of a home, he felt, a place that was his own, in which he might sit with his pipe, slippers on feet, slackly, but respectably, comfortable. He even looked forward to the social life, of which she had given him glimpses, into which they would presumably fit. Very different, he imagined it would be, from that of Campaspe. He wondered often how the two could be sisters. He remembered how they had appeared as strangely separate entities that afternoon in the little garden on East Nineteenth Street: Alice softly acquiescent, Campaspe radiantly benedictory, hovering like a bishop over some secret glory. How simple it all had been. He had expected strife, opposition, obstruction. There had been nothing of the sort. Oliver, apprised of his plan, had come forward with a sufficient sum to pay for a trip to Buenos Ayres, more than enough to cover an indefinite sojourn in this cottage by the sea. His father had telegraphed his congratulations, and had mailed a further cheque of quite an amazing denomination. Campaspe had presented them with this house. Paul had appeared to be rather melancholy, and he had shaken Harold's hand with an intensity which led the boy to believe that he must have misjudged his mentor. The Duke had sent the couple a set of Tennyson,[250] bound in half-morocco. Harold was not acquainted with the works of Tennyson, but he had sensed a derisory intention in this gift. Mr. Blake, in a letter, had hinted of future delights in store for the happy pair when they returned to New York. Persia Blaine had sent a great pink and white cake. Only his aunt, incomprehensibly, had not been complaisant. She had written a letter which Harold had found it difficult to understand, and which now he was finding it difficult to forgive. Nearly a month had gone by and he had not yet answered it. Scarcely a day passed, however, in which he did not read it.

> My dear Harold [the letter began in a manner which he recognized as not unduly formal for his decidedly formal aunt],
> I do not feel much inclined to write to you, but I suppose it is my duty, and duty is something that I never shirk. This letter, however, will be no bearer of congratulations. To be blunt, I feel that you are making a mistake. You should never have gone to your father. Had it been in my power, I should have prevented it. He is wrecking your life with his ego and his selfishness. He broke your mother's will, and he will break yours. If I had stayed with him in business, he would have broken mine. I have wept hot tears since I received your telegram, as I understand only too well what all this means. Poor ignorant boy, you have walked straight into the trap set for you. When you are through with this marriage, come back to me. Your

---

[250]   Alfred Tennyson (1809–1892), British Poet Laureate through much of the Victorian era, whose reputation suffered in the 1920s as a consequence of a modernist backlash.

father will be enraged that he has lost you, but I will be glad that I have found you.

Miss Perkins is here and sends her love to you. Persia has not been very well. You will remember that she always suffers from hay fever at this time of year. I cut my thumb a few days ago, paring peaches to preserve, and it still bothers me considerably.

I remain, with love,
your AUNT SADI.

Harold could explain this letter satisfactorily to himself on no other ground save the ground of jealousy. She is enraged because I am married, he thought, and she is blaming my father for something with which he had nothing whatever to do, to which certainly, in the beginning, he was opposed, for did he not send me to Paul and to a life which is the farthest removed from the life that I wish to live? Now that I have married Alice, he has accepted the situation with more grace than could have been expected from him. He said, Do anything you please, and apparently he meant it. How much broader and bigger in spirit he is than Aunt Sadi.

He had not yet showed the letter to Alice, but one day, when he had been talking about his childhood, he felt moved to do so. Drawing it from the pocket where he always carried it, he handed it to his wife, with a few words of explanation.

Do not let it hurt you, he said. She is an old woman, and what she says cannot matter after all. I have meant a good deal to her, probably, in her loneliness, and she thinks she is losing me. But she is wrong about my father. He has been very good to me.

He was not surprised to observe that she flushed as she read the letter. Handing it back to him, she stared at him in a peculiarly searching manner. There was an expression around her eyes that he had never noticed there before.

The letter does not hurt me, she said at last, only …

Only what?

Regarding him more intently still, she paused for a moment. Then, turning her head so that their eyes no longer met, she replied: Your father may have had some purpose in view, Harold, but he meant it for your good, I feel sure.

And now that I have done what he didn't want me to do he has forgiven me?

Ye-es, she replied, rather hesitantly, although he was not conscious of her lack of enthusiasm. Quite suddenly, she bent towards him and kissed his eyes. Let us go back to the house, Harold, she said.

They had been sitting on the dunes in the dying sunlight, for the day had been bright with a brightness, however, which merely served to accentuate the cold greyness of the place. A dragon-fly, shining purple and green, steered his course round and round Alice's head, like a miniature airplane. A flock of gulls swooped down over the sea, crying mournfully, and some of them disappeared under the grey waves, capped with white. A cool breeze was blowing in over the water and, as Alice rose, she drew the blue knitted scarf she was wearing more closely about her shoulders.

In the cottage, when they arrived, Emma, silent and stern, was laying the table with the gay variety of design which Alice instinctively hated. She especially detested the opaque white glass chickens of the Civil War period, consecrated to hold eggs, but the Spanish, Hungarian, and Brittany china offended her taste almost equally. She liked white plates with gold borders for the roasts, and engraved glass plates with gold borders for the salad and dessert. The cotton print curtains at the windows annoyed her, and her mind reverted to the consideration of some striped stiff taffetas she had examined at Johnson and Faulkner's.[251] Their magnificence, distributed at the windows and in the wall-panels, would almost serve to furnish the drawing-room. There would also be a great divan, upholstered in royal blue velvet, and a royal blue velours carpet on the floor. This maple! Mahogany was Alice's favourite wood. Some of these opinions she had uttered aloud at one time or another, safely enough, she thought, because this cottage represented her sister's taste. If Harold had been responsible …!

Harold was both pleased and alarmed by these discourses on the subject of interior decoration. Alice seemed so practical and matter of fact. He had not sensed these qualities in her before marriage. He was coming to believe, indeed — he was thinking in terms of fact and not of deprecation — , that he had known nothing whatever about his wife before marriage. He had hardly even conversed with her. But, fundamentally, he felt, she was his kind, and this interest in house furnishing, this passion for children, however incautiously and belatedly divulged, were part of what he wanted. They were fractions of a great normal entity to which he aspired. Yet, sometimes, with the cold breeze from the sea, a parallel psychic frigid wind had blown across his soul, an unknown terror had assailed him. His reason could not tell him what it meant but, instinctively, he understood, dimly enough at first, perhaps, that it portended disillusion. He was also amazed, sometimes, to find himself thinking — so little was he analytical — that a great part of Alice's charm for him, in this newly and none too securely established intimacy, consisted in the essential fact that she was Campaspe's sister, for, from that brief excursion into an alien world, he had borne away a perplexing but permanent affection for Mrs. Lorillard. She had seemed to him the only real person he had met in that world, and he never ceased to wonder why it interested her, what she got from it, for it was apparent, even to him, that it *did* interest her. Gradually, however, from Alice he had

---

[251]   Long-established importers and retailers of high-end decorative fabrics.

learned how closely Campaspe was bound to other more conventional circles in New York society, how in the fall she attended the Horse Show,[252] and during the winter was seen in the boxes of people whose names frequently appeared in the newspapers, how she gave dinners and dances for these people, and went to theirs. Very often there was mention of Laura, who, he gathered, with an adumbration of perception, would not have been altogether comfortable in the presence of the Duke of Middlebottom.

Laura and her children were the subject of a good deal of Alice's idle chatter. They were the most divine children, Alice asserted; she only hoped hers would be as good. She drew a showy picture of the nursery: Laura's Rollo-like[253] offspring eating at a little table with their Belgian governess, while Laura in a Bendel[254] gown received in the drawing-room below. Laura in most respects was obviously Alice's model.

At night, it was usually cold enough for a fire and, with the ruddy logs glowing in the great boulder fireplace, the pair sat on a wooden settle banked with cotton print covered cushions, facing the fire, holding hands. It was Alice who did most of the talking. She had so much to say. Harold was comparatively inarticulate; very few thoughts in his mind urgently demanded expression, and he had to search to find words in which to express even these. Half-comprehending, half-dreading life, he seldom asserted himself. He basked in the pleasant warmth of Alice's conversation, as she basked in the heat of the burning logs, enjoying Alice, talk, and fire, objectively. He, indeed, would have been glad to remain indefinitely at Provincetown, or near it, although they knew nobody and it seemed they never would, for Alice objected that she could not meet people from Greenwich Village, and, of course, she added, one can't know the natives. The Portuguese themselves, had she but been aware of it, would have taken the first step, had it been necessary, towards preventing any narrowing of this always ample breach. However that may be, although Harold and Alice crossed the dunes nearly every day to go to the post office or the market, they made no acquaintances of any kind.

Their intimacy was so complete and exclusive, indeed, that to the Provincetowners — both natives and visitors — they appeared to be a couple of youngsters revelling in their first illicit love. The married state, certainly, was never ascribed to them. Gossip was endemic among the Portuguese, and, as the rumour grew, biographies were invented to fit the happy pair. Letters passed back and forth as the gossip bubbled, gossip to which Emma added her unwholesome quota. Heartily disliking Alice, Emma permitted herself uncontrolled flights of the imagination once she met her friends in the village.

---

[252]   Key annual event of the social season for the elite held at Madison Square Garden.
[253]   Rollo was the hero of a series of nineteenth-century American children's books by Jacob Abbott (1803–1879), meant to inculcate New England Christian virtues and values.
[254]   See note 115.

Emma brought in the soup. They sat down to eat at two adjoining sides of the hexagonal table. Later, there was fish. Almost invariably, indeed, there was fish.

Alice's glance was directed towards the prongs of her fork.

Harold, she asked, shall we live here much longer?

The boy showed his astonishment. Are you unhappy, dear? he questioned her in return.

Not unhappy, no, but restless. You know it isn't my kind of place.

But New York in the summer....

We can't go back just yet, of course ... but in a little while. I suppose, too, that you will want to be getting to work. She observed his expression of amazement, but she hurried on: You are going to work, aren't you?

Of course.

He felt confused and embarrassed. Here was an aspect of the situation which had never occurred to him. Now that he was a family man he would be expected to make a living for his bride.

You can't, she went on rather sententiously, always live on your father, Harold dear. My daughters ... Well, dearest, they couldn't respect you.

What would he do? Harold helplessly interrogated himself. No more was said about the matter that night, but he tossed about restlessly in bed, his heart beating violently, revolving the idea over and over. It seemed that he could never accustom himself to the problems of life. As fast as the old ones were solved, fresh ones rose on every hand. Nothing seemed simple. How, for example, could he expect to get on sufficiently well to enable him to support his wife without his father's assistance? He could think of no possible opening in the business line except to go in with his father, and his father had expressly said that he did not wish him to do that. What could he do?

Alice, on her part, did not refer to the matter again for several days. She exposed the pleasantest side of her nature, wore her prettiest dresses. She even refrained from complaining about the plates. They took long idyllic walks together on the dunes. They bathed in the sea. The actual clouds drifted out of the sky and the tone of the atmosphere grew more mellow, less grey. Their evenings they passed on the settle. The morose Emma, having washed the dishes and arranged the neat punnets of berries in the ice-chest, left them alone, after fortifying herself for three hours of creative gossip with a nip of perry, a beverage she was skilful in brewing. In spite of the apparent calm, Alice's words ate deeper and deeper into Harold's consciousness. He felt that she was right and, finally, one night, he summoned up enough courage to broach the subject again.

Alice dear, I've been worrying about what you said....

She frowned, questioningly. What I said? she repeated, with an interrogative inflection.

About my going to work.

Dearest boy, I didn't mean to worry you…. Only — she was nervously switching her suede shoes with a willow-bough she had cut during her afternoon walk — , only, it has seemed to me at times that perhaps you are taking things too easily, too much as a matter of course; that was all. We can't stay here for ever, you know.

I understand. His tone was low and serious. I have been thinking about it and I know that you are right.

She brightened, and threw the switch into the fire.

I'm glad you agree with me, Harold. Now, what are you going to do?

That's just it, he groaned. I haven't the least idea!

Don't you think it's best for you to go in with your father? He would help you so much, and you would get on so fast, and we should all be so proud of you!

But my father doesn't want me to go into his business. I've explained all that to you.

Alice gazed at him intently for a little while, as if weighing him and the consequences of what she was about to divulge. As she began to speak, her glance dropped to the fire.

I think it's only fair that you should know something, Harold, she said at last.

He searched her face with some alarm.

Nothing serious. She grasped his arm and rubbed her cheek affectionately against his cheek. He has done it for your good, dear. Your father has been deceiving you.

My father! He sprang away from her in amazement and stood, helplessly, a little apart, trying to find some kind of meaning in her words.

It was a sort of plot or plan, she went on in a somewhat pedantic manner, as though she had been rehearsing this speech for a long time. You see your father had the feeling that, as you had been brought up by women, you were innocent and ignorant of life. He was afraid if he took you right into his business that you might break away, be misled — Oh! I don't know what exactly. Anyway, you said you didn't want to go in with him, and he hoped you would eventually decide for yourself that you did want to. So — she tried to approach him again but his manner warned her that this would be dangerous, or at least difficult — , he thought that if he threw you into the *wrong* kind of life in the beginning you would *hate* it, and come round to him of your own accord. That is why he made life unpleasant for you, as disagreeable for you as possible, hoping that a year of it would tire you. You were tired in a month. He was so pleased. He wants you with him, Harold — she was pleading now — ; he is expecting you. Only, you must *ask* him. He won't ask *you*. Don't you understand?

Harold was standing with his back to the fire, his face, in the shadow, almost green in its pallor. His head seemed to be reeling around and around. Suddenly he realized that he was excessively angry.

I'd see him in hell first! he cried.

Harold!

I mean it. Who's to blame for the way I was brought up? He didn't do much to prevent it, did he? the boy asked scornfully.

Harold!

And so, he went on, the whole thing was a trick!

Now, completely the prey of alarm, a suspicion of tears crept into Alice's voice. It was for your good, Harold, to make a man of you. She was whining, whimpering.

And who kept me from being a man? Who? I should like to know.

His voice had grown so incisive and cold that it scarcely seemed to be he that was talking.

Alice was really crying now. I shouldn't have told you, she sobbed. Only, it seemed to be the right time ... and ... and I thought you loved me, Harold ... I couldn't help telling you, Harold, because I love you.

He ignored this. How did you find all this out? was his next question.

She was trembling. Your father, she began.

Our meeting ... the stalled car ... arranged? He was sneering.

No, Harold, no! That was an accident. Only ...

Only what?

Only, you see, after we met ... Well, your father, of course, knows my father.... It seemed best to keep us apart.

You knew all this?

Why yes, Harold. It seemed all right. I loved you, Harold, and they told me ...

Did Campaspe know?

She stopped crying at once and her tone became petulant.

Campaspe? Why do you bring in Campaspe? Campaspe! Campaspe! Campaspe! Why are you questioning me? Why do you look at me like that?

Did Campaspe know? His tone was colder, more acid.

No.

Harold, who until now had stood as stiffly as a birch-tree, began to move about the room. Presently, he laughed.

So, he said, she's clean. They're all clean: Paul, and Bunny, and Ronald, compared with my own wife, my own father.

Harold!

You've tricked me: Your father, my father, you. At last I understand what Aunt Sadi meant in her letter. It doesn't matter. Only this — he grasped her shoulders firmly and held her at arm's length — only this, you can tell my father that I'm going straight back where he sent me!

Harold!

Straight back. They're clean. They didn't know what it was all about, but they were natural and real while all you rotters have been playing parts.

Harold, you can't mean what you're saying!

I haven't even begun to say what I mean! He threw her roughly back against the settle, relinquishing his hold on her shoulders. I'm through.

He crossed the room in great strides and rushed out through the door. Her screams rang in his ears as he staggered off across the dunes, black in the night, stumbling, falling even, in the deep sand. There was a distant rumble of thunder, faint flashes of lightning. A storm was arising over the sea.

Chapter X

On an afternoon in September, Campaspe woke up feeling a little ill, and decided not to go out. She did not, however, send for a physician. Campaspe cherished a peculiar superstition in regard to ill-health. She considered it as a visitation in the nature of a warning, a warning to take a rest. Any interference with the course of the complaint she held to be artificial and even vicious. The miraculously prolonged youthful appearance of her mother, who had never permitted a doctor to visit her since the days when she bore her children, confirmed Campaspe in this esoteric belief.

If I had a broken leg, she assured herself, I would call in a surgeon to set it, but a headache or a haemorrhage is natural. Decayed cells are breaking down and need to be replaced, or I am being punished by nature for some misdemeanour. When it is over, and the cells have renewed themselves, I shall be stronger than ever.

She glanced over her mail. A letter from Laura, which she did not open.... A postcard from the Duke, with a lithograph in colours of a cottage smothered in rambler roses, and a Nantucket postmark.[255] Inside quotation marks the Duke had written the following on the reverse side of the card: "Tu te prives de viandes, de vin, d'étuves, d'esclaves et d'honneurs; mais comme tu laisses ton imagination t'offrir des banquets, des parfums, des femmes nues et des foules applaudissantes! Ta chasteté n'est qu'une corruption plus subtile, et ce mépris du monde l'impuissance de ta haine contre lui!"[256] Ronald was amusing.... And so he had gone away again. She sighed, as she tore open an orange envelope with a Danish stamp. The contents were printed, but in such delightfully large type, in reds and greens and blacks and blues, that she was moved to examine the sheet more particularly. It was a prospectus, the preliminary announcement, of the Danish Colonial Lottery.[257] A whole ticket, five drawings, was available at

---

[255]   Island south of Cape Cod which, since the death of the whaling industry in the late nineteenth century, relied on tourism, serving as a retreat for New England city dwellers. Like Provincetown, it was a popular destination for artists and bohemians.

[256]   Quotation from the 1874 novel *La Tentation de Saint Antoine* (*The Temptation of St Anthony*), by Gustave Flaubert (1821–1880), spoken by Hilarion, who represents science and reason, and who tries to tempt St Anthony by sowing the seeds of doubt. It translates as: 'You deprive yourself of meats, of wine, of warm baths, of slaves, of honours? — but let your imagination offer you banquets, perfumes, women, and the applause of multitudes? Your chastity is but a more subtle form of corruption, and your contempt for the world is but the impotence of your hatred of it!'

[257]   The Danish Colonial Lottery was one of a number of alleged fraudulent schemes

$37.50. One might win 100,000 francs on each of the first four drawings and as much as 1,000,000 francs on the fifth drawing. The lucky number suggested by the agents was 38653. Mentally, Campaspe rapidly added these digits to see if the result conformed with certain figures on a chart that an adept in Kabbalism[258] had recently made out for her. She was a trifle disappointed to find that it did not.... Pushing aside the remainder of her correspondence, a mass of invitations and bills, her mind wandered to an article she had read in some magazine, picked up in a dentist's waiting-room, an article concerning the extermination of rats. The plan proposed was to catch the rats alive, kill all the females, and set the males free again. In time, as a consequence, the males would outnumber the females by such a high percentage that their persecution of the latter would eventually end in sterility and death for the whole race. In the same magazine there was a paper on hierba maté, the South American beverage, bitter and unpalatable until a taste for it is acquired, draughted from the leaves of the Ilex Paraguayensis. Genaro Romero, the Paraguayan, had rhapsodized regarding it: When we taste maté our energies are renewed, our nerves are comforted by the effect of the green sap, the juice of hope of the Paraguayan flora; and we experience strange impressions, we are nourished by an infusion of energy, and gilded dreams, possibly of good fortune, caress us.[259] Campaspe wondered, at this juncture, if Esperanto had any irregular verbs.... She made an attempt to define her impression of the work of Gertrude Stein.[260] She uses words, thought Campaspe, for their detonations and their connotations....[261] In the New York Times she discovered an account of a man who had devoted years to the engraving of the Lord's Prayer on the head of a pin.[262] Once this task was accomplished, he went first blind and then insane.... Out of the back of her mind she picked another detail: girls working in cordite factories use the explosive for chewing-gum. It acts as a heart stimulant.[263]

Campaspe began to feel restless and energetic. She was not, she now believed, ill enough to keep to her room; nor did she deny herself to callers, although

---

operating in this period that the US Postal Office had concerns about.

[258]   Judaic system of ancient mystical knowledge that influenced and was popularized by esoteric spiritual movements of the late nineteenth and early twentieth centuries.

[259]   These stories have not been traced to the same magazine, but the references are to actual articles of the period. The first, 'Rat Repression by Sexual Selection', is from *Eugenical News*, June 1922, while the second, 'Hierba Mate' by Andrés Blay Pigrau, is from *Inter-America*, April 1920, and includes the quotation of Genaro Romero.

[260]   Stein (1874–1946), American modernist writer and friend to Van Vechten noted for the complexity and obscurity of her writings.

[261]   Van Vechten himself described Stein's work in this way in a letter of 26 November 1914. See Stein and Van Vechten, *Letters of Gertrude Stein and Carl Van Vechten*, ed. by Edward Burns, 2 vols (New York: Columbia University Press, 2013), 32.

[262]   Though untraceable in the *New York Times*, this story appeared in regional newspapers in August 1922.

[263]   Practice developed during the war when women worked in munitions factories.

she was expecting no one in particular. Her mood was capricious, volatile, vibratory. She welcomed, therefore, the announcement of the arrival of the expressman with two large crates from Paris, and she ordered them deposited in the drawing-room, sending Frederika for the butler and hammer and screw-driver. The crates were not entirely a surprise. Fannie had written that she was shipping some pictures.

They proved to be unusually interesting pictures by Henri Rousseau and Marc Chagall, artists whose work Campaspe admired vastly.[264] The Chagall was a portrait of a girl with bangs across her forehead, long hair down her back, melancholy eyes (eyes which were uncertain, Campaspe noted), a sensual mouth, and an intellectual nose. She wore a tight-fitting yellow bodice with a frill, clasped by a brooch, around the throat, and deep indigo gloves. The background, too, was a rich blue. Campaspe considered the picture: fantasy, fable, colour. She would think about it a good deal more in the future, she was certain. She realized that Laura's first question would be, What does it mean? That was, perhaps, its chief charm, that it did not mean anything; it was as meaningless as Mozart's E flat major symphony[265] or life itself. The Rousseau was a splendid and definite jungle, with curiously exotic trees with long green fronds, plants with startling scarlet blossoms, monkeys, and a royal tiger.[266] She recalled that Rousseau had been a working-man, painting on Sunday, his only free day, how he had never left Paris, creating his jungles after visits to the Jardin d'Acclimatation and the Jardin des Plantes.[267] What a genius! This was not imitation but creation. And yet there were those who asserted that he painted in this sure way through naïveté. Looking at the picture, Campaspe realized that the artist had been entirely aware of what he was doing, that he must have been certain even on his darkest days that eventual recognition would come to him. Work such as this — Campaspe was irresistibly reminded of Lucas Cranach[268] — was assuredly no accident. She pondered over this idea. She was sitting on the floor in the centre of the drawing-room, still regarding the pictures, set up against the wall, when Bunny was announced.

Hello, Bunny, she called out, without rising, when he was shown in.

---

[264] Rousseau (1844–1910), self-taught post-impressionist painter whose naïve style served as an influence on the modernist avant-garde; Chagall (1887–1985), Russian-Jewish artist, an important figure across modernist art movements of the early twentieth century, though little known in America at this time. Both artists featured in the July 1922 issue of *The Dial*, a magazine devoted to modernism across the arts.

[265] Thirty-ninth symphony of classical composer Wolfgang Amadeus Mozart (1756–1791), composed in 1788.

[266] The jungle and jungle creatures are common images in Rousseau's oeuvre.

[267] Jardin d'Acclimatation, a Parisian zoo in the Bois de Boulogne, established in 1860; Jardin des Plantes, a large botanical garden on the Seine in Paris's fifth arrondissement.

[268] Lucas Cranach the Elder (1472–1553) and his son Lucas Cranach the Younger (1515–1586) were German Renaissance painters, specializing in biblical subjects.

Hello, 'paspe. His manner was solemn. What have you got here?

Oh! some pictures Fannie sent me. Aren't they divine? I could eat that tiger of Rousseau's.

They *are* good. There's something about that jungle which suggests to me what I have been trying to do in my rotten music.

Your music is as good as the picture, she retorted.

I can't compose any longer, 'paspe.

He had been standing, but now she rose to her feet and led him to the divan.

Poor Bunny.

I wish I'd never seen her!

Bunny! Don't forget the music she made you write!

I don't give a damn about that! I can't do it any more. I'm no good at all now. It's all gone ... with her. If I only had her back!

Campaspe changed the subject abruptly: What's Paul doing? He hasn't been near me.

Harold's father sent him another cheque; so he's happy. All he needs, for happiness, Bunny added bitterly, is money. Drains received a cheque, too, and he's gone off with the Duke.

Back to Ronald.

Everybody goes back to Ronald, Bunny remarked with some resentment. He bought a bulldog before he left town, he continued inconsequentially.

Whatever will he do with it?

Campaspe's mind reverted to the dog-fight in the garden. There was a moment's silence, during which she gazed intently at the Rousseau. Bunny's expression was most lugubrious.

A perfectly divine tiger! she repeated at last, as if speaking to herself.

'paspe, I don't believe you've been listening!

… heard every word.

Do you know what Zimbule is doing?

She rose slowly, still scrutinizing the painting which held her fancy.

No. What? Her manner was preoccupied.

Moving pictures. Angel. Apartment. Riverside Drive.

My dear Bunny, I believe you are a detective. Do you know who he is?

Yes, I do. His tone was hard and there was a challenge to interrogation in it. Nevertheless, Campaspe did not ask the question Bunny expected to hear.

Where is she living? she queried, lightly.

The Lombardy.[269]

---

[269] Fictitious name that nevertheless reflects the Italianate style of the luxurious developments on Riverside Drive north of Seventy-Second Street that emerged at the beginning of the century.

Campaspe smiled. I think I'll send her a picture.

She won't like it. She wouldn't understand *these*. He swept his arm around in a vague gesture. It was characteristic of Bunny's movements that they were never definite and forceful.

Oh! I wouldn't send her one of these. I like them too well myself. I'll send her the pictures I take down when I hang these.

I'm sure she has plenty of pictures. The boy was actually malicious.

No doubt, but one can always use a few more. Possibly she cares for change as much as I do.

Campaspe did not carry out her threat. Instead, she made a resolution to call on Zimbule in a day or so. She had heard the story of Harold's disappearance, or as much of it as she needed to hear, from Alice. Her father, too, had been voluble. Where was Harold? She must know; of that these two obtuse members of her family were firmly convinced. As a matter of fact she did not, and she was making no effort to find out. When he was ready he would come to her, and, subsequently, she determined, her family should hear nothing whatever about the visit. Her father and Alice had almost put her through three degrees in their effort to drag the information out of her which they were certain that she possessed. It required very little of this kind of thing to satisfy Campaspe. Her manner assumed a crisp frigidity which her family had encountered on occasion in the past. They knew the meaning of it, and, for the moment, they withdrew their brisk importunities.

She had considered the possibility of taking Paul with her when she called on Zimbule. After a little reflection, she decided to go alone. She dressed very carefully for the adventure, wearing a smart, grey tailored costume which had just arrived from Redfern,[270] and a black hat adorned with white wings. From her wrist dangled a cluster of crystal grapes, an inspiration of Marie El Khoury.[271]

As her motor bore her into the unfamiliar neighbourhood, already she began to smile. She was in her best humour as she stood before the telephone operator in the elaborate hallway, which reminded her, somehow, of a scene in a Theodore Dreiser novel.[272] She had, she was convinced, never before seen so much onyx all at once, such highly polished onyx, too. The electroliers of burnished gold, the tall gothic seats, with their rich, red velvet cushions, the purple uniforms and brass buttons of the black attendants, all played their parts in creating an

---

[270]   Fifth Avenue branch of a high-end British tailoring and couture house.

[271]   El-Khoury ran a bespoke jewellery shop on Fifth Avenue, The Little Shop of T. Azeez.

[272]   Dreiser (1871–1945), American author, whose novels often centre on characters with humble origins who are corrupted upon entering the realms of urban political and corporate power. *Jennie Gerhardt* (1911) and *Sister Carrie* (1900) concern the plight of working-class women in this realm, women much like Zimbule.

effect in which she could perceive no single flaw. She recalled a happy Spanish proverb, If you want to go to the devil, at least go in a carriage!

Once she had been admitted to Zimbule's apartment, she resumed her inquisitive appraisement, with some stupefaction at first, until she remembered that there was a trade called interior decorating. The room was Viennese (or München) in style[273] — an amazingly acute originality for New York in 1922, Campaspe thought. The walls were brown, the furniture heavy but extremely picturesque, in the fascinatingly tortured shapes affected by modern Austrian or Bavarian cabinet-makers. Campaspe cried out with delight when she descried a porcelain stove in one corner.[274] Over a particularly ornately constructed sofa hung a horizontal row of framed samplers, all the Scandinavian goddesses, Freya, Iduna, and the rest,[275] done in red yarn. There were other pictures, bright amazing dancers by Schnackenberg, portraits of Maria Hagen, Peter Pathe, Anne Ehmans, and Lo Hesse, more remote conceits in black and white by Alastair, a poster for a baroque ballet by Mela Koehler, and nude, graceful pretties with cats by Raphael Kirchner.[276] A great green and red and blue box of Baumgarten bonbons[277] stood on a table covered with a square scarf which resembled an Italian futurist painting. Over the mantelpiece, on which two heavy vases of garnet and gold Bohemian glass seemed very much at home, hung a large picture in pure design by Jean Metzinger.[278]

---

[273]   Zimbule's apartment is decorated in an Arts and Crafts style as manifested in the Austrian and German contexts by, for example, the Wiener Werkstätte (Vienna Workshop) movement. The Arts and Crafts style, popular in the late nineteenth and early twentieth centuries and pervasive across the arts, celebrated handcraft, beauty in everyday objects, and folk forms. In Austria and Germany, the style incorporated elements of Art Nouveau, notably its interest in curvilinear forms. There were some importers of modern Viennese goods in New York in this period, notably a branch of the Wiener Werkstätte on Fifth Avenue which opened in June 1922. See Christopher Long, 'The Viennese *Secessionsstil* and Modern American Design', *Studies in the Decorative Arts*, 14, 2 (2007), 6–44 (pp. 34–40).

[274]   In her best-selling *House in Good Taste* (1913, 1920), Elsie de Wolfe (1870–1950), interior designer for the rich and famous, extolled the usefulness and beauty of German porcelain stoves, which she used frequently in her decorating.

[275]   Norse goddess of love (Freya) and youth (Iduna). These folk art samplers are in keeping with the Arts and Crafts style of Zimbule's apartment.

[276]   Walter Schnackenberg (1880–1961), German graphic artist, specializing in poster-style art after the manner of Henri de Toulouse-Lautrec (1864–1901), incorporating Art Nouveau and Expressionist style with subject matter centred on the performing arts; Hagen, Pathe, Ehmans, and Hesse were popular German dancers who appeared in Schnackenberg posters; Alastair, pseudonym of Hans Henning Voight (1887–1969), artist whose black and white ink drawings combined Aubrey Beardsley's (1872–1898) 1890s decadent style with Art Deco; Koehler (1885–1960), Austrian graphic artist, associated with the Wiener Werkstätte; Kirchner (1876–1917), Austrian artist of Art Nouveau and erotic pin-up style work for postcards and magazines.

[277]   Candies sold in attractive Wiener Werkstätte styled tins by the Baumgarten Bonbonnière shop on Forty-Seventh Street off Fifth Avenue.

[278]   Metzinger (1883–1956), French painter and one of the founders of the Cubist style.

I wonder, Campaspe was thinking, if Zimbule lives up to this incongruous environment.

Zimbule, at last, came in. Her blond hair, turning at the roots, back to its natural colour, still framed her face in a nervous shock. She was wearing a négligé of coral sequins over Turkish trousers fashioned of gold cloth, and she plied a fan of ostrich plumes, unnaturally joined to prolong their length, of the colour of green jade.[279] She was, Campaspe observed at once, as much at her ease as ever.

Campaspe! I'm so glad to see you.

You never come to me; so I had to come to you. You haven't been near me since …

Out! The girl flung her fan across the room. I'm trying to forget him. Love! Nothing in it.

But … Campaspe looked around.

Yes, Zimbule remarked blandly, crossing her legs as she seated herself on a great stuffed ottoman, I've capitalized my talents. Why not? They all do. Probably you did it yourself when you married — Campaspe did not even trouble to shake her head in denial of this. There was a sudden and complete metamorphosis. Do you know where Harold is?

No, Zimbule, I wish I did.

I hear she's left him! Zimbule was eager.

You hear … Campaspe permitted an expression of light surprise to play over her features, an expression not unnoted by Zimbule.

Yes. I met Cupid in the Park. He told me.

It is true. They are separated, but *he* left *her*.

Zimbule ignored this echo of an event she had every desire to forget, and begged: Where is he, Campaspe? Help me find him.

I wish I could…. But tell me about yourself. You're doing pictures?

Zimbule was frankly bored. She pulled great tufts of down out of a quilt of colibri feathers[280] which she had drawn over her knee. Yes, she assented, I'm in the movies.

What company?

Zimbule O'Grady Incorporated. Capital $200,000. Zimbule yawned.

When do you start work?

Commenced a week ago. I'm not in the scenes today.

What is the picture called?

A Long Island Phryne….[281] Campaspe, please help me to find Harold.

---

[279]   Zimbule is dressed in the orientalist manner popularized in this period by the costumes of the Ballets Russes, as designed by Paul Poiret. See note 123.
[280]   A colibri is a species of hummingbird.
[281]   Phryne was an Ancient Greek courtesan of the fourth century. The term came to be applied broadly to courtesans and prostitutes.

I haven't an idea where to look. She paused. That's an interesting picture you have. She pointed to the Metzinger.

Yes, I got it because it has significant form.[282] He's sure to come to see you.

Campaspe adopted a more sympathetic tone. When he turns up, she said, I'll let you know.

Promise? Zimbule, with an instinctive gesture, thrust her hands forwards, and on one of her fingers Campaspe caught a glimpse of a familiar ring, a sapphire intaglio, set most curiously, and engraved with a banyan-tree, an ape, a cobra, and the motto, Fronti nulla fides.[283]

I promise. As soon as he comes to me I shall let you know.

She kissed the child.

Campaspe went out smiling, through the polished onyx hallway, past the black attendants, to her car, standing in the warm autumn sun. She consulted her watch. She would have time to get Han Ryner's Les Paraboles cyniques, Jean de Tinan's Penses-tu réussir, and P. J. Toulet's La Jeune fille verte.[284]

Go to Dorbon's, she commanded her chauffeur, 561 Madison Avenue.[285]

She settled herself comfortably back against the puce-colour cloth cushions as the car drove away from Riverside Drive.

---

[282] 'Significant form' was a term coined by British art critic Clive Bell in 1914 to refer to the manner in which formal qualities of art provoke aesthetic emotions in the viewer even when there is no identifiable subject matter (see notes 157 and 224).

[283] Latin, meaning 'appearances are deceiving'.

[284] Ryner, pseudonym of Jacques Élie Henri Ambroise Ner (1861–1938), French anarchist, philosopher, and novelist whose Paraboles cyniques (Cynical Parables) of 1912 consists of parables engaging with abstract metaphysical problems and issues of everyday life; Tinan (1874–1898), a figure in the literary and artistic avant-garde of fin-de-siècle Paris whose Penses-tu réussir! (Think Success!) of 1897 is a semiautobiographical account of a writer's attempt to produce an essay on the real-life celebrity dancer Cléo de Mérode; Toulet (1867–1920), French writer, whose 1920 novel La jeune fille verte (The Young Green Girl), in which green refers both to the girl's olive skin colour and to her inexperience, is a part sentimental/part cynical love story set against the backdrop of village life.

[285] New York City branch of the Parisian bookstore selling French books.

Chapter XI

If Campaspe had conceived the idea of making a search for Harold, she would have been hard put to think of a way to go about it. He seemed, indeed, completely cut off both from his family and from the group which had been charged, for a few weeks, with his education. She pictured him, like a kitten in a bath-tub half-full of water, struggling in an alien element. As it happened, however, one of Campaspe's most steadfast convictions was that nothing in life should be sought. People who were always seeking never found. Even if they discovered what they had been looking for, they discovered simultaneously that they really wanted something else. She held the theory that if Diogenes had stayed at home and attended to business, instead of prowling around Athens with a smelly lantern, he would have been visited by any number of honest men.[286] Everything comes to him who waits might be a trite proverb, but experience had taught her that it was a true one. Therefore, she followed her invariable custom in such instances, dropping the matter from her mind, arranging her days as pleasantly as possible, and waiting with as much composure as she could assume, taking into consideration the fact that Harold was probably the one person alive that she cared very much about seeing.

October came to New York warm and golden. The early days of the month, indeed, resembled the sultry daughters of midsummer. Nevertheless, in spite of the unusual heat, Campaspe's friends began to return from the country and from Europe. Every train, every boat, brought more of them back, and Campaspe's mail grew heavier with invitations to lunch and dinner. Houses on Park and Madison Avenues[287] opened their boarded eyelids and one encountered familiar and friendly motors in the Park.[288] The Ritz, Voisin's, Pierre's, and the Crillon at one o'clock were again crowded with gay, brilliant groups.[289] Mrs. Pollanger had even begun to plan a charity entertainment for the last days of the month. A bit of scandal enlivened, for Campaspe, the

---

[286]   Diogenes, ancient Greek philosopher, who endorsed the simple life against the corruptions of the artificial trappings of Greek society. One of the most famous tales about him concerns his daytime wanderings through Athens with a lantern searching for honest men.

[287]   From the 1910s, Park Avenue, a wide landscaped boulevard with luxury apartments, became as popular a residence for the city's elite as Fifth Avenue; Madison Avenue was an exclusive and strictly residential street until the late 1920s.

[288]   In the 1910s and 1920s, Central Park was more open to car traffic than today.

[289]   Fine-dining establishments specializing in continental cuisine located in and around the exclusive residences of Park, Fifth, and Madison Avenues.

monotony of this accustomed renaissance. Amy, having lost her Paul, had, according to report, found her Paula. Laura, of course, always correct, had come back with the others, and had opened her house in East Sixty-eighth Street[290] for a few weeks, long enough, at least, to afford her the opportunity of packing her boys off to school and arranging a few dinners before she went away again. The winter exodus was already a subject under discussion. Recurrence was a word that held few terrors for the members of Laura's conventional world, but fourteen consecutive winters at Palm Beach[291] seemed almost sufficient even to this group and there was some talk of a more novel hegira, a motor trip along the Italian Riviera or an excursion to Shepheard's Hotel.[292] Laura had begged Campaspe to join this comparatively radical party but, although Campaspe was still planning to go abroad a little later, she had no intention of travelling with any one else. Nor did the names of Spezia, Mentone, Monte Carlo, Nice, Cannes, and Genoa intrigue her. In the back of her mind were the happier alternatives of Trebizond, Chypre, Stamboul, Saigon, and Ronda.[293] She did not explain this directly to Laura, however. She did not definitely, indeed, refuse to become a factor in Laura's plan. It was part of her power and charm that she seldom said yes or no. At least, whenever she did say one or the other, nobody could be entirely certain that she meant it.

One day she went for a long course in her car, making several calls, stopping at Bergdorf and Goodman's to order a gown,[294] looking in at an exhibition at the Bourgeois Gallery,[295] and dropping off at the little shop of T. Azeez,[296] where she purchased a pair of ear-rings, clusters of sardonyx grapes to match the crystal pendants dangling from her wrist. On her return Frederika met her

---

[290] East Sixty-Eighth Street contained many late nineteenth-century single-family brownstone-clad homes. From 1920 on it was, like East Nineteenth Street (see note 84), subject to high-end redevelopment of its old-fashioned homes.
[291] Palm Beach, Florida, was established as a winter playground for the rich and famous in the 1890s and it continued to prosper in this period.
[292] A luxury hotel, formerly a harem, in Cairo, Egypt, established in 1841.
[293] Spezia, Menton (Van Vechten uses Italian spelling), Monte Carlo, Nice, Cannes, and Genoa are popular resorts of the French and Italian rivieras. Campaspe's preferred destinations are more eclectic and adventurous. Trebizond (Trabzon), Chypre (Cyprus), and Stamboul (Istanbul) were associated with the Ottoman Empire, which in World War I fought against the Allies, and were caught up in the Turkish War of Independence (1919–1922). In 1922, Trebizond was still suffering from the effects of war, impoverished and inundated with refugees, and there were tensions between Turks and the Pontic Greeks, who would be expelled in 1923. Chypre and Stamboul, meanwhile, were under occupation by the Allies in 1922. Saigon (Ho Chi Minh City), in Vietnam, was under French rule at this time and was European in appearance. Ronda is a Spanish mountain city, famed for bullfighting.
[294] A high-end couturier (still in existence as a luxury department store) which, in 1922, was located on Fifth Avenue.
[295] A Fifth Avenue gallery, specializing in modern art. In October 1922 the gallery was featuring a jungle painting by one of Campaspe's favourites, Henri Rousseau. See note 264.
[296] See note 271.

at the door with the news that Harold was in the garden. Throwing her sable scarf over a chair, she hastened out to join him.

Dear Harold, I *am* glad to see you. Why haven't you been here before?

She was shocked by the boy's appearance. Deep grey circles had formed under his eyes. His cheekbones seemed unnaturally prominent. He was thinner. And, Campaspe noted at once, he suggested, as usual, the dominant note of pathos. It was the one quality she had never been quite able to dissociate from him, or from any other very young person, for that matter. One never begins to be happy until one is thirty, she reflected, and then, sometimes, one only begins.

He did not seem able to muster sufficient poise to respond immediately to her greeting, and so she asked Frederika to bring out tea, and she moved freely about the garden, hoping to put him at his ease by the apparent carelessness of her manner. Her beloved Eros still aimed his bow at random and the nymph still lay prostrate on the marble sward, but the fountain had ceased to function and the basin was choked with yellow and red leaves, discarded by a neighbour's maple-tree. The pavement, too, was strewn with leaves, and the aged tortoise had burrowed under a heap of them in one corner. It was a setting replete with melancholy.

I wasn't sure you would want me, Harold replied hesitantly, at last.

He *was* pathetic.

Not want you! Of course, I wanted you. How, conceivably, could you get that idea?

You are her sister....

Bosh! I didn't arrange that.

She seated him in a chair beside her, adjacent to the table, on which Frederika was laying out pots and bowls and cups, slices of lemon and slim sandwiches.

Frederika, Campaspe said, will you please run around the corner to the grocery and order some gin. We're all out.... She turned to Harold: Lemon or cream?

Lemon, please.

His hand shook, she observed, as he took the cup, but he was beginning to look more comfortable, appeared to be surer of his ground.

You've seen her? he questioned Campaspe eagerly. She's told you?

I've scarcely seen anybody else, it seems to me, looking back. She has been here nearly every day. She is sure that I know where you live.

You won't tell her, he pleaded.

I don't know.

But you will....

Naturally, I won't tell her.

It was awful, Campaspe! he groaned.

A melodrama. It sounded incredible. But don't blame Alice. *She* didn't do it

... She isn't clever enough to think of it, she added.

But she knew all about it. I blame her for that.

She loves you. Campaspe's manner was as simple as it was possible for her to make it.

Even after ...

Yes. She put her hand on his wrist. I don't want you to go back to her, Harold, that is I want you to do what you really *feel* like doing, but it is the truth. She loves you. Of that I am certain.

Campaspe sipped her tea and nibbled a slender sandwich. Harold looked at her intently, searching her eyes.

Campaspe.... I don't believe I've ever loved ... Alice. It was the first time that he had spoken the name and the effort was apparent. I've been a fool. Sometimes, up in Provincetown, sitting on the beach, I have wondered if it didn't all come about — the marriage, I mean — because she was *your* sister.

But, Harold, you met her first.

It's very difficult to explain. I don't believe I can explain. What I want you to try to understand is that when I married Alice I had some kind of subconscious feeling that I was marrying *you*.

Harold, you delightful boy! Her expression was quizzical.

I don't know myself! I don't know myself! he moaned. That's the whole trouble.

You're young, boy.

So is Bunny. So is Paul. So is Ronald. So is — he hesitated again — Zimbule, but they do.

She remained silent.

Will I ever learn to understand myself?

I think so.

It's very hard. I've been trying to get on, to do something. I'm not used to it, but it seemed the only decent thing to do. He broke off suddenly and asked, Do you know how I was brought up? Do you know about my Aunt Sadi?

Alice has told me something. I think I understand.

The best woman in the world ... after you. It's not her fault. It's just my misfortune.

Campaspe brought him back. What have you been trying to do, Harold?

I don't want to talk about that ... ever. It hasn't been a success. I've got to begin all over.

What do you *want* to do?

It isn't so much that. The question is what can I do?

Can't you go back to your Aunt? Campaspe hoped for a negative reply.

Yes. She wants me. She wrote me a letter asking me to come back. But what would be the good of that? That would mean going back to what I began with and staying there. Probably I could never get away again.... He stared at her with some embarrassment for a moment before he said: I'd thought of the stage.

Her reaction to this was direct: But you're such a bad actor!

He groaned again.

I don't know that that makes any great difference, Campaspe reminded herself aloud. Then suddenly, she exclaimed: I have it! The very thing! The movies. You have a good appearance, and if you were a good actor you couldn't get into the pictures. Into the pictures you shall go!

Do you mean ...?

She cut him off: No, I don't own a company, but I know some one who does. She tossed the name lightly out: Zimbule.

He rose to his feet. I couldn't do that, he said.

Why not? she asked, her voice as even as usual. Why not? Don't be silly any longer, Harold. You are permitting your youthful pride and prejudice to govern you too much. You must take things just a little more as they come....

But ...

Try to realize, Harold, that some day you will get over some of your notions; you will even compromise with a few that you don't get over. Even Nana — Campaspe began to laugh — , even Nana, disgusted with ... well, with something new to her, reasoned that one should never dispute about tastes and colours because one never could be sure what one would like in the future....[297] And there is the story of the ship captain, related by Cunninghame-Graham. You see this water, he said. All my life I have loved water,... good air, good water and good bells, the proverb says, and yet, when I have been in an old sailing-ship out in the eastern seas, and when the water had run short been put upon two pints a day for drinking and cooking, I have stand round the barrel, and though it smelled just like the drainings of a tanyard, counted the drops when it was poured into my pannikin as if they had been gold.... Si, señor,... that is I mean,... how do you put it, eh? — it is not good to say fountain — out of your basin I shall never drink ... eh, no señor.[298]

Harold wavered. But will she want me?

That we must find out, was Campaspe's reply.

After he had departed, a half-hour later, Campaspe strolled back into the house and on to the drawing-room. A day or so earlier she had sent for some music by Bach,[299] in order to satisfy a certain intellectual curiosity. Bach!

---

[297] From chapter eight of *Nana* (1880), a novel about a high-class courtesan by French naturalist writer Émile Zola (1840–1902). In the scene described by Campaspe, Nana's laissez-faire reasoning is a corrective to an initial disgust at the sight of a woman dressed as a man who is the subject of attraction to a table of women.

[298] R. B. Cunninghame-Graham (1852–1936), Scottish writer and politician. Campaspe quotes from a sketch, 'Dagos', from his story collection, *His People* (1906).

[299] Johann Sebastian Bach (1685–1750), German Baroque composer. Bach, as Campaspe

Bach! Bach! She met the name, enshrined in extravagant encomiums, in all the writings about music that she read, but where was Bach played? Who played Bach? She was beginning to believe that Bach was one of the veiled gods, and she wanted to settle the question for herself. Among the Etruscans certain of the most powerful deities were never seen by the people.[300] The priests referred to these hidden idols as Dii Involuti, veiled gods. Their words were frequently quoted, but the gods themselves remained invisible. Certain savants have derived from this fact the explanation that the Etruscans may have held transcendental views in regard to the invisibility of the true god, but at least one commentator, whose work had come under Campaspe's eternally roving eye, had held that there might be a simpler interpretation of the phenomenon. The gods, he hinted, were concealed because they were no longer fit to look at. Rude tribes had carved them. Supplanted by more sightly idols, the only possible manner in which reverence might be preserved for them was to keep them behind screens, so that no comparisons could be made. And, as they were never shown, it was quite simple for the priests to aver that their splendour was so divine that ordinary senses would be overpowered by it.

In the temple of Isis at Sais, the inscription read: I am that which has been, which is, and which shall be, and no one has yet lifted the veil which hides me.[301] It is highly probable, thought this same sapient commentator, that the goddess was *black*, and as the fairer race mingled with the darker in Egypt this primitive Nubian countenance, if exhibited, would no longer inspire reverence, and so a curtain was hung before her altar. The Ark of Moses,[302] probably concealing objects which had lost their attraction for the eye, two scrawled stones, the

---

goes on to suggest, was undergoing a revival in America in this period. Van Vechten himself took a dim view of Bach, declaring that much of his music was 'below any moderately high standard' in 'Music and Supermusic', *The Merry-Go-Round* (New York: Knopf, 1918), 23–34 (p. 25).

[300] Campaspe's reflections on the Etruscan veiled gods are indebted to *Demonology and Devil-Lore* (1879) by Moncure Daniel Conway, the 'commentator' who is said to have 'come under Campaspe's eternally roving eye'. The section starting here and leading up to Campaspe sitting down to play Bach paraphrases this work. Conway (1832–1907) was an American writer, abolitionist, and religious freethinker, and *Demonology and Devil-Lore* is a two-volume survey that takes a rationalist approach to the study of the origins of the belief in gods and demons across world religions through history. Campaspe's scepticism about the reverence given to Bach parallels that expressed by Conway towards Etruscan, Greek, and Christian practices concerning holy relics.

[301] The goddess Isis was worshipped by the Ancient Egyptians and later by the Romans and Greco-Romans. This inscription, which identifies Isis with secret knowledge, was claimed by Greco-Roman authors to have adorned the temple.

[302] Biblical reference from Exodus. Also known as the Ark of the Covenant or the Ark of the Testimony, the Ark was a chest created according to instructions given to Moses by God which reputedly contained the Ten Commandments (described by Campaspe as 'two scrawled stones') and the other items described, and was carried, covered with a veil, by the Israelites in their wanderings.

bones of Joseph, a pot of manna, and the serpent-staff which is said to have
blossomed, carried this veil into the wilderness. To this very day, indeed, the
Ark is hidden. Twice the veil of the Temple has been rent: allegorically at the
crucifixion and actually by Titus,[303] but no Ark was discovered. The Jews, then,
must have been saying their prayers before a veil which concealed nothing. In
later days, as scepticism grew, there were those who had no desire to share the
deceit practised on the Jews. There is, for example, the case of the celebrated
bambino of the Aracoeli Church at Rome.[304] Alleged to have been carved by
a pilgrim out a piece of wood from a tree on the Mount of Olives and painted
by St. Luke while the pilgrim was asleep, this effigy is now bestowed in an
Ark, but, occasionally, visitors are permitted a view of a part of the face. Flat,
blackened, and rouged, this is a thing of ugliness, but it is set in jewels and the
walls are covered with pictures of the miracles it has performed, pictures which
have attracted the faithful in such numbers that at one time it is said to have
received more fees than all the doctors of Rome.... Campaspe seated herself
before the piano, opened the pages of the Wohltemperirtes Clavier,[305] and
struck a chord....

---

[303] The tearing of the veil coincides with Jesus's death upon the cross and is recounted in
the Bible as follows: 'And, behold, the veil of the temple was rent in twain from the top to
the bottom' (Matthew 27. 51). Titus (AD 39–81) was a Roman military general responsible for
quelling the Jewish Rebellion in 70 AD, when he captured and destroyed Jerusalem. He is
said to have entered the Temple and pierced the veil of the Ark with his sword.
[304] A fifteenth-century devotional image of baby Jesus, crowned, bejewelled, and wrapped
in gold swaddling.
[305] *The Well-Tempered Clavier* (Book I, 1722; Book II, 1742), Bach's collection of keyboard
preludes and fugues in all 24 major and minor keys.

Chapter XII

Harold had been working in the studio three days in the second week of November. It would be more accurate to say that he had reported for work, had made up and dressed for his part, but he had been kept waiting in his dressing-room, a tiny chamber, separated from the adjoining cubicles by thin walls of rough pine boards, which rose ten feet in the air and then suddenly terminated while yet some appreciable distance from the ceiling. A pine shelf served as a dressing-table, over which hung a mirror, framed in zinc, outlined with a blaze of electric lights. This was one in a long row of similar rooms on the second floor of a mammoth building which looked as if it had been put up over night and which probably could be destroyed by a brisk fire in considerably less time even than that.

A red and white sign vocatively adjured against smoking, and a poster of Zimbule in her costume as the Long Island Phryne, a veil of orange tulle and a rope of pearls, hung on the wall of this room, as it hung, Harold soon discovered, on all the other walls of this vast factory, for factory was what it seemed to him, but he had not yet caught a glimpse of Zimbule herself. Her dressing-room was located on the opposite side of the building and was approached by a separate staircase. He had taken it for granted that she would be working in the studio below and that was primarily the reason why he had refrained from wandering about downstairs, although he had been encouraged to do so by various actors, camera-men, and stage-hands, who had lounged into his room out of curiosity, ostensibly to light their cigarettes, or to ask the time. He had not taken advantage of their invitation to roam; instead, he sat alone in his room, waiting ... for what? he wondered.

Campaspe had oiled the wheels. He had found it incredibly simple to become a cabot of the silver sheets,[306] an epithet for his new profession dropped by one of his visitors, an assistant director named Rex MacGregor, a lad about seventeen years old, whose thin white face was profusely sprinkled with pimples, and who wore ridiculously tight shepherd's plaid trousers over his extremely thin legs, a waistcoat which exposed about as much of his shirt as the similar garment of a Spanish matador, and a coat in which the pockets were cut at angles which would have thrown a cubist painter into a delirium.

---

[306]   John Cabot (*c.* 1450–*c.* 1500) Venetian sailor, reputedly the first European to discover America; silver sheets was an early expression for cinema, akin to the better-known silver screen.

Harold had called one morning, following instructions, on the casting director, and when he encountered that superb individual, with his shirt-sleeves rolled back to the shoulder, exposing the lumps of muscle which distorted the contour of his hairy arms, a huge black cigar between his teeth, sitting before a desk littered with papers and stills, he had not felt encouraged. This ruffian apparently had forgotten that Harold had been announced, and after leaving him standing for half an hour or so while he conversed, in a language of which Harold could only understand one word in ten, with a blonde lady, massive and buxom in the style of 1896, the figure tightly corseted and swelling with curves like a Bartlett pear, he turned suddenly and savagely on the boy and asked him his business. Who are you and what d'ye want? he growled. But when Harold had repeated his name, the man's manner considerably altered. His face became wreathed in equivocal, nay blandiloquent, smiles and, without a single further question, he pushed a long sheet of printed paper over towards Harold, and asked him to sign it. The man never laughed, Harold observed, and even his smile he controlled in a curious and disgusting way with his tongue. There was something about this smile, indeed, that Harold did not quite like. Nevertheless, before he signed the document, which he took to be a contract, his natural honesty compelled him to explain that this was his first job in pictures, that he was wholly inexperienced, that he hoped, etc. But the casting director, alternately biting his cigar brutally and removing it to give vent to one of his enigmatical and unsatisfactory smiles, waved away this attempt at reason with a That's all right. I know. I know, pronouncing these I knows with a downward inflection which gave them, perhaps, a richer meaning. Sign here. He indicated a dotted line and Harold signed.

A little later, when alone, it occurred to him to read the document and he discovered, to his amazement, that his salary was to be $400 a week and that he was engaged to play leads. He was employed, apparently, by the Zimbule O'Grady Film Company, Incorporated, to appear in a picture entitled The Passionate Flapper. He endeavoured to satisfy his conscience by assuring himself that he owed this turn in his fortunes to Campaspe, but his uneasy conscience retorted that Campaspe had arranged his easy ingress only through the influence of Zimbule. How could he, he asked himself, accept the position under these humiliating circumstances? The fact remained, however, that he had signed the contract, and a certain clause provided definitely that in case the contract should be broken by either party, a large sum of money was to be forfeited. It was too late, then, to listen to his conscience. Besides he was not sure. Perhaps Campaspe had friends among the directors of the company. It was possible, indeed, that she, herself, in spite of her denial, had put money into the project. It was like her to wish to help Zimbule and, if she had bought stock with this intention, it would be unlike her to seek any recognition for her good deed.

As the days passed, he grew more uncertain still. Zimbule had made no effort to approach him. If my contract had been arranged through her she would have come to gloat, he argued, or she would send for me. As a final mode of relieving his tortured mind, he determined to make good. If I do satisfactory work in this picture, he reasoned, if I do what I have to do well, it doesn't matter who got me the job. In any case, then, I will be earning my salary. With casuistry of this nature he held daily communication with himself.

Passionately, he wanted to make good for his own sake, for Campaspe's sake, even for Alice's sake. He would show Alice that he could get along on his own. He had to confess to himself, however, that as yet he was not on his own, that in taking this position he had been obliged to make as great a sacrifice of his principles as if he had accepted his father's shameful offer. Principles! He was beginning to wonder if he had any left! And then alleviation came again in the thought that what he was now doing he was doing independently, of his own free will. He had not been tricked and driven into this corner. He had listened to Campaspe's arguments and, with his eyes open, he had walked voluntarily into it. If he succeeded, Alice might never know, perhaps, how the chance had come to him. She might even credit him with initiative in the matter.

As for Campaspe, she was more in his thoughts than any one else. Without professing to understand her or her motives, he thought of her as a consistently kind and sympathetic person. She was more than she appeared to be in the somewhat ribald crowd with which she so strangely associated, of that he was sure. His sympathy for her, as the weeks had gone by, had deepened into a kind of affection, in which, even he, with his naive reasoning powers, recognized a filial element. In some respects, he realized, he regarded her somewhat as he might have regarded his mother, but this, for him, who had never known his mother, was a dangerous affection, the most dangerous of all. Again, the inexplicable tangle confused his thinking: how, inconceivably, he had married Alice with the idea of Campaspe paramount. And there was much more that he did not understand at all.

He wondered if Zimbule would show resentment, turn spiteful. Towards her, from her point of view, he had, indubitably, behaved in the shabbiest possible manner. She had gravitated towards him naturally. She did everything naturally. Campaspe was right: Zimbule was a little animal. Why had he rejected her attentions so forcibly, so rudely? He could not tell. He knew only that he was subject to extravagant reactions, insane impulses. Everybody around him seemed to take life as a matter of course. He, alone, seemed to regard it with suspicion, a suspicion, he was horrified to discover, which seemed to aggrandize with every new opportunity. He was afraid of life; that was it, afraid of life! Nothing seemed to be easy for him. Another, perhaps, even more thin-skinned than himself, but less obstinate, less timid, would have put up with his father's

stupid joke, have fallen in with his father's wishes. Paul would have done so, he
reflected. To Paul, with his sense of irony, one course would have seemed as bad
or as good as another. There was, apparently, a great gulf fixed between any two
generations, the way people have lived and the way they live now. Youth must
bridge this gulf. Others did; why couldn't he? Why to all intents and purposes
did he still belong to his Aunt Sadi's generation rather than to Paul's? Paul
seemed to have nothing in his nature which resisted, which *revolted*, while he
seemed to have nothing else but resistance and revolt in his nature. He could
accept nothing unaccustomed without an internal struggle. What was it: pride
or stupidity which held him in its vice, so that he felt unable to turn in any
direction without a sense that he was shaming some older and more honourable
intention? He did not know. All he knew was that he was that way, and he
had begun to realize that, at bottom, no one changes. As one is born one is ...
always. The only growth possible lay on the side of increasing comprehension of
oneself. He did not understand himself, or Alice, or Campaspe, but Campaspe
he accepted, as he accepted his aunt and Persia Blaine. These three, alone, in
the world with which he had yet come into contact, did not arouse him to
resistance. These three and one other. Paul, he could understand after a fashion,
and Zimbule, a sheet of flame burning a path before her desire, he understood
only too well. In the past he had avoided this flame, only, it would appear, to
walk voluntarily into it in the present. And the question he asked himself, so
much had his experience already taught him, was whether it was worth while
to struggle against this flame any longer, whether it would not be better to ...
But did Zimbule still cherish her old desire? That doubt assailed him fifty times
a day and it had lodged in his mind afresh when he heard a voice down the
corridor calling, Mr. Proowit! Mr. Proowit! He started guiltily as he bade the
boy come in, and he was in a perspiration of dread and fear when Rex entered
to tell him that he was wanted at once in the studio below.

He quickly rubbed a little more flesh paint into his cheeks — the first day,
following the advice of some ancient thespian, he had used yellow powder, but
a lad in the next room who visited Harold to borrow towels, rabbits' feet,[307]
matches, soap, and eyebrow pencils, had informed him categorically that the
employment of yellow powder was obsolete. This ain't a Pearl White serial,[308]
he explained. Them days is over.... Harold drew on his dinner coat, examining
himself once more in the mirror, catching therein a glimpse of the impertinent
and grinning Rex gazing over his shoulder, and then started out.

As he entered the enormous studio, crowded with actors, stage-hands,
carpenters building sets in various corners, producing a deafening racket

---

[307]   Once used to apply theatrical makeup, rabbits' feet later became lucky charms for
actors who would keep them in their makeup boxes.

[308]   White (1889–1938), stage and film actress of the 1910s, most famous for the sensational
serial *The Perils of Pauline*.

with their hammers, he felt as though everybody were staring at him. As a consequence he could scarcely walk steadily. Rex guided him to the proper set and once he was there he found that no one was aware of his presence at all. The director, the cameraman, and the art director were in the midst of a heated argument. It can't be done, the cameraman was yelling. I ain't never done it before and anything I ain't never done nobody can do. I tell you it can, declared the art director, with the finality of a person who knew. Well, it won't be. See! put in the director, setting his square jaw high. Not if I have my way. And I'm going to have it. It's my job to arrange the sets. What do you think I'm getting paid more'n anybody else around here for? To argue with a bunch of fish? By God, I'll see you all in hell if you don't do what I want!

At this seemingly crucial moment — to Harold the men seemed on the verge of murder — , round a corner of the scenery, set to represent a moving picture art director's idea of a somewhat flashy Parisian apartment, Harold saw Zimbule approaching, leading a leopard by a silver chain. She was wearing a costume fashioned entirely of strands of rhinestones. On her head waved a forest of yellow feathers, secured in a crown of brilliants. Her bare arms were encased nearly to the elbow in a succession of circles of diamonds, emeralds, sapphires, and rubies. On her bare right ankle — her feet were casketed in sandals — , she wore three more of these circles. There was a heavy impression of muguet[309] in the air.

Are you all cuckoo? the girl demanded of the belligerent group. This ain't a bull-fight or a baseball game! What d'ye think y'are, she inquired shrilly of the art director, Babe Ruth?[310]

Zimbule passed the silver chain, with the leopard attached, to her Negro maid, who followed her. The men were apologetic.

I was jest tellin' 'em it couldn't be done, explained the camera-man.

That's right, Zimbule sneered. You tell 'em, Sweeney, you're the biggest. Suddenly she saw Harold. Hello, she said, in a friendly enough tone. So you're here.

As she walked towards him he advanced to meet her, thinking at the same time that never before had she appeared so beautiful. He hesitated for a second as to whether or not he should offer his hand and she, observing his confusion, held out her own. Curiously, she too seemed a little ill at ease.

I hope, he stammered, that you'll find me all right. You know — he patted his face with his handkerchief; even in November the studio was a hot-house and he was perspiring freely — , you know how little experience I've had.

She regarded him quizzically, but when she spoke her tone was careless. I hope so, she echoed, her mind apparently elsewhere. Then, more seriously, Of course you will. Even the wops can do it. Never look at the camera. Look at me.

---

309   The scent of lily of the valley.
310   Ruth (1895–1948), the highest-paid baseball player of the era.

I'll *make* you act.

Scene, Miss O'Grady, please, cried the director.

Zimbule took Harold's arm and propelled him into the flashy Parisian apartment. Now the lights, full on his face, were blinding, suffocating. The strands of gems which hung from Zimbule's shoulders and waist flashed blue and white messages to his eyes. He seemed to have lost his vision. His head began to ache and, in the intensity of the heat, he could scarcely breathe. Behind the camera he vaguely caught a glimpse of a knot of bystanders, men and women in evening dress, waiting, probably, to appear in some ball or fête scene. Zimbule did not seem to be conscious of their presence.

I haven't the least idea what I am to do, Harold whispered in desperation. I haven't seen the scenario.

I haven't either, she laughed. It doesn't make any difference. That's what that stiff is paid for. He'll tell us what to do.

Now we'll take the temptation scene, the director shouted, in a tone suggesting that he was advising a crowd of ten thousand people in Madison Square Garden to vote for Debs.[311] Hey! Cut that! This to the carpenters who had now begun to pound at double the rate they had hitherto employed. Rex dashed off to the further end of the room to repeat the injunction. Soon there was comparative silence, only about as much noise as in the Stock Exchange on a fairly busy day. The director continued: Harold — Harold was a trifle startled by this familiar approach from a man he had never seen before — , you are alone with Dolly, the passionate flapper. She is determined to seduce you, and you are almost ready to yield when you see that picture of the madonna on the wall. The picture reminds you of your good wife, calls you back to your senses, and you cast the vamp off. Now, try it.

Harold sat down, as directed, and Zimbule approached him.

Register the beginning of passion! You are fascinated by the sigh-reen, screamed the director, through a megaphone.

Harold had the air of a man who has just been told that he will die within the month. On the arm of his chair, Zimbule smoothed his hair with her right hand. He felt her warm breath on his cheek. His heart was beating violently in an irregular rhythm that Stravinsky[312] would have given his right ear to have invented.

Nothing like it! NO-THING LIKE IT! drawled the director in a hoarse wail of dissatisfaction. Passion! PASSION!!! You aren't saved yet. You haven't seen the picture YET! Snuggle! SNUGGLE!

Harold tried desperately hard to snuggle. He put one arm tentatively and

---

[311]   Eugene V. Debs (1855–1926), famed union leader and socialist, noted for his fiery oratory.
[312]   See note 187.

awkwardly around Zimbule's waist. With valiant cozenage she fell limply into his lap. Now the gods had not given Harold any talent for acting, but he was not entirely bereft of natural feeling. Quite unexpectedly he began to sense the spirit of the scene.

More like it! shouted the director. Now, look at the madonna and think of your poor little wife at home. Harold obeyed. The blood rushed to his face.

Push her away!

Harold pushed. Zimbule fell before him, pleading on her knees. She wept, she wrung her hands, she clasped his legs.

Keep your eyes on the madonna! Sp — URN the gurrrrulll!

Harold kept his eyes on the madonna. His nails were digging into his palms as he held his arms tight against his sides. His brain began to reel. Quite suddenly he had realized that he desired wildly to take Zimbule in his arms, to caress her, to kiss her violently, to crush her, to beat her. So love was like this. All that was needed to set one afire was propinquity and opportunity. Alice one week; Zimbule the next. He began to have a glimmering of understanding and he recalled Campaspe's story: It is not good to say fountain — out of your basin I shall never drink … eh, no señor.

The scene was over.

Great stuff! said Zimbule, picking herself up. I knew you'd do.

Go over it again! the director ordered.

This time, when Zimbule touched his head with her hand, he half rose, and drew her towards him. Pulling her down into the chair, he covered her face and throat with kisses. Their lips met.

That's eeee — NOUGH! Look at the madonna. Think of your WIFE!

You love me! Zimbule whispered.

As he looked at the picture and pushed her away, Harold nodded. This time, Zimbule fell with her back to the camera and in her eyes, as she gazed at the man who was trying hard to register rejection, there was an expression of triumph.

We can't see your face, Miss O'Grady!

As she turned, she burst into a fit of hysterical sobbing. Then she fell back on the floor, laughing and crying, her lithe, young body shaken with convulsions.

Great! commented the director. Great! We'll take it.

Zimbule, still crying, staggered to her feet. Her maid, having passed the young leopard on to Rex, approached with a mirror and a powder-puff, but Zimbule, unable to control her emotion, rushed off to her room.

The kid's gone too far, commented the cameraman. She's wore herself out.

You're the goods, boy, the director said to Harold. Valentino[313] himself couldn't do better.

---

[313]   Rudolph Valentino (1895–1926), Italian-American film star and sex symbol.

Harold was dazed. He scarcely knew what had happened and apparently it had to happen again. He tried to get his bearings. After a long wait, during which nobody exhibited any surprise or impatience, Zimbule reappeared.

Scene 62, cried the director. Title: Reginald remembers his wife. All ready! Camera! The camera-man began to turn the crank and the scene progressed, its course accented by the shouts of the director: Register passion! Look at the ma-donna! Spurn her! SP-URN her! Kick her! This time the scene went even better than before. It was carried through with abandon on both sides, but in the emotional scene, Zimbule was a little more artful. Her tears and her hysteria were no longer natural but they were magnificently feigned. She wept and grovelled. She wrung her hands and clasped Harold's knees. And, finally, she flung herself prostrate on the floor, apparently in a faint.

Take it again!

For the fourth time Harold clasped Zimbule in his arms and kissed her.... Good. That's all for you two today, said the director. We'll take the ball-room scene.

Come with me, Zimbule whispered to Harold. She hastened on ahead, followed at a few paces by her maid and Rex, leading the leopard. Harold brought up the rear. Once in her dressing-room, having seen the leopard fastened and Rex dismissed, Zimbule kicked the door shut with her foot. Then, pressing Harold's head between her hands, she guided his lips to hers. The maid, grinning like a black demon, hovered over them.

Harold!

Zimbule!

Why did you go away ... that night?

I don't know ... I was afraid....

You love me?

I adore you!

Zimbule caught sight of the black Mephistophela in her mirror.[314]

Here, you Desdemona, she cried. Take these, sign 'em, and mail 'em. She shoved a pile of photographs into the Negress's arms, and pushed her into an adjoining room.

---

[314]   Mephistophela is the name of the female devil in Heinrich Heine's (1797–1856) ballet of 1851, a version of the Faust myth, *Der Doktor Faust: ein Tanzpoem* (*Dr Faustus: A Dance Poem*). Mephistophela bewitches Faust with the use of a mirror. It is also the title and main character of an 1890 novel by French decadent novelist Catulle Mendès (1841–1909) about an alcoholic, drug-addicted, nymphomaniac lesbian. Van Vechten expressed familiarity with both these texts in his critical writings.

Chapter XIII

It was the morning of the third day. Harold awoke, immersed, as usual, in a vast sea of rose satin and lace, and looked up at the rococo Cupids high over his head. Through an open window the bright sunlight entered. Presently, he knew, Desdemona would appear with their breakfast on a tray. Zimbule was still asleep. He wondered if he could get out of bed without waking her. A mild form of curiosity impelled him to attempt this feat, but no sooner had he lifted a corner of the covers than Zimbule cast her arm across his body. Smiling, he fell back into the soft bed, and she, content once more, ran her slender fingers through his thick hair.

They had been lovers for two days. Zimbule had telephoned the studio that she was ill, too ill to work, and had kept Harold with her in this Riverside Drive apartment, which she had furnished for Love, but until now Love had not abided there. Now, however, He seemed to have entered into every object in the place. Not only the gilded plaster Cupids were instinct with life; the silver and ivory on the toilet-table vibrated with passion; the needle-point chairs invited to it; even the pictures took on new meanings. When they had entered this amorous bower two days earlier, passing through the Viennese room, Zimbule had frowned at the Metzinger.[315] It no longer seemed suitable. It was more in the mood of the interior decorator than her own. She had tried, on this initial evening, with Desdemona's and Harold's assistance, to turn its face to the wall. They had not been successful, but their united efforts finally dislodged the wire from the hook and the great canvas in its massive frame crashed to the floor, smashing the frame and shivering the glass. There it had lain ever since, for Zimbule was superstitious regarding an incident that had happened immediately after the entrance of the new master, and she refused to have it removed. But they had scarcely gone into the Viennese room since.

Harold was very happy, happier, he realized, than he had ever been before. An aureole of happiness seemed to radiate about his head. They had talked very little together. They had eaten, they had slept, they had kissed.... With her lips upon his, his conscience died. He felt secure in this new happiness; never had he felt secure before. He was even a little proud of himself.... Love! So this was love, the love that he had avoided, fled from, rejected.

The days had been so saturated with this novel feeling that all that had happened before seemed a little vague to him, like a series of half-forgotten

---

315   See note 278.

dreams. Places he had known came to his mind surrounded by a haze; even people, faces, were only pale shadows of things no longer familiar. All he really knew, all he really felt, all he was conscious of was before him, within his reach … within his reach!

Hal!

Yes, dear.

I'm so glad you're here.

Yes, dear.

Desdemona, grinning broadly, brought in a tray of coffee and steaming buckwheat-cakes, a passion in which Zimbule was indulging herself now that she had the opportunity. They taste, she commented, like angels' saliva. The cackling Desdemona catered to all the girl's whims. Meals were served at irregular hours and their composition was lacking in rhythm. Zimbule entertained fancies for old-fashioned scallop broil, for spumoni, for curry, for chicken à la Maryland, for apple pie smothered in Welsh rabbit.[316] Sometimes, an entire meal would consist of one of these; sometimes, a strange group would be served in a strange rotation. Whatever Zimbule wanted was all the same to Desdemona and Harold thought this wanton self-indulgence part of the girl's fascination.

Desdemona closed the window and turned on the steam. Presently she came in with a great bouquet of huge white fluffy chrysanthemums.

Zimbule clapped her hands. Like geese's bottoms! she cried.

A number of rolled magazines arrived in the morning mail. While Harold and Zimbule were eating their breakfast, Desdemona opened them with a butter-knife: Motion Pictures, Photoplay, Picture-Play Magazine, Shadowland, Screenland, Movie Weekly….[317]

Is my picture in any of 'em? demanded Zimbule.

I'll see, Miss Jimbool, Desdemona answered. She turned over the pages with her long brown fingers. Suddenly she emitted a howl. Yah t'is! Yah t'is!

Gimme! Gimme!

Harold looked over her shoulder and saw the portrait of his bride, the familiar picture of the Long Island Phryne, which, as a poster, had hung in his room at the studio. Zimbule, impatient, grabbed the lot from the darkey and began to examine them herself, making comments as she flipped the leaves:

---

[316]   Chicken à la Maryland is fried chicken and gravy, while Welsh rabbit (original spelling for Welsh rarebit), is a savoury melted cheese sauce served over toast. Presumably, Van Vechten is thinking of the cheese sauce only as an accompaniment to apple pie.

[317]   Titles of a range of weekly, semi-weekly, and monthly fan and industry magazines that emerged in the 1910s and 1920s. Of these titles, *Shadowland* had a slightly wider remit, including features on art, dance, music, and theatre, as well as film.

There's that sheeny[318] vamp. She had a beak but a doctor took a knife to her and gave her a pug. Cut off her nose to spite her race! Kitty Grandison: you know how she gets her drag.[319] Senators will be boys. He went to Paris with his wife and Kitty was there ahead of him. She called him up and told him she wouldn't have him travelling with his legal wedded. Bad for Kitty's reputation.... Olly Waters: Director's wife, 'nough said. Looks like a piece o' pie cut on the bias. Couldn't get a job as a waitress at Coney. They make me sick, the poor boobs! Kiss me, Hal!

A package of books arrived from a bookshop.

Oh! I know what they are. Henderson told me he'd send 'em. Got to read 'em to see if they'll do for a picture. She cut the string and removed the wrapper. The Glimpses of the Moon, Babbitt, The Bright Shawl, The Vehement Flame, December Love, and a few others fell out.[320] Zimbule tore open the uncut edges of one book with her finger, rapidly turning the pages, glancing at a line or two, and muttering Um — Um. Then: You read 'em, Des, you're stronger'n I am.

Why don't you do a snake-charmer picture? Harold suggested.

I don't want to see any more of those monsters.... Want to watch me take my exercises? She leaped from the bed, slipped out of her thin night-dress, and stood, her back to Harold, nude on the rose carpet, her palms on her haunches, arms akimbo, her tousled head turned coquettishly. Then, lifting her arms straight over her head, she began her exhibition of chamber athletics, stooping to touch the floor with her finger tips without bending her knees. She counted ... twenty-seven, twenty-eight, twenty-nine, thirty.... Desdemona called out from the bathroom: Youah baff am suah ready, chile.

Wait for me! Zimbule pecked Harold's cheek with her lips, and skipped off to her tub. Presently shrill little cries, mingled with the clucks of the good-natured Negress, scrubbing her mistress's back, could be heard.

Harold lay back in bed. He was wearing a suit of yellow silk pajamas which Zimbule had unaccountably discovered in a chest of drawers. They were, it may be said, too small for him. The little gilt French clock on the mantelpiece struck two in clear bell-like tones. Harold realized that he was losing track of time, that he was drifting. The voyage to Cythera[321] had proved unexpectedly pleasant.

---

[318]   Sheeny, a pejorative slang term for a Jewish person.

[319]   Drag, an American slang term for influence.

[320]   Novels of 1922 by Edith Wharton (1862–1937), Sinclair Lewis (1885–1951), Joseph Hergesheimer (1880–1954), Margaret Deland (1857–1945), and Robert Hichens (1864–1950), respectively. Popular fiction of the period was often turned quickly into films. Of these titles, Wharton's, Lewis's, and Hergesheimer's were made into films within a year or two, while Deland's was purchased by a film company but appears not to have resulted in a production.

[321]   Greek Island associated in mythology with Aphrodite, the goddess of love, and with the kind of idyllic, erotic, and languorous existence Harold is invoking. In Baudelaire's 1853

The voyage back? Why go back? he asked himself. Why not continue to live on Cythera, a joyous, careless island, with a quaint little animal in the shape of a fascinating woman leaping about in the shadows of the great trees, plunging in the pools, lying with him on the banks of velvet moss? Why go back? Harold tried to think what back would be like. Again, as before, it all seemed hazy, dreamlike. He could not see any of the figures in his past very clearly. His father's face he could not recall at all. Alice seemed a conventional figure, any conventional figure, a type. Paul had assumed the veil.... Even Aunt Sadi and Persia Blaine and Miss ... what was her name?... Perkins. Only Campaspe emerged from his memory complete and definite. Campaspe! He must go to call on her, thank her. They must go together. She would understand. Approve? She would not disapprove; of that he was certain. He could not remember that Campaspe had ever disapproved of anything or any one.

In a few days, a week, whenever Zimbule was ready, they would return to the studio, resume work. His heart ... Zimbule interrupted his revery. Play a tune, Des! she was crying. Desdemona emerged from the bathroom, wiping her eyes. Her head was dripping with water; Zimbule had spattered her. All right, honey chile, all right. She moved, flat-footed, across the room. Harold noted her thin legs, her long, narrow feet.... No use crying! shouted Zimbule from the bathroom, and then, No! I've got what it takes, but it breaks my heart to give it away![322]

All right, Miss Jimbool! Desdemona was arranging the disk in the Viennese room. The strains soon filtered in through the open doorway. Zimbule, nude, reappeared in the bedroom, and moved to the rhythm across the rose-carpeted floor. Perching on the bed, she kissed Harold's eyes and ears and throat, while he lay perfectly still, entranced with delight.

When are we going back to work? he asked.

Oh! I don't know.... Tired?

Tired! His tone was reproachful. I don't care if we stay here for ever!

Then we will. She kissed him again.

It breaks my heart to give it away! She dragged him to the floor. Come on! Let's dance. Dancing, as it happened, was not one of Harold's accomplishments, but he tried to follow her as she guided him.

Clumsy! she cried. Come on! Let's go in where the music is.

She pulled him after her into the Viennese room, where the Metzinger, the back of the canvas uppermost, still lay prostrate on the floor.

---

poem titled 'Un voyage a Cythère' ('A Voyage to Cythera'), however, the island takes on an ominous tone, revealed as a place where men are tortured, castrated, and hanged.
[322]   Two popular songs of 1922: 'No Use Crying (If your Sweetheart Goes Away)', a foxtrot dance number (Hugo Hirsch, composer; Alice Mattullath, lyrics) and the ragtime, 'I've Got What It Takes' (J. Russell Robinson, composer; Roy Turk, lyrics), a suggestive song performed by African-American Broadway celebrity Florence Mills (1896–1927) in *The Plantation Revue* (see note 238).

There's that damn picture! What *are* we going to do with it? Come on, Des, something swifter ... Bandanna Land....[323] Come on, Des! She snapped her fingers. The Negress chuckled as she replaced the record, cranked the machine, and set the needle.... Come on, Hal! She bounced him about the room, as if he were a heavy rag doll. Desdemona, with a great expanse of white ivory and her red tongue protruding, beat time with her long, narrow feet. Ta-ta-ta-ta, Bandanna Land! Shake your shimmy,[324] Hal.... The entrance-bell sounded.... Not at home, Des, cried Zimbule, to *any one*!... Desdemona shuffled off, closing the drawing-room door behind her. Zimbule did not stop the phonograph. She continued to circle the room with her willing but inefficient partner.

Desdemona, no longer smiling, came back into the room, again closing the door. Zimbule caught her expression.

What's the matter, Des?

The Negress was silent. Zimbule walked over to her and the black whispered something into the girl's ear.

The cheek! I told you I was home to nobody, nobody! she shrieked.

He hab heard....

What the hell ... Tell him to get out.

Desdemona was propitiatory. He hab brought a chinchilly coat.

Tell him to leave the coat and get out! Zimbule's face was pale with fury.

Desdemona left the room. The phonograph disk continued to revolve: Ta-ta-ta-ta, Bandanna Land! The door reopened slowly. Zimbule, in a towering passion, advanced to meet the intruder. Harold watched the moving door with his eyes. It was not Desdemona who entered, but Cupid Lorillard, a heavy, expensive chinchilla coat over his arm. Ta-ta-ta-ta, Bandanna Land!

---

[323] Ragtime number (Will Marion Cook, composer; 'Mord' Allen, lyrics) that featured in a Broadway musical show of 1908 of the same name, the creation of the renowned African-American producers and actors Bert Williams and George Walker.

[324] A term deriving from the slang for chemise. Its origins as a dance term can be traced to descriptions of female vaudeville performers in the 1910s, whose dances involved shaking of shoulders and hips, i.e. shimmy-shaking. In the 1920s, the shimmy was associated with flappers.

Chapter XIV

One morning, late in December, Campaspe was awakened by a revolutionary assault on her privacy. A lady wrapped in a long sable mantle, with a shako[325] of monkey-fur standing erect on her head and fitting so closely that it gave the curious effect of being her own hair, exploded into the room.

Campaspe, my darling!

Rudely awakened, Campaspe found herself in her mother's arms.

Fannie! My precious Fannie!

My own!

My beloved!

My favourite daughter!

Did you have a good crossing?

Awful! I feel nine years older.

Campaspe contemplated this woman who had the indecency to be her mother: an exquisite oval face without a single line; narrow eyebrows that arched like some architectural masterpiece; eyes as blue as velvet pansies; a straight, slender nose; and a mouth that invited kisses. The open mantle revealed a figure as pimpant[326] as Mary Garden's,[327] and the ankle-length skirt exposed a foot like Cinderella's. An inciting scent, perhaps Bichara's Ambre,[328] evaporated from the furs. It was obscene of this woman, Campaspe reflected, to have the effrontery to look five years younger than her eldest daughter.

Do you mind, Fannie, if I drink my coffee while we talk? Without waiting for a reply, Campaspe pressed the jewelled head of her bed-table tortoise. Fannie was seated in a comfortable chair before the grate in which the hot coals glowed.

You still know, dearest Fannie, what belongs to a frippery![329]

Lanvin and Vionnet[330] tell me, Mrs. Blake demurred. Then: How's Cupid?

Just the same. He's keeping a snake-charmer.

---

325 Military cap in the shape of a truncated cone, topped with plume or 'pom-pom'.
326 French, meaning 'dashing' or 'dapper'.
327 See note 157.
328 Exotic fragrance by the famous Paris-based Syrian perfumier.
329 Campaspe quotes Trinculo's remarks to Caliban in *The Tempest* (Act 4, scene i). In the Shakespearean context, a frippery is a place where cast-off clothes are sold. It is not clear that Campaspe means it in this way, as the term was used in fashion advertising of the day to refer to accessories and ostentatious embellishments.
330 On Lanvin, see note 179; Vionnet was a haute couture label established in 1912 by Madeleine Vionnet (1876–1975), a pioneer in designing modern, uncorseted, women's clothing.

Fannie laughed. A snake-charmer!

Well, just at present she is a moving picture star. I am a little sorry for her. She deserves something better than Cupid.

How *can* you let him, 'paspe?

Let him, Fannie! I *encourage* him.

Mrs. Blake was powdering her face. We are so different, she said, you and I, and yet you are the only member of my family with whom I can get along. I don't understand you, but I adore you. As for me, in such a case, I would be jealous. A man must belong to me.

I know, Fannie dearest. We want different things, but in the end it is the same. Our bond is simple. We both get what we want and we admire each other for it.

Frederika was laying a small table with the breakfast-paraphernalia.

Will you have some coffee, Fannie? Campaspe queried.

Thanks, no. I shall never eat again. How's your father? Not that I care.

Campaspe smiled. I don't know, Fannie. You know I never see him.

Alice? Mrs. Blake made a wry face.

Oh! Alice married.

I heard something.... Mrs. Blake's face assumed a vague expression.... I think she wrote me.

Campaspe sipped her coffee. He left her a month later, she announced.

Mrs. Blake looked annoyed. Why didn't you let me know? I would have cabled Bravo to the boy. What a dreadfully priggish little snob Alice is! Where is the boy now? I'd like to meet him.

I don't know where he is, said Campaspe.

Mrs. Blake shook out her monkey-fur muff. Well, I shan't see Alice or your father. I doubt if I see anybody but you, dear 'paspe. I only came over to consult my lawyer. I expect to sail Saturday. The present rate of exchange makes it more convenient for me to live in Paris. Besides, you know, I don't like New York.... She paused for a moment.... I'm going to be married, 'paspe dearest.

Fannie!

Yes, 'paspe, your old mother is to be married again!

Fannie, my baby!

I met him in London last summer and was immediately seized with the most unbelievable béguin.[331] His name is Cohen, Manfred Cohen.

A Jew!

Yes, darling.

Laura will not receive you! Campaspe shouted with laughter.

That moron! Do you still see her?

Sometimes ... enough to keep in touch with ... Campaspe waved her hand in a vague gesture.... Oh! you know, WITH.

---

[331]   From the French colloquial, meaning 'infatuation'.

But how can you tolerate her? Cette femme est ridicule.[332]

Chère[333] Fannie, she's here so little. She summers in the Berkshires. She winters at Palm Beach. She opens the Horse Show and the Opera[334] and then she goes away. Tell me more about Mr. Cohen.

I have no intention of being so simple, her mother responded. When you come over you can examine him for yourself. Tell me about your boys.

They are coming home from school today.

You like them?

Campaspe reflected. I may. I am waiting.

All life is a gamble.

Not, dearest Fannie, if you put your money both on the red and black and never take it out.... Keep on putting it in. There will always be plenty in that case. I never lose and I never break the bank. Sometimes, I think I own the bank.

I draw my winnings.

Clever Fannie! Where will you and Mr. Cohen live?

Cadenabbia: Lago di Como.[335]

You always go there.

I'm always happy there. I even enjoyed my honeymoon there with your father.

My angel!

They embraced again. Mrs. Blake rose, gathered her sable mantle about her figure, smoothed out her muff, and stooped to pick up her ebony cane, with a head sparkling with emeralds, which had fallen to the floor.

It's wonderful to have such a mother! Campaspe cried. It gives me courage! I hope I can do it too!

Do what, 'paspe?

Learn to be as beautiful as you.

It was noon when Fannie departed. Campaspe rose and, after her bath, arrayed herself carefully in a négligé of lilac velvet, filmy with a rich Spanish gold lace. She glanced over the envelopes on a tray, but was not tempted to open one. Presently Frederika brought in a great box, bursting with calla lilies and tube-roses with a card from Paul.

---

[332] French, meaning 'that woman is ridiculous'.
[333] French, meaning 'dear'.
[334] The Horse Show and the opening of the Metropolitan Opera House season were key events in the New York social calendar.
[335] Resort on Lake Como, popular with British and Americans since the nineteenth century.

I am marrying Mrs. Whittaker, the card read. II faut tant d'argent pour être bohême aujourd'hui.[336]

Nice old Paulet! However you toss him, Campaspe reflected, he lands on his feet.

She walked over to the window, and looked down upon the pavement covered with a thin film of ice, the heaps of white snow in the street. It had begun to snow again. The warm room now seemed more comfortable to her. Her mood was idle, listless, and she sat for some time before the fire, thinking about her mother.

At one o'clock a strange thing happened. Cupid returned for lunch. She could not remember that this had ever happened before.

The boys are coming home, he explained, sheepishly.

But not until late this afternoon, she countered, not unsympathetically, however. The poor man looked troubled, worried, harassed. Was it, she wondered, money?

Cupid, is anything the matter? If it's money, I could help you....

Her words threw the gates open. Money! he flared up. Money! It's you. Can't you ... Won't you ... Campaspe, do you hate me?

Looking at him, she noted tears in the poor creature's eyes. No, she didn't hate him, she reflected, but he was very tiresome, and more than a little ridiculous.

Don't be romantic, Cupid, was what she said. It seemed to her that she had thus adjured him several thousand times.

He faced her. Is it, he asked, because of ... Zimbule?

What nonsense, Cupid. Go ahead enjoying yourself.

I'm not enjoying myself, he muttered morosely. I hate her.

Well, Cupid, she rejoined, smiling, and with as much kindliness as she could assume, taking into account her slight interest in the matter, I don't hate her at all. I like her.

He stood before her, perplexed. I don't understand you, Campaspe. What do you want? A divorce?

No, Cupid, I don't want a divorce. Do you?

Campaspe!

Well, there we are. Neither of us wants a divorce. We are a happily married couple like ... Laura and her husband. Suddenly, she began to laugh. Cupid, she said, Fannie is getting married again.

I don't give a damn about Fannie! His face was red. It's you that I want to talk about. You're like a cake of ice! I don't believe you even have a lover!

Immediately this affront had passed his lips, he was apparently aghast that

---

[336] French, meaning 'It requires so much money nowadays to be bohemian'. Paul does indeed marry Mrs Whittaker and both make an appearance in *Firecrackers* (1925), a sequel to *The Blind Bow-Boy*.

he had let it slip out, but Campaspe's manner was not indicative that anything untoward had been said.

You are quite right, Cupid, she remarked quietly. I haven't.

Forgive me, Campaspe!

And now Cupid made another unusual move. He invaded her sacred bathroom. More curious — had he, she wondered, succumbed to emotion? — than annoyed, Campaspe slowly crossed the room and peered through the crack left at the hinges by the door slightly ajar. Cupid stood before the mirror combing his hair. Life, she assured herself, grew more amusing all the time. She was certain that she would remain young as her mother had. Getting bored was what aged people, and she was never bored.

The boys arrived about five, quiet, well-behaved, handsome lads. Esmé, with his great dark eyes and his curly brown hair, had charm. He might turn into something. They *were* nice, both of them. Campaspe discovered that she was really fond of them and she was so kind to them that they stood before her transfixed with delight. They adored this mother of theirs and they saw so little of her.

A little later, Basil, alone with her, became confidential, sought advice. A Spanish boy, who shared his bedroom, had made a curious request.... Should I, mama? Must I?

Do you want to?

No, mama.

Then you don't have to.[337]

On the stairs she re-encountered Cupid.

I forgot to tell you, Cupid, she said, that I'm sailing on the twenty-third.

But that's two days before Christmas. You won't be here with the boys on Christmas day.

No, Cupid. I no longer believe in Santa Claus, and you can amuse the boys. There is too much mothering going on in the world. What our boys need — what all boys need — is independence. As she spoke she realized that it was curiously ironic that Esmé and Basil should prefer her to Cupid, who worried about them constantly.

Cupid did not argue. He took her tone: When are you coming back?

I don't know.

The little man groaned. Campaspe, he pleaded, we can't go on living like this. Will it always be like this?

Yes, Cupid if you wish. Always. I am content. You are free, of course, to do what you like.... Yes, it will always be like this, unless you change it.... She passed him and continued on her way upstairs.

---

[337] In the British edition, the lines running from 'A little later' to 'Then you don't have to' were expurgated.

Before dinner they all met again under the lamps in the drawing-room. Cupid was reading This Freedom.[338] The boys were playing a game of halma.[339] Campaspe felt a certain amount of pride in contemplating this scene. The American home, she mused, as she sat before the fire, smoking a cigarette. I have achieved it ... along with something else.... But presently her thoughts drifted to her garden, her dear garden, which she must bid good-bye; Eros, blindfold, his bow hanging with icicles, the nymph below buried in the snowdrift....

A week later, Campaspe, wrapped in a heavy moleskin cloak, walked the ship's deck. It was Christmas morning, bright, clear, and cold. The ship sped on through the frigid, green waves. Presently, Frederika appeared with the rugs, and a pile of books. Well tucked in and protected from the crisp December ocean wind, Campaspe sat idly in the bright sunlight, watching sky and sea. She knew, she fancied, nobody aboard. There were, indeed, few passengers.... She examined the books she had selected for this journey: Marmaduke Pickthall's Oriental Encounters, Le Livre de Goha le Simple.... She had some faint intention of visiting the Orient.... Stendhal's Armance:[340] she could not read these now. She had no desire, she found, to read at all. Then, immediately, she regretted that she had brought no book by Huysmans, Huysmans who had said: There are two ways of ridding ourselves of a thing which burdens us, casting it away or letting it fall. To cast away requires an effort of which we may not be capable, to let fall imposes no labour, is simpler, within the reach of all. To cast away, again, implies a certain interest, a certain animation, even a certain fear; to let fall is absolute indifference, absolute contempt....[341] Some time or other, she said to herself, we all drift into the Sargasso Sea,[342] where the wrecks of all the past thought in the world are caught in the rotting sea-weed. I have escaped from this sea.... The only triumphs in this life are negative. I get what I want

---

[338] Bestselling 1922 novel by A. S. M. Hutchinson (1879–1971), critical of women's increasing demands for independence.
[339] Halma, Greek meaning 'jump'. A strategic board game invented in America in 1883/84, similar to, but more complex than, Chinese checkers.
[340] Campaspe's first two selections suggest her desire to whet her appetite for Eastern travel. Pickthall (1875–1936), a British scholar who converted to Islam, whose Oriental Encounters: Palestine and Syria (1894–1896) are semi-autobiographical travel sketches reflecting his view of Middle Eastern culture as inspiring and freeing after a rigid British upbringing; Le livre de Goha le simple (Goha the Fool) (1919) by Franco-Egyptian authors Albert Adès (1893–1921) and Albert Josipovici (1892–1932), concerns common life in Cairo before the spread of Western influence; Stendhal, pen name of Marie-Henri Beyle (1783–1842), an earlier practitioner of literary realism, whose Armance (1827) is a tragic psychological romance of thwarted love.
[341] Joris-Karl Huysmans (1848–1907), French decadent and naturalist novelist. Campaspe quotes from his novel En route (1895), in which the protagonist, Durtal, converts to Catholicism. In this passage from chapter six, a priest advises him as to how to resist Satan.
[342] Region of the North Atlantic, the site of four converging currents that serve as a trap for masses of seaweed.

by wanting something I can give myself. That is my ultimate security.... She recalled Gabrielle Delzant's wise remark to Vernon Lee: We must be prepared to begin life many times afresh.[343] How true! Perhaps, for this new beginning, she would see no more people. Some lines of La Fontaine impinged on her consciousness:

> J'étais libre et vivais seul et sans amour;
> L'innocente beauté des jardins et des jours
> Allait faire à jamais le charme de ma vie.[344]

She had a snug, comfortable feeling that all was well. The past was the past and the future was the future. Only the present occupied her, and it delighted her to remember that the present was as blank as a white sheet of paper. She could write on it what she wished. For the moment she was content to contemplate the white sheet.... Later ... later, she might seek a new pen ... fresh ink.... Campaspe drew her scarf around her face and dozed.

When she awoke the great disk of the fiery sun was sinking into the cold sea. The ship was plowing its way through furrows of foam. She felt a little chill and numb. Where, she wondered, was Frederika? Presently she became aware that two men in heavy coats stood just in front of her, their backs towards her, leaning over the rail. There was something familiar to her in the contours of these backs; there was nothing strange about the timbre of the men's voices. At this moment the two men, who had not yet seen Campaspe, turned, and stood facing each other, their faces clearly silhouetted against the sky. They were the faces of Harold Prewett and Ronald, Duke of Middlebottom.

New York

October 28, 1922[345]

---

[343] Delzant (1854–1903), French author who was suffering from a fatal illness when Lee (1856–1935) befriended her. Lee shared with Delzant the essays that would form her volume. As Lee explains in her dedication to *Hortus Vitae: Essays on the Gardening of Life* (1904), this maxim was one passed on by Delzant to Madame Blanc, a mutual friend of the two women, and is a sentiment that Lee claims informs her book.

[344] Jean de La Fontaine (1621–1695), French poet and fabulist. Campaspe quotes his poem for Mademoiselle de Poussay (1667). The lines translate as, 'I was free, living alone, and without love; | The innocent beauty of gardens and days | would forever form the charm of my life'.

[345] The date marking Van Vechten's completion of the final draft of the novel. It was Van Vechten's practice — for his novels and critical writings — to indicate composition dates in this way.